Casanova,

CURATOR

OF

MEMORIES

PRESTON JAMES METCALF

AUGUST WORDS PUBLISHING!

unique books by exceptional authors for select readers

 **August Words Publishing**

www.AugustWordsPublishing.com

www.augustwords.org

Cover design & portrait of Casanova: Cricket Freeman, © August Words Publishing
Book design: © August Words Publishing
Author photo: courtesy of the author

ISBN: 978-1-942018-14-8

Author's Note

This novel is a work of fiction, only loosely based on the historical figure, Casanova. Throughout the novel, many famous paintings and sculptures are reproduced as introductions to the main character's memories and tales of loves past.

To learn more about the art, the artists, and explanations of references and allusions made throughout the story, please visit PrestonJamesMetcalf.com.

For Kay

my Katerina

Chapter One

*G*iacomo Casanova lay dying, his diminished eyes set upon a flickering candle drowning in its own wax, ebbing into darkness. The splendors of the Venetian sun had long since set, its final rays stretching across the room all too briefly for the dying man before abandoning day to give way to the inevitable night. Shadows danced against timeworn walls like spirits in some distant cave, ignorant of Plato's proxy crumpled on the not distant bed. Giacomo resisted, denying their pull into worlds beyond.

"Not yet," the old man whispered to the fleeting ghosts of dark on dark. "Soon, but not yet."

He turned his head away from the sputtering wick towards the window set high in the wall to the side of his bed. At his instructions the uneven glacial panes remained open to the city outside. His niece, Zanetta had protested. Though fall was calling, the hazards of a late Venetian summer remained. Dangerous vapors might yet linger on the canal below or he might catch a chill with the cooling weather, she warned.

Giacomo scoffed at such notions. What did he care of summer miasma? Too late for that to be of any concern, he thought. And besides, he told her, it was yet unseasonably warm, despite the fact that his withered frame seemed unable to retain any heat, causing him to feel unrelentingly cold. Even the layering of down-filled covers did not warm the bone deep rime. His niece reasoned, threatened, and cajoled, but in the end he got his way, as he knew he would, and the window remained open.

Only the faintest pins of light pierced the early night sky, otherwise dominated by the indigo black of a moonless view. Giacomo strained to hear what his bedridden sight denied. In the quiet of his room he allowed the sounds of the night fallen city to reach him. What was earlier a cacophony of merchants plying their trade, housewives elbowing their way through a nearby market, fishmongers calling, soldiers strutting, babies crying, and angry workers drifting their way back to their homes, faded as the city retired with the coming of darkness. Into their houses they retreated, closing their doors to all but their own. Evidence of their existence reached the bedridden old man through the smells that wafted along the night breeze coming off of the canal latticed lagoon. The sultry smoke of home fires carried on the wind, an occasional elongated finger wisp curling into his chamber through the open window. It was a smell of comfort. A fragrance of memory. The tang of the sea air rested in his nose, as ever it does in Venice, while in some nearby household the harvest of that same sea was prepared for meal, the odor of cooked fish escaping the kitchen fires.

The cawing of a thousand scavenging birds and the random barking of dogs now slept. Gone were the hollering calls of youths running in carefree abandon along the waterways or dashing into narrow alleyways to avoid the unwanted glare of the authorities, perhaps to spy the passing of one of the city's elegant courtesans or a local girl who may have caught their eyes. Gone were the sounds of day only to be replaced by the changing character of night.

But not all was silence. In the distance Giacomo heard a late returning tradesman shout a farewell to his departing coworkers. A boat creaked up the canal, followed by the bumping grind of its docking. The gentle lapping of water against stone filled his room. Somewhere in the far away Giacomo heard, but could not make out, the hurried, muted voice of a woman and the equally stage-whispered response of a young man, an early evening transaction, no doubt, for services to be rendered.

The city changed at night, as Giacomo knew only all too well. The night dwellers would soon be out to join the early enterprising whore and her eager customer. Gamblers and drunks would make their way about in the torch lit darkness, each seeking his or her next escape. Thieves, ever with their sights upon their next potential victim, would trail the hapless orgyers, waiting for their opportunities. Ruffians would brawl and somewhere in this glorious city of glamour and vice, someone would die. A knife in the back, a boozy fall and drowning in the canal, or an angry lover revenging himself upon a rival, followed by shouts and cries, the arrival of the guard, and then silence would resume.

Giacomo welcomed all of these sounds, the buoyancy of day and the sinister of night. This was his city and he sought to savor it all until he could no more. Even the fetid dank stench of the canal that reached his nose pleased him. As the end neared, every morsel of life was to be cherished. He would miss the sounds and sites of his beloved Venice, its Palladian villas, stately palazzos, and elegant grime of worn splendor.

This was the Venice of his youth and of maturing man, and though still vivid in his memories, his Venice was changing. The world was changing. In less than two years the century would roll, as if turning a page on former chapters in a book still being written. He would not see the new century, but that didn't really matter. The changes were already here.

France, his once and second home was already forever transformed by revolution. The dynasty of his former patron, Louis XV had bloated under his grandson, Louis XVI's rule, until the common classes rose to assert a new order. It was a bloody affair headed by madmen with noble intents, consumed by power lust. It had been less than six years since Louis' grandson met his end on Dr. Guillotin's device, and only four since the bloodthirsty lunatic Robespierre met his own fate on the same table. But things would never go back to the way they were. They never do, mused Giacomo. Democracy was on the rise and powers were shifting.

He had outlived the notables of his generation. His friend, the sage Voltaire was gone some twenty years past, though younger minds like young Goethe had picked up the Humanistic torch. *I should write to him once more, before...* Giacomo thought, though he knew he would not. He would have liked to have met Dr. Franklin when he was storming Europe with his Yankee ways of common sense and lighting mind. That is the future, Giacomo realized, not for the first time. New ways of thinking were afoot. New powers on the rise. And what of Mozart, that flashing genius with whom he shared more than one raucous evening? Had it really been less than a decade since his brilliant flame extinguished?

It is time, Giacomo thought. *I have outstayed my welcome. I will miss Venice, though,* Giacomo thought with a pang of sadness, should such lamentations be allowed wherever his next journey was about to take him.

In his mind, the only venturing his frail body now afforded, he floated down the Grand Canal, guiding his memories like a gondolier coursing the myriad waterways. How many times he passed under the Bridge of Sighs, just as he had once traversed the bridge itself from the Doge's Palace to the state inquisitors and prisons beyond. Pleasure and pain both left their marks on his remembrances.

Image blended into image as he recalled the buildings of his life. He called to mind the massive basilica of San Marco with its golden interior and towering campanile, and its iconic four horses, the *Quadriga* charging from its façade. Looted from the Hippodrome in Constantinople during the Fourth Crusade and brought to Venice, they were a favorite of his. Many times he had climbed the interior stairwells to the overlooking balcony of the cathedral to admire them and to look out over the bustling piazza.

He thought of Santa Maria Gloriosa dei Frari, with the celebrated *Assumption of the Virgin* by Titian, a work of glowing wonder, the massive oil painting that was the largest altarpiece in the city. He thought of the times he drifted under the Rialto, the most magnificent bridge in Venice, and his visits to the small isle of Murano, with its closely guarded clandestine secrets of glassmaking, and his personal favorite, Santa Maria della Salute, the magnificent Baroque cathedral erected a hundred and sixty years or so earlier as a votive offering for the city's deliverance from a deadly outbreak of the plague, the Black Death, with its domes and scrolls and scalloped buttresses protecting a trove of masterworks by Titian, Tintoretto, and others. It was a meander he knew well.

A knock at the door shook Giacomo from his reveries.

"Uncle." The door creaked open a way and a young man peered in, holding a lamp in front of him. "Uncle, are you awake?"

Giacomo grunted. "Don't you mean are you alive?" he said, more caustically than he intended.

The young man looked crestfallen as he stood in the doorway.

"Why, Uncle, I, I would never…"

Giacomo softened his tone. "Oh, I know you wouldn't. Don't be so glum. You look like death entering my room."

"Uncle!" the young man exclaimed as if shocked, but smiled at the old man nonetheless. Lorenzo was seventeen, just three months past, and idolized the old man, now but a shell of his former self.

"Don't dawdle, Grandnephew," Giacomo said. "Come in, come in."

Lorenzo entered, the light of his lamp chasing the shadows to the far corners of the room. He approached the large four-poster bed with its richly woven valance at top and set the lamp on the nightstand next to the flickering candle.

Giacomo eyed the young man as he fidgeted by the nightstand.

"So, what brings you up here this time of night?" he asked.

"Mother sent me, to see if you ate the soup she brought up earlier, and to see if you needed anything."

A rasping half laugh, half cough escaped Giacomo's lips. "I need many things my boy, but the one thing I need most you can't give me, unless you can turn back the sands of time."

Lorenzo shifted uncomfortably from foot to foot.

"No, I didn't think so." Giacomo continued. "Here now, grab that pillow and prop me up."

Giacomo cringed as Lorenzo elevated his back and head and inserted the pillow behind, then lowered him to a slightly sitting position.

"Unh," Giacomo groaned. "That's better." He labored to catch his breath.

"Believe it or not boy, but there was a time when this old body could sit up on its own, and a lot more."

"I know, Uncle."

Giacomo glanced around the room in the light of the glowing lamp. There was little there to identify it as the abode of the once celebrated Giacomo Casanova. An old sword in its scabbard hung from a hook on the wall behind the door. Giacomo couldn't see it clearly, but he knew it was covered in dust. Even before confinement to his bed the sword hung unused and neglected. The days of ceremonial swords and gallant preening were long past. Many times young Lorenzo had admired it, but he never dared to touch it. That was all of his former life that remained in the room. That, and of course, the books that made him famous, and rich.

His memoirs, twelve expansive volumes, sat atop the high chest of drawers, their gilded leather spines facing him. Giacomo was inwardly pleased at the thought of them. Between those leather covers was his life, the life he once knew, or at least his life as he chose to tell it.

He looked back at the boy. Many were the times Lorenzo asked to read them, devouring their pages with enthusiasm, much to his mother's dismay, and Giacomo's delight.

"Sit down," he said, tired of straining to look up.

Lorenzo pulled the nearby chair closer to the light by the bed and sat.

"So, what is it you wanted to talk about?" Giacomo asked knowingly.

"As I said, mother wanted me to check on your meal."

Giacomo looked at the bowl of soup still sitting on the end table, untouched and cold. Lorenzo followed his gaze.

"Mother will not be pleased."

Giacomo sighed. "Your mother is rarely pleased when it comes to me."

"Uncle, Mother loves you. It's because of you we live in such a nice home. We owe you everything. She only wants what's best for you."

Giacomo considered the earnest young man. "Familial love does not always ensure approval. There is much about my life and the way I chose to live it that does not meet with your mother's approval," he glanced again at the books on the chest of drawers, "but yes, you are correct, she does love me, in her own way.

"Her mother though, my sister and your grandmother never had a disapproving thought about me. It simply wasn't in her. She had such a great heart, as does your mother in her ways." Giacomo allowed his mind to drift back onto one of the fluid memories of his sister, as he did with increasing frequency over the past months. "You remind me of her, my sister that is."

"I do?"

Giacomo nodded and reflexively cringed at the effort.

"You even look like her, though maybe not as pretty," he said with a slight grin.

Lorenzo looked embarrassed at the compliment and the gentle ribbing.

"Mother says I look like you." Lorenzo spoke with a hint of pride.

Giacomo closed his eyes. Just a fortnight prior he asked his niece for a mirror. What he saw shocked him. The face looking back through the silvered glass was not the face he knew. He had long since accepted that he was no longer the vital youth of his memoirs. His lined face and white hair proclaimed as much, but the emaciated countenance framed by stringy, limp wisps of bleached straw that stared back at him from the mirror was of some other creature, a creature touched by death. That is when he knew this was to be his final illness.

It wasn't so bad, really. When living becomes harder than surviving, it is time to let go. He would miss his beloved Venice, however, and the boy sitting here to whom he had grown especially fond. And yes, he would miss his niece Zanetta and her disapproving scowl, which she always seemed to blend with loving concern. Everyone else of any importance to him was already gone.

He pulled himself back to the boy beside him.

"Yes, I suppose you do, at least as I did long ago. A very long time ago. Now, why are you really here?"

Lorenzo shifted in his seat.

"Uncle," he hesitated, "tell me about them."

"Them?" Giacomo asked. "Whom do you mean?"

Lorenzo blushed brightly before answering.

"The women, your lovers."

"Ah, *them*." Giacomo chuckled. "I suppose they would be of interest to a young man of your age."

Lorenzo's color deepened.

Giacomo continued, "You read my memoirs. You know all about them."

"Is it true?" Lorenzo asked in a rush. "Did you really, well, all of them?"

"What do you think?"

"Mother says it is true. She says you will probably burn in Hell, though she hopes not."

Lorenzo stopped abruptly realizing with a shock what he just said.

"Oh, I'm sorry, Uncle! I didn't mean…"

"It's alright my boy," he said ruefully. "She may be right, though I hope not as well."

After an uncomfortable silence Lorenzo asked again, "Tell me about them?"

Giacomo raised a feeble hand and pointed to the twelve volumes. "It's all there. Read them again if you like."

"I know what you wrote, Uncle, but what was it like? I mean, what was it really like? You've had so many, so many…"

"Conquests?" Giacomo completed the statement for him.

Lorenzo nodded.

Giacomo exhaled deeply as he assessed the earnestness of the young man and his request.

"My life was full of adventure and excitement, not all of it concerning women, you know? I was a soldier in the Venetian army. Nearly got myself killed. Would you like to hear about it?"

The young man stared at him with an anxious expression.

"No? How about my time as a spy in the employ of King Louis XV of France? Now there was an adventure. It all came about after my escape from prison where I was incarcerated on charges of Freemasonry, a complete misunderstanding I assure you. It was forty-three years ago and I still remember it like it was only just past. I was one of the few to pass over the Bridge of Sighs only to revel in its beauty from the canal below years later. Legend says that lovers who kiss beneath the evening glow of this bridge will be granted eternal love.

"Do you know why they call it the Bridge of Sighs? Midway across there are grilled windows set in the walls, out of which the escorted prisoners are allowed one last look at our beautiful floating city, and it is said that here they each sigh at the realization of their loss. I can tell you with assurance that this is true. I thought never to see Venice again. But of course, I escaped, or I wouldn't be here with you now, all these years later.

"It was all very bold. I scavenged a metal rod and spent weeks scraping it on the stone wall to sharpen it, then weeks more gouging my way through the floor to the room below, but wouldn't you know it, before I could take advantage of my ingenuity the guards moved me to another cell. I was crushed, but not for long. I was able to conceal my iron rod in the move, and with the help of a fellow prisoner, a renegade priest named Father Balbi, a rather disagreeable cleric to be sure, residing in a neighboring cell, we cut a hole through the wall separating us and together we made our way up through the ceiling and from there to freedom. And then there was my subsequent flight to Paris where I founded the first lottery in that country. My newfound wealth afforded me the perfect opportunity to move in circles that the King found to be…"

Lorenzo continued to stare at him with an expectation that clearly did not include tales of daring escape and royal espionage, embellished, no doubt, with the varnish of time.

"This is not what you want to hear about?" Giacomo asked.

"I have heard these stories before, Uncle."

"Yes, so you have."

"Please, Uncle," Lorenzo implored.

Giacomo snorted, "Your mother will not be pleased."

"Mother is rarely pleased when it comes to me," Lorenzo replied, echoing his uncle's words.

"Something else we have in common then," the old man replied.

Giacomo considered the young man at his bedside. How like his dear sister he truly was, great hearted, yet totally unaware of the impact his goodness has on others. So like her, he mused. And then there was Zanetta, his niece, Lorenzo's mother. She was another matter altogether.

How old is she now? Giacomo quickly calculated. Thirty-seven? Yes, not even yet forty years and already she has given up on the wonder of life. Not that this made her uncaring. Far from it. Zanetta was as giving and caring as her dear mother had been. No, it was not generosity of spirit she lacked, it was something much crueler to the soul. She lacked faith in her own humanity. Somewhere along the road she lost the ability to believe that life had something more for her, and with that loss any hope of personal happiness also fled. Happiness, she now believed, resided only in what was reflected from others. Lorenzo was her mirror on life. His success would be her goal. His fulfillment would be her purpose. His happiness would be her reward. But it never quite works that way, does it, Giacomo thought.

Zanetta's caring extended to others as well, Giacomo chief among the recipients. For the past ten years she and Lorenzo lived in his household, accepting Giacomo's invitation after the untimely death of her husband. She quickly assumed the management of Giacomo's personal and business affairs, showing an acumen and dexterity that relieved his burden just as his own abilities lessened. Then there were his illnesses, each turn of health worse than the last, until this final confinement. Through them all, Zanetta was there, caring, nursing, and devoid of any spark of self. It pained Giacomo beyond the infirmities he endured to see the personal emptiness of his niece, and the greatest pain was that Giacomo understood the why of her withdrawal. She was, after all, though she would be loath to admit it, more like him than not. Not in life's exploits perhaps, but in depth of feeling she was his equal. This was, perhaps, the reason she retained such a reticence regarding Giacomo's influence on Lorenzo. She wanted better for her son. She would spare him the mistakes of his elder.

Giacomo grimaced at the thought. Mistakes, yes, but each one was of value in his journey. And now that his journey's end was near, he had to ensure its continuance in another.

He eyed his eager Grandnephew assessingly. Time was short. What did he have left? Weeks? Days? He was ready to depart this life, but there was yet one more transaction to be made. A mantle to be passed. He was nearly out of time, but would his successor be ready for the role they must now assume? Giacomo wasn't sure, but he knew he had to try. And then there was Lorenzo.

"Telemachus," Giacomo said, almost to himself.

"What?" Lorenzo replied.

"Telemachus. Homer? *The Odyssey*? Good lord boy, have you forgotten your Greek already?"

"Um, no, Uncle. I'm just not sure what that has to do with it."

"Are you ready for what you are asking?"

Giacomo focused his gaze on Lorenzo, who appeared to be puzzling his way through his uncle's question.

"For your stories? The women, they are in your books."

"Are they?" Giacomo asked. "What you are asking is not a simple thing, Lorenzo. I need to know if you are ready."

"Ready for what?"

A spasm of pain pierced Giacomo, causing him to gasp and catch his breath. He forced himself calm before he resumed speaking.

"When Athene appeared to Telemachus there was more to it than just an order to go find his father. She had to know that he would be ready for what he would find. The truth can be a daunting thing."

"Do you mean finding Ulysses, his father?"

Giacomo nodded his head.

"Before undertaking such a journey Telemachus had to be prepared. Fear, trepidation, prejudice, social constraints, all must be left behind. Are you ready for what you will find?"

"I'm not sure I understand."

"Never mind. I doubt if Telemachus did either. You have an open heart. Perhaps that is all the preparation you need. Time is short." He gaged the anxious and confused expectation in his grandnephew's face.

"Very well." Ultimately Giacomo was both resigned to and delighted by the request. "What is it you wish to know?"

Lorenzo leaned forward in excitement.

"There were, well, so many!"

"So many, indeed," the old man repeated barely above a whisper.

Giacomo turned his gaze back towards the open window and the deepness of night.

"So many indeed."

Women at Play

Jean-Honoré Fragonard
The Swing
1766
oil on canvas

It is a frolic. Antoinette's frolic.

She is abandonment and laughter with a promise no greater than tease. She sighs a wistful pleasant sigh too intimate to be shared, too shared to be mine alone.

Our eyes dance throughout the day, first meeting then away, always followed by a glance meant both to draw and deny. She knows what she is playing, this one. Am I ready to play her game? Can we dance with more than eyes knowing that it will not last?

"You are Antoinette," I say by way of introduction.

"So I have been told," she lobs back.

"Is there some doubt?"

"Not on my part," she says. "I am quite certain of who I am. And you are?"

"Giacomo," I introduce myself with a bow.

"Ah, I have heard of you."

"Nothing untoward I hope."

"Nothing disqualifying," she corrects.

A man next to her clears his throat and she turns to him.

"Darling," she says in her most charming lilt, "I need champagne."

He tips his head in reluctant acquiescence and gives me a sharp look before departing to address her whim.

"Husband?" I ask with a touch of sarcasm.

"A means," she lets out with a sigh.

I watch him cross the room, a clueless aristocrat accustomed to getting what he wants. He is out of his league with this one.

"My congratulations then."

"Pity," she says.

"What is that?"

She looks away while answering.

"I have heard that despite certain charms, you are not a man of means."

"You have been asking about me then?" I say with feigned hopefulness.

"Idle gossip about the local downtrodden," she responds.

"It's true, I have yet to make my fortune. I do try to compensate with other virtues," I say. "As for the trajectory of my fortunes, give me time."

She sighs again. "Time. Perhaps another time then?"

"Another time, perhaps. Until then, I wish you and your returning mouse all the best."

The clueless wit returns and hands her the champagne, requested and retrieved. I bow my exit.

"Take me to the swing. I must swing," she pouts prettily to the man who has reappeared and again holds her attention. He is a dullard fool who thinks her dancing eyes and wistful sighs are for him. He will be disappointed, but only when she has no more use of him. He thinks to find a bride, while her search is of an earthier sort. You cannot capture a breeze; only let it tickle your flesh in its passing. He will be denied even that.

Another glance, another innocent batting of eyes not innocent at all and I watch her disappear through the glass paned doors from the magnificence of man's palace creation to the even greater cathedral of nature. Neither is strong enough to contain her for long.

I watch them leave then hasten my way to another door, another path. I will be there before them. I am her match in this game we play.

The gardens are luxurious full this time of year. They burgeon with vitality. Hyacinth and ivy and wild rose compete along paths pressed by strolling lovers seeking solitude for a stolen kiss.

In the middle of the garden is a clearing canopied by oak, and beyond by Rococo clouds made white warm in the airy spring day. Roman marbles aged to a dusky cream by centuries of watching over the fleeting, carefree spirits whose frolic they inspire, peek through the brush. Cherubs embrace at a marble bench and Cupid looks impishly across at the eros that unfolds before him. From a great branch hangs a swing with velveted ropes and cushioned seat awaiting her.

I hear them nearing, her voice preceding her up the winding path. She giggles and coos and lures him along with an ease he obliviously follows. Sad for him, but he is a witless purse and nothing more. He should be home courting a wife rather than chasing a wisp. He will learn, after she is gone.

I am hidden at Cupid's base. Nature has been kind in providing me concealment. Two can play at her game. I ready and wait.

The rustle of clothes and the sound of her enticing voice announce their arrival. The fluttering leaves above tell me she and the swing have found one another.

"Push me! Higher. Higher!" Her commands are followed with eager simplicity.

Unknowing, she tempts me. It is her nature, and my good fortune. A glimpse of white and pink disappears as quickly as it arrives, and each new passing offers me a greater spectacle as she arcs higher to reach her own peels of joy ringing through the trees.

That is when she sees me looking up at her. Pleasant surprise lights her face and she vanishes again from my sight. Her expression changes with each new arrival above me. At one such advent she raises an eyebrow as if to say, "Oh really, you think so, do you?" At another she rolls her eyes in mock exasperation, while yet again she feigns shock, but still the only sound is that of her laughter and occasional renewed commands to her unwitting fool. It is a performance worthy of her skills.

Pink satin and silk billow and flail. White lace flutters at her sleeves and across the bodice of her dress that pushes her corseted breasts upward soft. She kicks her feet and her skirts expose, promising me a token whisper of what is beneath. I am gifted a picture of white stocking-clad legs that her wealthy mouse will only dream of seeing. She pretends not to notice that her dress is revealing beyond her control, but of course it is entirely by her design. How is it that she can make it obey her will, while her hat remains placid still and not a strand of hair strays from allowable boundaries of ruliness?

When next she appears her face is sweet and promising. She kicks off her shoe and points her foot away. Her intent is clear, and it does not include her swing pushing fool. I will leave before I am found out, but with the knowledge that the game has changed. We will meet again and dance with more than our eyes. I away to wait.

Our joining will be like the fullness of the gardens, but it will not last. As she does on the swing she will back out of my view. I look forward to what is to come, but already I know she is gone. You cannot capture a breeze; only let it tickle your flesh in its passing.

Women Who Hunt

François Boucher
Diana Resting After Her Bath
1742
oil on canvas

"I can see you Giacomo!" Diana calls out.

"No, you can't."

"I can Giacomo. You are behind the big oak."

"No, I'm not."

"Yes, you are! And you have been there for several minutes. You came tromping through the woods like a bear through a garden."

"No, I didn't."

"Oh, honestly Giacomo! Why do you argue with me? I heard you coming a mile away. Now come out from behind that tree before someone mistakes you for a hiding stag. A spy can get shot that way."

I step out, smiling broadly.

"I wasn't exactly hiding," I say from my position leaning against a massive oak tree, enjoying the scene.

She shoots me a doleful look.

"You were lurking," she says with amusement.

"That's not hiding," I reason.

"This is your defense?" she asks, incredulity dripping from her voice. "From denial to semantics?"

"Hiding would seem to indicate I was doing something wrong. Lurking sounds more like I was just hesitant to walk away from something far too lovely to abandon."

"Humph. Hiding, lurking, it is all very sneaky if you ask me."

My eyes widen in innocence and I hold up my hands to indicate the lack of any malintent.

"I like what I see," I say simply.

Lurking can be excused with such a spectacle. Diana is seated at an embankment on a tumbling curtain of satin blue, the sun warming her smooth bare skin. Her clothes are yet abandoned as she prepares to adorn herself with a string of pearls, a hundred orbiting moons to halo her slender neck. Her pretty servant, Egeria sits at her side having just dried her mistress after her bath.

"How long have you been there?" she asks.

"I thought you heard me arrive," I say.

"Careful Giacomo. I still might determine you are a stag, and I am a hunter after all."

"A stag that talks?"

"A stag that lurks and those are the easiest kind to hunt. How long have you been there, lurking?"

"Long enough," I shrug again.

"Were you watching while we bathed in the creek below?" Her question is accusatory.

"Do you mean the creek in which you stood by a large rock that you steadied yourself against as the current coursed between your thighs and Egeria bathed you with handfuls of rose petals and water until you stretched your arms high above your head and you gave yourself to the cleansing massage? No, of course not, that would be spying."

"Shame on you Giacomo, taking advantage of an innocent girl's need to bathe after the hunt."

"I wasn't taking advantage. I just stumbled upon this spot as I tromped through the woods raising all kinds of ruckus like a bear or what have you. How was I to know I would find you here clothed in nothing but sun? And once I did, quite by accident of course, I didn't want to interrupt. You seemed to be otherwise occupied."

"You just stumbled upon this spot? It's more than a league from my home, and you have been here before. You know this is where I stop after the hunt to bathe."

"Oh, yes, I thought it looked familiar," I say with all the innocence I can muster.

"Really? And what tipped you off? The two naked women bathing in the stream?"

"Well, I am no expert hunter, but that did seem to be a pretty good clue."

"So you decided to lurk a while?"

"It seemed a reasonable thing to do."

"And you are a reasonable man, Giacomo."

I hold out my hands as if this a self-explanatory fact.

"Would you have me any other way?"

Diana smiles seductively.

"I would have you any number of ways."

Hmmm… Who is hunting whom?

I see that her hunt was successful. Game is set aside, her bow resting on top of it, her quiver full of arrows nearby.

"The hunt went well?" I ask the obvious.

"I managed to find you," she replies.

"So you did, but I wasn't hiding."

"That's right," she says, "nor were you spying. You were lurking and busy not interrupting two girls bathing."

"Something like that."

Egeria giggles as she hands her mistress a cloth to dry off a bit more.

"Yes," she says at length, "the hunt went quite well. The moon-grove is rich with game."

For all of her feminine charm, Diana is any man's match in the hunt, a true twin of Apollo. How many men have made the mistake of believing this woman's place was hearth and home and nothing more? How many men so erred to think this woman could not be anything she chose to be? To them she is forever virgin.

"It's a shame you weren't with us," she continues.

"The hunt is over then?" I ask.

"Well," she explains, "we have already bathed."

"So I see."

"So you do. And really Giacomo, you should be punished for intruding upon what was an entirely private and chaste activity."

"Perhaps, but I can assure you my happenstance encounter has left me with purely chaste thoughts."

Diana laughs.

"You are a poor liar, Giacomo."

"Really? And I thought that was one of my better lies."

"No doubt. Nevertheless, the hunt is over," she sighs.

"And you are chastely bathed."

"Yes."

"And clean," I helpfully offer.

"And clean," she concurs.

"And natural as nature's child," I add.

"Careful Giacomo," she warns. "I may have to sic my dogs on you. They'll chase you like Actaeon."

"Wasn't he torn apart like a stag in the hunt?" I ask.

"Yes, he was caught spying."

I rub my chin as if deep in thought.

"I see, then it's a good thing I was only lurking."

Diana whispers something to Egeria who happily grabs her dress and strolls off around a bend in the trail, Diana's dogs gamboling after her.

Diana motions to me with her finger and says, "Come here, Giacomo, lurk a little closer."

I leave my leaning tree. The hunt is back on.

Natural Women

Antonio Allegri da Correggio
Jupiter and Io
1530
oil on canvas

It is a forbidden encounter.

It is an old and oft retold story. A disapproving father. A family opposed. Their plans are not her plans. They see in her a means to their own advantage, but she is to be no one's pawn. Her happiness should be their joy, but the selfish rarely see it that way.

"Shh! We'll get caught," she whispers, while furtively pulling me towards her.

Deep in a garden recess, far away from prying eyes we meet. A small path mostly untrod opens to a small clearing fit for such a rendezvous. Dappled sun and mossy ground make for an inviting chamber between the trees. It is our private place, Io's and mine.

"No one will catch us," I reassure her. "Not in this forgotten corner."

And if they do?

I am not afraid of discovery. I can take care of myself. It is Io for whom I fear. She deserves more than to be a player in her family's script. She deserves her own happiness, her own fulfillment, but that is a decision she must come to on her own. I can only support her way. To do more would be an expectation of my own scripting, and she deserves more.

Io exhales a nervous little chirp that is cut short by the eager meeting of our lips, tasting, swelling, touching. Hands seek and find the tender places that excite our passions even more. Our bodies press against each other, heat rising.

"I've missed you so."

Her words are rushed and hoarse with anticipation. I kiss her neck and up to her blushing cheeks. She tilts her head back receptively and submits her rosy face to my probing mouth and hands. After our first devouring kisses we pull apart, as if to savor what is to come.

"You may be right," I continue. "We should be cautious. A clandestine meeting such as this may not be proper or acceptable for a daughter of Argos. It is probably more befitting a wood nymph," I say.

Io brightens.

"A wood nymph? How intriguing. And how would a wood nymph act if she was in my position?"

"That's a good question."

"You don't know?" she asks. "Then perhaps a wood nymph I am!"

I look her up and down appreciatively.

"Well, I've never actually met a wood nymph before."

"Ah, then I am your first?" she teases.

"So it would seem," I counter.

"And am I everything you expected?" she asks.

"Yes and no."

"That is rather indecisive," she points out.

A diplomatic answer here would be apropos.

"Yes, in that you are even more radiantly beautiful than ever a Nereid has been described."

Io flushes deeply and bestows another long kiss upon me, then stops suddenly as if remembering something.

"And no?" she asks.

I consider my response.

"Far be it from me to say how a wood nymph should appear, but I rather would have thought to meet you, how should I say it, in more of a natural state."

"And what could be more natural than this place?"

"It is not the location to which I referred."

"What then?" she asks.

"Well, I doubt your average wood nymph would have the finest dressmakers in the land," I say, indicating her expensive gown.

"I am not average then?"

"Io, you are far from average."

"But not adorned like a wood nymph?"

"Not the wood nymphs I have imagined," I reply.

"Ah," she concedes and stands back a step. "Far be it from me to disappoint."

Io unbuttons her dress and lets it fall to her feet, stepping out if it. She lowers her underclothing and tosses it onto a protrusion of stone near an aged krater.

She faces me, one arm covering her breasts, the other hand shielding her nakedness. Never has she been so sumptuously adorned.

"Is this more of what you had in mind?" she asks in her most innocent voice.

I am entranced by her pale tender flesh, desiring her even more.

"I never conceived such perfect beauty," I say.

"You are pleased?" she asks. "Do I surpass your average expectations?"

"Only if I had the hundred eyes of Argus could I be more pleased."

"Then love me," she says, opening her arms to me.

I move to cover her like a cloud, enfolding her. Her body responds to my touch and moves beneath me.

She whispers invitations in my ear as I descend like a morning fog, obscuring her from all but me, revealing her all to me. She throws her head back as if lost in erotic rapture. I have never loved a wood nymph before.

For a long time we laze on the ground, exhausted by our tryst.

"Giacomo?" she says, breaking the sated silence between us.

"Yes?"

"This isn't enough."

It is not the tryst she is talking about.

"No," I agree.

"I have been thinking," she says.

"Are you sure that is wise? Thinking may lead to decisions."

"And what is wrong with that?"

"Nothing, as long as it is a decision I want to hear."

She let the moment pause.

"My family. They have plans for me."

"And those plans do not include me."

"No.

"Then what are we to do?" I ask.

Io's fingers trace their way down my chest.

"I'm not leaving you," she says.

"Your family will not be pleased."

"Probably not, but I have plans of my own."

"We will have to leave this place."

Io nods.

"The sun came out," she says at last, feeling the warmth of its diffused rays through the trees. "It feels nice."

"So it has. Is that a sign we should be getting back before you are missed?"

"I'm not missing. For the first time in my life I know right where I am. I am with you. However, I suppose we will have to return soon, if only for a bit."

"Shall we dress then?"

Io blushes again and says, "Not yet. I enjoy looking at the clouds," and happily, I hover once more.

Women of Pleasure

Kitagawa Utamaro
Lovers in an Upstairs Room
from *Utamakura (Poem of the Pillow)*
1788
woodblock print on paper

"Is this your first visit to the floating world?" she asks, a slight lisp to her soft luring voice.

Ours is not her first language, and she is more fragile in the speaking, like an eggshell thin porcelain vase, tiny and rare. She is kneeling demurely on a tatami mat, her legs folded under her. I am entranced by the subtlety of her features. Her raven black hair is piled high, a wooden comb holding it in place. It sweeps up exposing the tender nape of her neck. She is alluring.

"My first time here, yes," I answer.

"Then welcome," she says with a deep bow, her forehead touching the mat. "My name is Mariko."

"Yes," I affirm again, "I was told you would be here."

"*So desu.*"

A demure nod and her painted lips animate her softly powdered face.

"Please," she continues, "be seated."

She motions to a cushion opposite her. I remove my boots and step up onto the woven mats and sit.

A window at the wall is open to the warm spring air. A plum tree is in bloom, the perfume from the blossom full branches filling the room. I hear water running through a small fountain in the yard below. That and the sound of birdsong are all that mask the pounding of my heart.

"You have traveled far?" she asks.

"I'm not from around here," I joke, but she does not understand my attempt at humor. She puzzles at it as if my answer is a curiosity she is trying to comprehend.

"Very far," I add. "Very far indeed. I came as part of my duties."

"Ah," she nods. "You are a, how do you say it, a *samurai?*" she says in her own tongue.

"A soldier?" I ask.

"Yes, that is it, a soldier?"

"At times," I admit.

She eyes me curiously. In her land a soldier is a soldier, a farmer a farmer, a priest a priest, an artist an artist, and rarely do they change.

"You came by ship?"

"Yes, many weeks by ship, and many more on horseback to arrive here."

"Your business brings you far," she says.

"Business, and pleasure," I explain.

"Pleasure is the purpose of this place," she says, indicating her surroundings with a graceful passing of her hand. "You are welcome."

I hear muffled footsteps at the door and shadows appear upon the paper panes of the wooden frame. Softly the door slides open and a young servant girl enters carrying a tray. She approaches and kneels beside the low table, setting the tray upon it. She bows deeply to her mistress, then to me and silently retreats.

"Please," Mariko invites, "you must be hungry."

I am, but not entirely for the savoring morsels on the nearby tray.

She selects three or four items and places them in a small dish, deftly manipulating the food with two sticks. She hands me the plate and sticks, with which I proceed to fumble. She kindly ends my frustration and retrieves the awkward implements from my unaccustomed grip.

"Please, allow me."

She plucks one of the small foods from the dish and holds it to my hungering mouth. It is delicious, and my throated expression of satisfaction tells her so. She brightens with delight and serves me another. She continues feeding me like a nesting bird until nearly all of the morsels are gone.

She lifts a ceramic vessel from the table.

"*Sake?*" she asks. "Rice wine," she adds by way of explanation.

I have had sake before and nod my head in assent.

She pours a small amount into a miniature cup and offers it with both hands. The warm liquid goes down smoothly and she pours me another. I drink, but with a sudden flushing sensation in my head I determine to slow down.

As if on cue, the door slides open and the young servant girl pads in to remove the dishes and tray, leaving the bottle of sake and cup behind. She returns with a musical instrument, a three-stringed lute, and hands it to her mistress. The girl leaves and closes the door behind her.

Mariko moves away from the table and kneels again, arranging her scarlet patterned kimono around her. She holds up the instrument and with an inquisitive incline of her head seems to ask, "Would you like to hear?"

I nod, not wanting to damage the preluding silence with my coarse words.

She begins to pluck at the strings with a wooden blade. The notes are alien, discordant at first, but somehow proper and in place here in this willow dream. I allow myself to be lost in the notes, finding a melody and harmony that carries me. I am now of this place, floating on notes played by a delicate geisha.

Mariko finishes her song and I open my eyes to her radiant expression.

"Thank you," I say, and she beams with delight.

"You like the music of this house?" she asks.

"It is unlike any I have ever heard before. I like it very much," I add.

"It is *Sakura*, a song of the cherry blossom. It is a song of spring. It is played soft and slow to remind us of the gentle ebbs of life. Winters come and end, but always to be warmed by new life, new blossoms, floating on an evening air."

"And you are one among the blossoms," I say, believing.

"So, now you know," she says, her voice soft like a whisper.

"What do I know?" I ask.

"Why they call this the floating world," she explains.

I ponder for a moment.

"Yes," I reply.

"Then now you are ready," she says, lowering her eyes.

"Ready?"

"For pillowing," she answers, her words spoken in reverence.

I catch my breath. It is why I came, only now it seems so much more.

Mariko meets my eyes and slowly she unties the sash at her waist. She parts her kimono, baring breasts and legs and blossom flesh. She encourages me towards her and together we lay until we meet the rising sun.

Women of Metaphor

Yakshi bracket figure
on the East *Torana* of the *Great Stupa* at Sanchi
Early Andhra Period, mid-1st Century BCE
stone
Sanchi, India

I am tired from my travels. I thought to explore, to learn new truths, but history repeats and everywhere the foibles of man find new voice. I wander from the palace confines of inexperienced youth to witness the same travails from land to land. The poor are in need, the sick in pain. Death touches all, and I feel helpless before it. It is a prose history that echoes through time. I am hungry to understand why.

In the torana she waits, like a personification of the waters, flanking a garden mound. She is like no other woman I have ever met, and yet my entire life seems to have been directed to this very point, this time, this place. She greets me with an angeli, with downcast eyes and a sensuous trim of her lips.

"I am Yakshi," she intones.

"A sign of prayer?" I ask, referring to her steepled hands and dipping bow.

"Is it so in your country?" she asks, her voice a lilting caress, like the trickle of floral scents down a birthing stream.

"It is a sign," I reply, "from when I was a child. It is how I was taught to pray, hands thus." I mimic her angeli.

"Ah, so it is here as well." She beams at the affinity. "I pray."

"But not the same," I hasten to add. "Our prayers were to God."

She frowns at my words, trying to comprehend the differences of which I speak, and in her frown I see the questioning girl beneath the woman's mask. Her face brightens and once again she speaks.

"Yes, so it is here," she repeats. "Thus I greet you."

She repeats the angeli and bows.

"But Yakshi," I say, "I am not a god. I do not deserve such reverence as your greeting implies."

For only the most fleeting of moments a frown again darkens her expression, then composure returns and she explains.

"The divine is in you. Out there," she says, "is just an illusion. A form we give for what is truly within. Do not mistake the form for the divine, which is beyond all forms."

She dips her head again. I am trodding holy ground.

"What is this place?" I ask.

Her black almond eyes widen at the question.

"The stupa?" she inquires, as if my asking is a surprise.

"Is that what this place is called? I have never been this far before. All is new to me."

"Ah," she says, understanding dawning. "This is Sanchi, an ancient site. The stupa is behind me."

I note the earth dome structure in the distance, loathing to lose sight of the bountiful girl.

"A temple?" I ask.

"A resting place," she corrects. "It was built by a king, ages past."

"His tomb then?"

"No," she says simply.

"Then who's?"

"In it he who awakened, sleeps, never to sleep again."

"I do not understand," I say with a shrug.

"No matter," she says. "It is the center."

"The center of what?"

"All."

"Your words are an enigma, Yakshi."

She first questions the unfamiliar word, and then laughs as comprehension dawns, and in her melodious voice there is none of the questioning young girl. She is ageless and beyond the confines of time.

"I speak to you in metaphors," she explains. "The stupa, it is the center of the universe, but then again, so is where you now stand, and here, beneath my tree."

"They are all the center?" I ask.

"As are all places where the divine is perceived."

"*Axis mundi*," I say, comprehending.

"Now it is I who does not understand," she says.

"I think you understand more than you say."

"Words are words. They are part of the illusion. Truth exists beyond the words. How can mere words describe that which is beyond all forms?" she asks.

I have no answer. Only questions.

"But words are all we have," I say. "How else shall we express ourselves?"

"Perhaps you are correct," she says. "Perhaps not. Words can illuminate. They can also deceive."

"I do not understand."

"The truth of the universe is poetry, which is metaphor. Reduce metaphor to history, poetry to prose, and words deceive. Wars are fought over history. The form of one land's God is not another's, though both speak of the same truth, even born of the same book. Martyrs die and saints kill for the perceived rightness of their histories. Countries and peoples divide when they cannot agree on the prose. I choose to see the poetry in all."

"You are a scholar?" I ask.

She looks at me with a tilt of her head.

"I am a seeker of truth, like you."

I indicate the cardinal gate. "Do you guard this place?" I ask.

She looks at me as if considering how to answer and I feel as if the source of all life embraces me in her goodness.

"I am of this place."

"You live here then?" I need to know this coal-haired Kali.

"I am here," she says without further explanation.

I have traveled far. I have witnessed many customs and sights both strange and new, but I have never seen such abundance of life in such a lovely form.

Yakshi moves beneath her tree. One arm entwines like a bracket support, the other reaching for a branch above, as if plucking a star from the umbrella sky. The swelling of her arching curves is echoed by the undulating strand of pearls between her breasts. A golden ornamental girdle pulls low at her hips, framing the lotus of her sex. She leans daringly and with the heel of her foot she kicks behind at the illuminating tree, striking it with life infusing force. It flowers at her touch. Like dangling fruit she is ripe, voluptuous, and full. In her the cosmic waters meet the celestial realm. I have traveled far to find her. She is the poetry I seek.

"You are an epiphany," I exclaim.

"I am a metaphor," she smiles.

Arriving Women

Sandro Botticelli
Birth of Venus
c. 1482
tempera on canvas

Love floats as if on a gilded scallop shell. Jade waves scull towards a sandy shore, licking at my feet. Uncounted tiny grains wash away beneath my toes, with each receding wave causing me to feel the unsteady earth while she approaches in a state of casual modesty. The windy seas carry her to me, yet I am the one adrift, seeking sure footing where even the ground gives way before her beauty.

Her head tilts in silent acknowledgement of my presence, yet her face is serene. Long auburn hair eddies downward to her hand that clutches it at her sex, concealing and revealing. Her other hand is at her breast in a languid putica pose. I am dazzled and reverenced by her milky flesh, Simonetta's flesh. She is a new land born of an unknown sea. She is the discovery of new worlds to be mapped and explored.

It has been so long. I all but gave up on ever finding one such as her, one with whom I could spend eternity. Life has been a succession of seductions, false romances promising fulfillment, but delivering only empty gratifications that could not last. And now that she is here I wonder at my worthiness.

Her arrival is mythic and seductive. Her innocence radiates. Simonetta's gift is a birth of purity and beauty, her arrival ripe with promise.

"How long have you been waiting?" she asks, the morning sun highlighting her unflawed cheek.

"A lifetime," I answer. My voice sounds unfamiliar to me, deep and hoarse, as if emanating from the center of my being, a place untouched until this daughter of the sky came ashore gifting my tided life with a giving of her all.

Her tone is gentle as the summer breeze.

"You haven't known me for a lifetime."

But I have. Hers is the image of woman whose beauty transcends the deceiving contours of the physical and proclaims the splendor of her nature.

"I've known of you for ages past," I boldly proclaim.

"Have you? So much for the appearance of youth." She places her hand on her hips, removing the sting from her reproach.

It is time for an artful retreat.

"You are the embodiment of beauty, youthful to the eye, mature in the perfection of grace."

She is delighted by my words.

"Hah! Well played Giacomo. You at once stroke my vanities and ease my insecurities."

"I perceive no insecurities."

"Ah, if only that were so. You see me as I arrive and a picture captures your imagination, as if I was forever held in this state like a crowding delight in a Florentine gallery. It is an illusion. I see every change, every alteration. Age and life, Giacomo, they touch us all."

"I see only malleable perfection, each minute change a new chance to experience a new beauty."

"You see too much in me. I may not live up to your expectations. It is a long fall from an Olympian mount."

"I do not see enough." My words betray the anticipation I feel. "There are worlds you have yet to reveal."

"Now I know you exaggerate," she replies. "I come to you bare of anything, save my hope and love."

Love. I stand on consecrated ground, between the waning line of water's shore and a baldachin of orange-scented trees, where each stem and leaf is lined in gold. Or is it the sacred grove of the Hesperides, laden with the golden fruit of eternity? If I bite this fruit will I find eternal life?

"You are an arrival worth waiting for," I say.

"Are we back to the passing of time then?" she asks with a gleam in her eye.

"Only in regret for that which has passed without you, and joy for what is yet to come."

"Well answered, Giacomo. Time is an unforgiving sibling, yet without its passing vengeance we would not be meeting here, now."

I muse openly. "Cronos castrates Heaven's vault and timely love is born."

I look beyond Simonetta's wake to the seething foam from whence she sprang. Waves, diminutive beneath her feet, echo the mons above of her legs and I am wrapped again in the reflection of her grace.

Zephyr plays at Simonetta's hair and I feel the warmth of fair Chloris's breath upon my brow. In my mind I detect roses fall, scattered by their whispering currents, each adorned with a golden heart. They are blossoms of the perfect love that came into being with the arrival of this Venus bare.

"Would it surprise you to know that I have been waiting for you?" she asks.

"You? Waiting for me?"

"Do you think me so different in my longing? What you see in me I cherish in you. The chase, the games, these things are fun, of a sort, in our youth, but they wear. It is the sad person who sees in only these the aim of life. They will never know happiness. They will never be whole. They think they are experiencing life, but what they miss is the experience of being alive. It is I who has been waiting for you."

I cannot help but shake my head in bewilderment.

"I am not the one descended from the heavens," I say.

"Don't you know, Giacomo? Heaven is not a place. Eternity is not a time. They are here. They are now."

She steps ashore and into my waiting embrace. In her, all time dissolves. We love with a passion I have never known. Is this the eternal moment of the Hesperides' promise?

But even eternity must give way to time's adamantine sickle. In the future is a ready nymph adorned in spring flowers, a garland of myrtle and sash of roses beneath her breasts, waiting to wrap her garment around this daughter of the sky. Perhaps we are not meant to look upon love unclothed, merely touch her beauty in a single moment of forever.

Chapter Two

"*I*n the name of all that's holy, Giacomo, what did you tell him now?"

Zanetta was staring in at the rousing Casanova, filling the low beamed doorway with her arms akimbo, fists resting on her hips.

"What?" he stammered in his disorientation. "What is it?" he muttered.

"Oh, don't 'What is it?' me," she shot back. "You know damn well it is me and you know damn well what I'm talking about."

"Oh, Zanetta dear. What's wrong?" Giacomo eyed his niece through a feigned expression of waking confusion.

Zanetta responded with something close to a growl and strode into the room.

"What's wrong? What's wrong! You know damn…"

"Zanetta! Whatever it is there is no cause to come in here swearing like a Corsican pirate."

"Hmph!" she sniffed.

"Please, dear girl, help me up. I am at rather a disadvantage lying here like a workworn courtesan at dawn."

"Something you would know about, I should think!" she snapped back.

Zanetta moved to the bed and lifted the old man forward, propping pillows behind him, making great show of punching the down cushions into place, while at the same time taking care to be gentle with her uncle.

"There," she said smartly, once he was settled in. "Is that better?"

"Yes," he shifted some more, bracing himself for what he knew was coming. "Yes, thank you."

"Good." The sarcastic solicitude left her voice. "Then maybe now you will tell me what you have been saying to Lorenzo."

"Lorenzo? Nothing. I, we, that is, we just talked, like we always do. What has gotten into you?"

"No, not like you always do. You said something. Told him something."

"I said many things," Giacomo replied as if innocent of any storytelling that could merit her disapproval.

Zanetta sank into the chair beside Giacomo's bed, crossed her arms, and began tapping her foot in a rapid staccato.

"Honestly my dear, I haven't a clue what you are talking about."

"The women, Giacomo. I am talking about the women."

"What women?" He was toying with her now.

"You know perfectly well what women. Last night Lorenzo came down going on and on about someone on a swing and a huntress bathing, and even some woman you met in the Orient. You've never even been to the Orient!" she exclaimed, her voice rising, and then seemed to reconsider.

"Have you?"

"Ah, yes, I can see how that might have upset you, given that you have made your feelings on the subject of my memoirs quite well known. But honestly, Zanetta, it wasn't like that."

"Wasn't it?"

"No. I mean, yes, Lorenzo came to me last night and asked me about the women in my life."

"So you told him? Isn't it enough that you let him read all about your sordid past? Did you have to start filling in the gaps?"

Giacomo laughed a gentle laugh and reached out for his niece's hand.

"Lorenzo is seventeen. He wants to know."

"He is just a boy," she sniffed.

Giacomo shook his head.

"No, he's not your little boy anymore. He is quite grown up and ready for the world."

"But that's just it, he's not ready. Not yet!"

Giacomo took a deep breath before answering.

"I seem to recall a girl of only sixteen, headstrong, determined, fully convinced she held the reins on life, marrying the man of her dreams, setting out to establish her own life."

"It's not the same. Times were different."

"Times are always different, my dear, but people? People remain much the same as ever they were."

"I was young."

"Too young?" he asked.

Zanetta slightly shook her head before gathering herself.

"You shouldn't be telling him more of your lurid stories," she said without conviction.

"I can assure you Niece, I am leaving the lurid parts out." He smiled.

After a quiet interlude, Giacomo asked softly, "Now tell me, what is really troubling you?"

He kept his gaze on Zanetta who, after several moments appeared to slump deeper into the chair.

"I'm tired Giacomo. I am so tired."

"You work yourself too hard," he said. "You try to do too much."

"No, that's not it," she replied.

"Zanetta, you take care of this family, all of my business dealings, and now you have me to care for. That is more than enough to make anyone tired. And as far as I can tell, you haven't let up on your other good works, a sick neighbor here, a friend in need there. You are wearing yourself too thin."

"I'm tired Giacomo, but not just because I am worn out. I am tired of life."

That was it. His concerned observations on his niece summed up in one telling confession.

"Yes," he replied simply.

Zanetta looked up, startled at the response.

"What?"

"I see that what you say is true. And it has been true for quite some time. Oh, you go through all the motions of someone engaged in their activities, but you aren't really, are you? You are sleepwalking through life."

"I just don't want Lorenzo making the same mistakes I did," she said, "or Heaven forbid, the same mistakes you made!"

Giacomo laughed out loud at this.

"Lorenzo will make his own mistakes, rest assured."

"That's hardly comforting."

"Zanetta, I am an old man and by virtue of having lived longer than most I have made more mistakes than most, but we cannot confine young Lorenzo because we fear he might experience what every human experiences, the lessons of life."

"Yes, but do they have to be the lessons of your life?" she asked with a roll of her eyes.

"Who are we really talking about here? Lorenzo or you?"

"Me?"

"What are these great mistakes you so fear Lorenzo might emulate?"

"You mean if he avoids turning into you?" she asked, the sarcasm creeping back into her voice.

"Just so."

Zanetta hesitated and Giacomo could tell she was weighing whether or not to confess the real reasons for her concerns.

"I was too young Giacomo. I thought I was in love. I thought I was ready for life."

"Weren't you?"

"I wasn't ready."

"You were in love," he said. "Your husband was a good man. You were happy. He gave you Lorenzo."

"And then he died." Her voice was flat.

"Yes, he died, far too soon. You were his queen. He would not want you to feel this way."

"I was too young. I was foolish and naive." Tears began welling in her eyes.

"You were sublime."

She let go of Giacomo's hand and fished for a kerchief from her pocket.

"Oh Giacomo! You always do that."

"Do what?"

"Say something that comforts and confuses all at the same time. What does that even mean, sublime?"

Giacomo thought for a moment before answering.

"Your husband would have gone to the edge of the world for you. You were his divine in the tabernacle. You were his bliss. And then he died.

"You weren't too young for love, Zanetta. You were too young for loss. We always are."

Zanetta dabbed her eyes and composed herself.

"And now I am tired. Old, worn out, and tired," she said. "I could sleep for an eternity."

"Hmph. Do you forget to whom you are speaking? And you don't even have the decency to look chagrinned. Old and tired indeed. You are still sublime."

"Me? Look at me!"

Giacomo did look. Zanetta did look tired, but it was an exhaustion that ran deeper than the expression on her face or the weight she appeared to bear upon her slender shoulders.

"I see a beautiful woman, not yet old."

"You think every woman is beautiful. It's what makes you such a charming lech," she replied with a sniff.

"Perhaps, but what I say is true. You are still beautiful."

"My hair," she said. "Look at my hair."

Giacomo assayed her hair, pinned up behind her head, loose curls dangling down the sides and back. It was still deep brown, albeit with dozens of gray strands coloring the flow.

"I see hair that shimmers with silver threads, like filaments of moonlight readying a halo for your crown."

Zanetta snorted.

"And the wrinkles?" she added.

Giacomo could see the tiniest of wrinkles at the corners of his niece's eyes, and a relaxing of tone at her neck and jaw.

"I see the rewards of the years of laughter you enjoyed with your son."

Now it was Zanetta's turn to laugh.

"You really are a luscious old fool, Giacomo. No wonder Mother tolerated you so."

"Your mother adored me," he added.

"Yes, she did. I miss her."

"So do I," Giacomo nodded. "You know, she named you after our mother, a most formidable woman. An actress. Very much frowned upon, but she was determined to forge her own way in life, and so she did. How different from her your mother was. A rose from among the thorns."

He looked again at his niece, trying to see some of his beloved sister in her, but it was not to be seen in her countenance. She looked nothing like her mother. No, he thought, she has the crispness of her father's features, strong and angular. And yet, what appeared severe in her father was softened and attractive in the daughter.

She was quite unlike her mother in other ways as well. Giacomo recalled that while his sister was open, warm, and trusting to a fault, Zanetta was, here too, more like her father, reserved and even aloof. This, Giacomo knew, was just a perception harbored by those who did not take the time to get to know her, assuming of course that she allowed them the time. Giacomo knew that his niece could be quite matter of fact in her demeanor, and even appear cold at times, but this was not the case. Zanetta was a woman of deep passions and emotions. So potent were these in her that she feared to let these fires be seen by others, and so she kept them in reserve, save for those closest to her.

"Sleeping eternal in a ring of fire," he murmured without realizing he was speaking aloud.

"What?" Zanetta asked.

Giacomo stared back quizzically.

"You said, 'Sleeping eternal in a ring of fire.'"

"Did I? Well, I was just thinking of Brynhildr. She was a goddess. Teutonic. She was brave, giving, yet severe at times, not unlike some others I could mention, but won't."

"A wise decision," she said.

Giacomo continued, "She was made mortal and cast into an eternal sleep, surrounded by shielding flames."

"Eternal sleep. Sounds nice," Zanetta said.

"Yes, well, between the two of us, you and me, this has become the house of sleep, and time has sealed us away."

Zanetta sat up straight and shoved the embroidered kerchief back into her pocket, as if she suddenly remembered she had something else to do.

"Maybe, but it hasn't sealed Lorenzo away, and your stories are not helping. Please Giacomo, can you ease off on the stories just a bit. Lorenzo is young, and I don't want to see him running off to be his great uncle."

Giacomo considered her words. Zanetta may indeed fear the time is at hand for Lorenzo to step beyond the bounds of hearth and home, though they both knew he would not write a new volume in the memoirs of the great Casanova. This is not who Lorenzo was. But Giacomo also knew that things would change. They always did. There was no stopping the force of life, only, perhaps, influencing its course, and there was a course he desperately needed to influence. No other could write new volumes of Casanova, but when he was gone a void must yet be filled, and he had chosen his replacement. She must be awakened to the role.

"There are things I need to say, Zanetta, and while time may have sealed each of us away, it is not eternal. My time is running short."

Zanetta dismissed him with a wave of her hand.

"You're too devious and sinful to die any time soon," she said.

"Moments ago you asked me to look at you. Now I ask you to look at me."

Their eyes locked.

"I am dying."

"No…"

"I am afraid so. And you know it too."

"I know no such thing! And I won't hear any more of your foolish ramblings. It's all that miasmic night air coming in off the canal, addling your brain, because you are too … too stubborn to be sensible and sleep with the window closed."

"Time, Zanetta. There is not much time."

Zanetta stood abruptly and strode to the door, turning back sharply.

"You are a scoundrel and a libertine, Giacomo Casanova! And if you must keep recounting your sordid affairs, please at least have the decency to censor your delight in reliving them."

She turned away and slammed the door behind her.

Giacomo sank back into his pillows and said to the closed door, "Sleeping eternal in a ring of fire."

Giacomo's spirits rose whenever Lorenzo arrived for his daily visits. They took on added significance after the previous evening, with Lorenzo's open expression of desire to learn more of his great uncle's history. Giacomo was well aware that the initial interest for Lorenzo was activated by thoughts and feelings that came naturally to a young man of Lorenzo's age, but it was an opportunity more than he could have hoped for. It wasn't until his earlier visit with Zanetta, however, that he realized his grandnephew's curiosity would be the key to achieving his one great remaining desire before he died. Despite Zanetta's fears, Giacomo would see his successor prepared.

He relished the exchanges between him and his grandnephew with the awareness of one who knows such visits are to be few and then no more.

Lorenzo was nearly breathless when he came in for his visit that evening.

"Uncle, are you well?" he asked in a rush.

Of course he wasn't well, he was dying, but Giacomo knew that what the young man really meant was, are you well enough to tell me more stories.

"Well enough," the old man replied.

He motioned for Lorenzo to come forward and sit himself beside the bed. He regarded his grandnephew for a few moments.

"You have the look of a young man hungry for adventure."

"I was wondering, Uncle, about the women you described. I don't recall them from your memoirs."

"Ah, so you noticed. Yes, well, not everything in a man's life can be written. The most precious can only be experienced, and maybe, only maybe, told."

"Then these women, they were precious to you?"

Giacomo mulled this over before answering.

"The most precious, yes."

Lorenzo seemed to consider this new information and though every moment now had the import of a rare commodity, Giacomo was content to let him approach the subject in his own course. Lorenzo was drawn and Giacomo had his boon to deliver.

"I am not sure I understand," Lorenzo said. "If they were so precious to you, why didn't you write about them in your books? You told me those books were your life."

He glanced at the top of the chest of drawers where his twelve volumes stood at attention like soldiers arrayed at parade.

"After a fashion, yes, that is true, but one's entire life cannot be fully told, even if it were to comprise a hundred such volumes."

"Mine could," Lorenzo said. "In one volume."

"Perhaps, but you have much life to live. An entire universe lies before you and you have no idea what treasures await."

"I doubt I will ever see as much as you have."

"No? I think you may see more. Much more. The world is bright and new and you will see wonders that I never imagined."

"I have read about some of your wonders."

"Ah, yes, back to the women."

"Why haven't you talked about them, the women you told me about before now?" Lorenzo asked.

"I suppose," said the old man, "because you never asked. And I didn't think you were ready."

"But I am now?" Lorenzo eagerly asked.

"That is hard to say. Only you can know that, and only after you know that you know."

"Uncle, you are talking in circles."

"Yes, well, it is something of a circle, isn't it? Life is a rounding way to be puzzled and discovered. Sadly, most people muddle their way along the well-worn public byways, never looking side to side, and miss the partially hidden paths leading them to life's great mysteries, and discoveries. What lies beyond is the great mystery yearning to be discovered."

"Did you take those paths, Uncle?"

"Oh yes," he replied with a bow of his head. "There was a midway time when I found myself off the well-travelled and blinding path, alone in a dark forest grove. It is a fearful place, but necessary if you ever wish to see life's wonders."

"Where is this place?" Lorenzo asked.

"You have put your finger on the point, my boy. It is no place. It is a forest within. Life's greatest journeys are not out there, in some distant land. They are in here," he said, tapping his chest, "and in here," he pointed to his head.

"But if it is inside you, how is it fearful?"

"Ah, how so indeed? We create our greatest monsters, and only we can defeat them. I answered the call."

"And that is when you met the women you described?"

Giacomo raised an eyebrow at his grandnephew.

"You are thinking of it too literally."

Giacomo watched as Lorenzo tried to make sense of his words. He tried to explain.

"Do you see the valance crowning the posts of my bed?"

"I've seen it hundreds of times," Lorenzo replied.

"You have noticed it, but have you ever really seen it?" he asked.

Lorenzo sat back in the chair, craning his head upwards to get a better view of the tapestried fabric frieze surrounding the top of Giacomo's bed. Multi-colored threads wove in and out to create a narrative that stretched from bedpost to bedpost. Age showed in the woven cloth, threads frayed here and there, the once bright colors faded to muted hues, the valance sagging slightly in the middle stretches between the corner posts. The narrow running backdrop was of forested trees, with medieval horsemen riding its perimeter. One horseman, in the center of the expanse between the posts at the head and foot of the bed was turning inward, riding into the darkened woods. Lorenzo knew that each side had a similar scene.

"It's a hunting scene," Lorenzo announced.

"Is it?" Giacomo asked. "What are they hunting?"

Lorenzo looked again. Giacomo was amused as the young man first searched then registered that despite the presence of men on horseback, there were no traditional signs of a hunt.

"Well, I mean, men are riding around a forest, and some of them are riding into it."

"Ah, now you are beginning to see. Why do the horsemen mostly pass the forest by, while but a few enter its realm? Never mind, I will tell you why. It is only a few who can hear the forest's call."

"The forest's call?"

"The forest is life's unknown abyss, dangerous and dark. One must not enter lightly. Each knight entered the forest at a point he had chosen, where it was the darkest and there was no way or path. It is the legend of the British King Arthur, sending his knights off on a quest to find the elusive *Sangral*, the Holy Grail."

"Is that the scene on your bed?" Lorenzo asked.

"Indeed, it is," Giacomo replied. "It is always a reminder to me."

"Reminding you of what?"

"The need to listen, to be ready for life's calls."

"Is this what you did, Uncle?"

"I tried," he said simply.

"And what did you find?" Lorenzo asked.

"Why, the Holy Grail, of course."

Lorenzo laughed with his uncle.

"Uncle, how did you, I mean, the women, you make it all sound so easy, so exciting."

"Exciting, yes. Romance is always exciting, especially when it is real and new. But easy? No, love is never easy."

Lorenzo fidgeted in the chair beside him, picking at the gold braid at the edge of the velvet, worn to a dusty rose that upholstered the arm.

"What is it?" Giacomo prodded.

"What, I mean, who was the most exciting?" his grandnephew asked, his face reddening at the question.

Giacomo chuckled. The question was not unexpected. Lorenzo was a young man enticed, and Giacomo's tales were a siren's lure.

"Hmmm," he mused. "That is difficult to say. I suppose that depends on how ready I was for the love to come."

A confused expression creased the young man's brow.

"You have to be ready for love?"

"One must be prepared for the adventure. The forest is dark and deep."

"Prepared? How so?"

"Romance is a quest, and the hero must always prepare himself for the quest."

"The hero?"

"Yes, quite. Heroes prepare themselves for quests into the dangerous unknown, and what is more dangerous and unknown than the ways of love? Only the brave of heart, someone willing to suffer the torments that inevitably accompany the joys of romance will ever survive to know true love."

"I never thought love would be dangerous," Lorenzo said.

"Dangerous, yes, and exciting," Giacomo replied.

"If it so dangerous, why would anyone pursue it?" Lorenzo asked.

Giacomo laughed more deeply than his fragile body was accustomed to before replying, "Did you forget about the exciting part?"

Women Who Dance

Aubrey Beardsley
Salome with the Head of John the Baptist
illustration from *Salome* by Oscar Wilde
1892
ink on paper

"Shall I dance?" Salome asks.

"You dance too fast," I say.

"I'll dance slowly."

"You are too wild for me."

"Isn't that how you like me?"

I ask her, "Wild?"

She smiles seductively.

"It is an ancient dance. Perhaps you know it?"

"Am I so old?" I ask.

"Not too old, I should think."

"Then why an ancient dance?"

"Sometimes those are the best."

She moves to a rhythm of undulating hip and inviting grind.

"Nice dance. Is that how the ancients danced?" I ask approvingly.

"Mmn hmn," she intones. "Some did."

"Anyone I know?"

"Inanna, for one. Did you know her?"

"I think she was a little before my time," I say.

"So I should hope," she says, "or I might be wasting mine."

"I can assure you, it is not wasted on me."

"You like it then? The dance that is."

"Those ancients were on to something," I say.

"Inanna knew her way. She was a goddess, after all."

"Knew her way to where?"

"The underworld."

Salome winks her sensuous delight.

"Is that where she learned to dance? It would explain much."

"So they say.   Through seven portals, an article of clothing discarded for passage through each"

She peels away a scarf and drops it at my feet.

"A revealing dance then?" I ask.

"Just so. Seven portals, seven veils."

"A dance of seven veils. Sounds enticing."

"In a manner of speaking. Shall I demonstrate?"

An open blouse drops to her feet.

"I like where this dance is going."

"I thought you might."

"You are taking me to the underworld then?"

"Under. On top. There is pleasure to be found in each."

"Are we still talking about dancing?" I ask.

"That depends. Will you give me what I ask?"

"What do you ask?"

"Nothing more than you are willing to give."

"Seems a dangerous bargain." I consider my options, but only one appeals.

"I fear I'll lose my head," I say.

"Which head?"

"I have only one head."

"That hasn't been my experience."

"You have me confused with someone else."

"I don't think so."

"I'm sure you do."

"Wasn't that you in my bed last night?" she asks. "He looked just like you, and he was more than willing to give me what I asked. Don't you recall?"

"It was me, I'm sure of it. It was very memorable, but with only one head," I reply.

A third silk drops.

"Like compass points, I saw two, one North and one South."

"I count only North."

"But you were thinking with only South."

"The North is larger."

"The South is more adamant."

"Then it betrays me."

"You don't like it then?"

"Not if it betrays me."

"Pity. I was quite fond."

"Of a traitor?"

"No traitor to me, or to you as I recall. Where the South led, you eagerly followed."

Four and five leave each leg bare.

She glides across the floor with graceful carriage, as if floating above a lily padded pond.

"Come back to bed," I ply.

"I'm dancing," she replies. "Where would Inanna be if she stopped midway down?"

"At just about the right location, if my calculations are correct. Come back to bed."

"Who's asking, North or South?"

"North while he can, but he'll be betrayed by the time you return."

"Hah. You are a battle, but in the end, I will win."

"What makes you think you will win?"

"Because you like the dance."

She laughs and continues.

"Mother was right about you," she says.

"Your mother hates me."

"Only because she knows you."

"She's never met me."

"She knows your type."

"I have a type?"

"You have a type."

"Pray, tell me."

"You are a lone voice, crying in the wilderness."

"And what am I crying?"

"Of one yet to come."

"You?" I ask.

Number six bares breasts, which arms and hands revealingly conceal.

"Hah! The North has fallen. The South rises again!"

"Come, civil me."

"You could use some civiling."

"That isn't even a real word."

"Oh? Who are you going to believe? You, without the blood to think, or Inanna, with or without her seven veils?"

"That's a tough choice for one who cannot think. You confuse me with your big words."

"I know lots of big words."

"Any that apply to me?"

"Mother says you are a harbinger."

"A hat seller?"

"That's a haberdasher."

"I could use a good hat."

"And a codpiece I dare say."

"What do I harbin?" I ask.

"Sin."

"Sounds about right. For or against?"

"Mother would warn you are for, but she's a hypocrite. She's no descending dove."

"How do you know?"

"I'm living proof."

The last veil falls.

I beckon her. "Born of sin, let's sin again."

"Do you even have a North with which to think anymore?"

She shoots me a mirthful look and skims her fingers across the heated rings of water in the waiting tub.

"What do you expect?" I reply. "I've been in a veritable desert."

"You are parched. You need water."

"I need you."

"I'm in the water."

I watch as first one silky leg and then the other step into the steam escaped wetness. Slyly she lowers herself and her body disappears beneath the depths. A curling finger entreats me and I obey. I am quickly at her side, my hands sliding across soap and flesh. A new dance has begun.

As I bathe her, Salome sings a song.

"J'ai baisé ta bouche,

"Iokanaan,

"J'ai baisé ta bouche."

"Suggestive song."

"I learned it in Sunday School."

"You went to Sunday School?"

"Only on Sundays."

"Is that where you learned about hat sellers?"

She licks her lips.

"It's where I learned about sin," she says.

"What did you learn?"

"I think you were mentioned."

"I'll baptize you."

"To cleanse me of my sins?"

"To make room for more."

"Careful," she warns, "you're about to lose your head."

"You dance too fast."

Sweet Women

Jean-Étienne Liotard
The Chocolate Girl
1744
oil on canvas

"I have heard it said that in the New World this was a deadly drink," she says in a voice full of sweet mischief.

"Not the best of enticements," I say, inspecting her tray suspiciously. I sniff at the piping liquid, its heady aroma filling the air between us.

Between us. What is it that is between her and me, aside from the refreshment she offers? Is it the drink I suspect, or is it her, this otherly woman?

Wars have been fought between our kin and kind. Our fathers were taught to hate and we are the inheritors of that divide. Never trust the monsters beyond the Alps, so I was told. They are not like us. They do not value life as we do. They do not value God as we do. They do not share the values that we do. They are below us. And yet, here she stands defying all that I was told.

"It's true, or so I hear," she continues. "Cultures far older than ours revered what you are about to drink."

"This deadly drink?" I ask.

She snickers at my discomfiture.

"The drink itself was not deadly. It is made from the extracts of a bean and was given to those whom they were about to sacrifice," she explains ominously. "Human sacrifice!"

"Oh, I am much relieved to hear it. Am I to be sacrificed then?"

She answers with a touch of mystery.

"After a fashion. To those distant peoples, the Incas I believe they were called, this was the food of the gods. A bittersweet draft of this was given to sanctify the souls of those who were about to lose their lives."

"A cheerful thought," I mutter. "It sounds bittersweet indeed."

"The way they served it, I suppose, but I think you will be pleasantly surprised. My version is milky smooth and sweet to the taste."

"Is that before or after the human sacrifice part?"

"It's good. Try it."

"I don't know," I say, my suspicions asserting themselves. "From the Incas you say? Weren't they some kind of savages?"

"Giacomo! I am surprised at you. How far have you ventured, how many new things have you seen, and now you turn your nose up at this? Wasn't it you who said that I should keep an open mind about you? Where is your open-mindedness now? Or was that all just a part of the seduction?"

"What? No, of course not," I protest.

Or was it?

It's true, I have been to many new lands, visited many new cultures. Why then am I so resistant to what she offers now. I harbor no prejudice against the Incas, whoever they may have been. At least none that I am aware of. Or is it that she offers it to me? She who embodies that which I was taught to hate.

How can this be? I don't hate her. She is lovely and intelligent and sweet. Her humors are my humors, her wants my wants, so how is she different.

In experiences, yes. In traditions, no doubt, but these are trivialities when set against the ways in which we are alike. Am I, a man who prides himself on his knowledge and taste of the world, so bigoted that he cannot accept in his heart that which he so readily lusts with other parts?

We are no different, she and I, not in the ways of humanity. Our differences are but costumes to be savored, not denied, but beneath the costumes we are of the same flesh and soul. The realization is hard. It is not she and her kin and kind that are below us, below me. It is I who am reduced.

"Would it help to know that those same savage peoples also believed the extract of this bitter bean was an aphrodisiac?" she asks seductively.

"It does promise a better ending for the drinker."

"I suppose it does," she agrees. "Will you taste what I have for you?"

There is comfort in the familiar. It is what we seek and, if not careful, it is the veil that blinds us to the wonders of the other. I choose to savor what I see and smell, this Swiss maid, *mes petite* Coco.

Taking the tray from her, I set it aside and turn my attention once again to what she truly has to give. She is a confection, tempting and indulgent. I wonder at what new surprises I will find.

I begin to unwrap this sweetest of treats. I peel her clothes like papers from a truffled cream. Her flesh is silky and soft like the most-savory soufflé delight.

In a thrice she stands before me, bare, a candied Lady Godiva, waiting to be devoured.

I kiss her, kisses upon kisses, and each kiss of hers dissolves into my mouth. A little satisfies, yet still I want more. I taste in her a richness that fills me with desire. If I am to be sacrificed, then let me first partake of her. Food of the gods.

I touch her, and she melts beneath my hands. I take her and together we consummate the sacrifice, the desserts of our flirtation.

For a time, we rest, my senses consumed as I consumed her. Time passes, and I know that I will forever recall our indulgent feast. At length she leans on one elbow.

"So, you like what I have to offer after all."

I prop myself up and see beyond the dividing Alps to the individual before me.

"You are different."

"Hmmm. Is that a good thing?"

"It is the best, especially when in all ways that really matter, we are the same."

Coco laughs in a velvety trill.

"Now will you drink?" she asks, proffering a cup of the still hot liquid.

I sip the heated chocolate, tentatively at first, then with increasing greed.

"Does it satisfy?" she asks delightedly.

"Delicious," I reply.

"Then you want more?"

I set the cup aside.

"And more," I pull her to me, "and more..."

Women in Reverie

Jean Auguste Dominique Ingres
Odalisque with a Slave
1842
oil on canvas

In Neoclassic splendor she drifts, as in a hashish haze, lounging on silken sheets. She is an academic's dream of romantic theme. I have waited for this time, a time I feared I had lost forever.

I look across the seraglio at the orientalizing tableau. She is a golden-haired image of anticipation, her lucent skin warming her bed with inviting glow.

It was a day not unlike this when I first saw Caroline strolling past the isolated court, forbidden to all but the women of the harem, turbaned eunuch guards, and me.

I was a young man then, given to desire and ever consumed with seeking its immediate gratification. It is the folly of youth, this inability to see beyond one's own urges. It saw me into trouble on more than one occasion and yet I still fell prey to its self-gratifying trap. I was immortal then, absent the sting of mortality's proximity as only youthful brash can be. And then I saw her and everything changed.

Aquamarine skies expansed overhead, touching the earth somewhere beyond trees and mounts. Feathered brushes of white floated across the arching sky, delicate clouds, like the wisps of flowing silk that now cling to Caroline's softly curving hip and thighs. The tinge of orange blossoms filled the air, mingling with hints of jasmine and coral petaled rose in a fragrant heady dance. It was a cloistered abode set within and apart from the bustling markets and denizens of this Eastern realm.

Beyond lay streets and alleys filled with pungent spices and burning coals, charred foods, tanning leather, labor's sweat, hay and waste of horse and hog and ox and sheep, each serving its master or awaiting the butcher's ax, stale perfume, lye drenched laundry, baking bread, soured milk, dust of grinding stone and smoke of blacksmith iron being beaten and forged. And with these came a thousand sounds, assaulting the ears in a cacophonous melee, laughter and cries, voices raised in bartering banter, the squeal and squall of fowl and man and dog and cart and all manner of industry, but none of these, not the sounds or smells or hustled day reached this separate world, this oasis of calm repose.

Caroline was a girl no longer a girl, but not yet aware of the woman she would become. I watched her pass, an earthen jug balanced on her head as she attended to her chores. There was no attempt to catch a young man's eye in this girl who set about her duties as she did each and every day. Hers was a ritual of tasks to be fulfilled, and this she did in daily obligation, unaware of her own allure.

I made it a point to learn her ritual. I knew when she would pass on her way to the cool Alhambra wells, convinced she never noticed the young scholar seated on a marble bench in the shadowed arcade, head buried in a scroll or book or quill in hand, never realizing that he was as oblivious to the studies before him as she was to his ever-growing attention.

In truth, I was not much older than she, though the age of boy felt to be a long distant past, one I had left behind before setting off to see the world and learn its mysteries. For Caroline, this was her world, this protected shell. She had not yet experienced the wonders and joys and frights and marvels of the world beyond. She was still a girl no longer a girl.

I did not plan our meeting. Or perhaps I did. I knew where she would be. I knew when the eyes of others would be elsewhere, and she would be free to speak, and maybe more.

"Hello," I said one day as she casually approached my unplanned walk across the gardens.

"Oh," she said, startled at the greeting, "hello."

She quickly lowered her eyes and the young girl appeared along with the young woman unaware of her maturing allure.

"You're Caroline, aren't you? The cook's daughter?"

She nodded her head, allowing a peek at me.

"I am Giacomo," I introduced myself.

"I know," she said.

Her words set off fireworks within me. She knew who I was? Everything I imagined about this girl was suddenly shifting.

"You do?" I asked somewhat incredulously.

"I've seen you reading your books," she explained. "You like to sit over there, in the shade of the colonnade." She pointed to my perch, my imagined blind.

"Ah, yes, it's a nice place to read," I fumbled for an explanation.

"You read a lot," she said, a statement of fact.

I smiled at this. "I suppose I do," though for the life of me I could not remember a thing I had read in weeks.

"What do you read?" she asked.

I was perplexed for an answer.

"My studies. You know, the philosophers, astronomy, histories."

"Do you ever read stories?" she asked, now giving me her full attention.

"What kind of stories?"

She shrugged slightly.

"I don't know, stories of heroes and ladies."

"Romances?" I suggested.

She shrugged again and diverted her eyes, but not so fast that I missed the color blushing he cheeks.

"Sometimes. Do you like romances?" I asked, feigning a boldness I did not entirely feel.

"Sometimes," she echoed my words.

A distant movement caught her attention, and mine.

"I had better be going," she said, turning to leave.

I watched as she started to walk away, not the walk of a young girl.

"Wait," I called. "Will I see you again?"

She hesitated and gave me a sidelong glance, the young woman fully replacing the girl.

"It depends. Will you be in the colonnade pretending to read again?" She laughed and walked away.

I knew then, as I know now, that she will be mine, and more than concubine.

Our meetings became a part of our daily rituals. Minutes, precious to us both were spent getting to know one another. I brought her tales of romances from books and little by little she revealed her own dreams of life beyond the cloistered walls, and romances awaiting her. Our days revolved around each meeting, a daily secret we kept, which meant that the entire court knew every detail.

It was little surprise then, when the old sage Roques took me aside. He guided my studies, and said nothing of my apparent interest in the romances I sought in the expansive court libraries.

"She is in love with you," he said.

"In love with me? Who?" I asked in my most innocent voice, to which he only laughed.

"I am not a blind fool. Young Caroline, of course. And so you have a decision to make."

"What kind of a decision?"

Roques mulled this over before responding.

"A woman new can be a brittle delicacy. Touched too soon and she is a like a flower withdrawn into the cold confines of darkened night, neglected too long and she scatters to the winds like a flower spent.

"She is in love and will give herself to you, this is no mystery. But what will happen to her should you rush into this passion you feel? You must ask yourself, are you ready for the commitment of love, or are you merely interested in the momentary satisfaction of lust? Would you steal her future from her by denying her the commitment you are not yet ready to give?"

"But I am ready," I said.

"Are you?" he asked in return. "Youth seeks happiness of the now. Maturity seeks happiness of the forever. Which do you seek?"

"But what if I lose her? What if she does not love me later?"

"That is the risk of love over lust," he explained, and my world was cast into a torrent of despair.

Many such conversations followed, and with each I realized he was right. I loved Caroline, but our futures were more than bedded sport. If I ever wished to truly have her, I would have to wait until we were both ready, even if waiting meant I might lose her. I lost any vestiges of my own boyhood with the lessons and love in the cloistered court.

Our goodbyes were furtive and painful and buried in devouring kisses and hands barely restrained. She cried, but I knew, for the first time in my life, that short-term pleasure was not good enough for one who wished for lifelong happiness. It was a lesson neither of us wanted to embrace in those moments of goodbye.

Time passed, as it always does, and I returned as I knew I would. The world had made me a different man, but my love never waned. I returned, and Caroline was waiting for me. Ours was a love that survived the denial of momentary lust.

Caroline has blossomed into her potential. She knows her dreams and is ready for the world beyond this haven court. This time is ours and we are ready for the commitment of love.

A eunuch strums a lute, plaintive notes harmonizing with the bubbling rhythm of a nearby fountain and the song of birds lured to the effulgent gardens.

Line defines her Neoclassic beauty.

She does not know that I see her, or so I think until I recall a girl no longer a girl, but not yet aware of the woman she would become, all too aware of a boy pretending to read in the shadows of a colonnade. I leave her to her reverie. Tonight she will be brought to me, a sultan's bed, but she will be no mere dalliance. I know the woman she has become. I have watched and waited, and it is I who am slave to this odalisque, my harem bride.

Women of Names

Théodore Chassériau
The Toilet of Esther
1841
oil on canvas

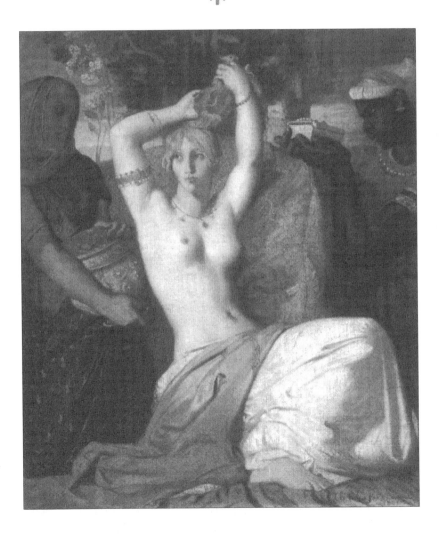

Her name is Esther and she is my Persian star.

She came to me through the good offices of her cousin, to whom I owe my life. It was he, Mordecai who brought the girl Hadassah, she who would become Esther, to me. She is not the first, but now she is all.

Vashti was before her, a spouse unfaithful to her position. In her there was no unity, no meeting of man and wife. To her I was but a means of position, opening doors to her options. She would not, could not see me as one to love. Such is the nature of arrangement. I bid her come to me. She would not. Her refusal was the end of us, but then came Esther. It is said she is the beauty of a kingdom, and I believe it to be so.

Vashti elicited neither love nor jealousy. Her ways were known, her ambitions expected. Not so with Ester and for this some feared. A good heart and generous soul are alien in the Court. They cannot understand one whose interests are not oneself. Especially Hammon, he who would be my advisor. He would betray me, betray all in the pursuit of his own interests, even if it meant the slaughter of a people, were it not for Esther.

I look on as Esther casually piles her spun gold hair in preparation for the banquet to come. Her attention is averted, her pale blue eyes taking in movements far removed from her immediacy. It is an aspect of her, this burning curiosity that intrigues me so. She hungers to see all around her, to know all around her. It is not idle curiosity. For her knowledge has a purpose.

Even after the time we have spent together, her beauty arrests me. Bare to the waist, Esther lifts her arms, firm, strong and smooth above her head. Her skin is like cream, befitting a princess or a queen. Her bridal gown is folded loosely across her lap, soon to be fitted to her. I am as captivated by her now as I was the first time I saw her.

"You shouldn't be here," she chides. "They say it is bad luck to see the bride before the ceremony."

"I have seen you before," I say in a conspirator's voice, "quite intimately as I recall."

"So you have." Pleasant memories are reflected in her eyes.

"You are truly beautiful," I say to her.

"Thank you," she says with neither conceit nor false humility.

Two handmaids attend her, one presenting her with jewels to adorn her neck.

"And keen," I add to the compliment. "You notice everything, don't you?"

"I notice enough," she says with just a hint of coyness.

It was Esther's eye that saw Hammon for what he truly was, an opportunist. It is a weak man who must destroy others to elevate himself. Esther saw this, and by seeing she saved a race. She is more than lover. She is trusted.

Esther's clear blue eyes meet mine.

"You have renewed my life," I say.

"Our life," she amends. "We are to be wed."

"Our life," I repeat. "Yes. A ceremony you mark with a new name."

She smiles.

"Is that not the tradition from times long past?" she asks. "I once read that Esther was the name given to the high priestess chosen to represent the goddess in the King's ceremonial marriage rite."

"And so you take this name?"

Esther considers.

"It seems appropriate."

"If I recall my lessons, however, didn't they used to kill the surrogate king after consummation?"

She gives me a bemused look.

"Perhaps, long ago, but I think you have nothing to worry about. Fortunately for you we no longer regard the king as a sacrificial necessity."

"A dubious honor indeed," I agree.

"Old ways or not, we will have a consecrated marriage."

"And you will be my Esther, my Astarte, my Ishtar."

"I will be her, and all of them, for you."

"You are my greatest honor. Just the same though, I am pleased that I will not be sacrificed after the ceremony."

She runs her tongue seductively over her lips.

"Actually, I had something more pleasurable in mind."

"I see."

"So you do," she says. "You see more now than you should. You shouldn't be here."

"Yes, you said that before. Very well, I shall be content to wait."

Turning, I head towards the door.

"Husband to be," she says.

I enjoy the sound of that. I give her my full attention.

"Thank you."

"For what?" I ask.

"When I first came to you, when Mordecai first brought me to your attention, I did not think to fall in love with you."

"Is this a confession?"

"Of my love? You already have that. No, what I mean to say is that I feared emerging in Vashti's shadow. She was first."

"First in time, not first in love."

"I know that, now. But it was a daunting thing."

"So why are you thanking me? It is I who should be thanking you."

"You listened," she says simply.

"And this merits thanks?"

"Growing up in my uncle's household, my voice was seldom heard. Mordecai is a good man, a noble man, but he is a man of his times. And like men of his time, he loved me like family, but with a purpose. I was, like so many other women of his time, a card to be played when the opportunity was ripe."

"And I was that opportunity?"

She nods.

"Esther, this is the world's way."

"But not your way," she says.

I consider the import of her words.

"No, you are not a commodity. You are wise and your heart is great. I would be a fool to ignore what walks before me."

"You listened to me."

"You advised me."

"You have advisors."

"But none like you. Hammon learned as much."

"I had to say something. Death was on his mind," she says.

"And in speaking you saved a nation. Speak always, Esther."

"It is not the world's way."

"You are my world, and it is our way."

"Thank you."

I prepare to leave and as I do I hear Esther stand as her attendants arrange her gown. Without further comment I depart, knowing that once evening comes I will experience the full passion of my Persian star.

Modern Women

Gustave Klimt
The Kiss
1907-08
oil and gold leaf on canvas

It is the end of one century, the beginning of another, and the modern waits. It is a golden period of glittering change and innovation. It is an era of the new. I am not ready.

Emilie is with me, as she always has been, but somehow seems far away. She is by my side as we lie in bed or address the mundanities of life, but inwardly she has moved beyond me. I am left behind.

"I am not the same girl I was when you found me," she says in one of our many confrontations stemming from my inability to see her as she is, now. "Things are not as they were."

What things? I am the same as ever I was. How did this grow beyond my control?

"What do you mean? Don't you love me anymore?"

It is a cheap ploy, invoking love as a bludgeon. I am ashamed even as I say it, but I do not back down from the impossible question.

Do I really want to know?

Emilie looks at me with caring eyes. She knows I love her, as I know she loves me. It is not love she needs, it is understanding.

"It isn't that, Giacomo. Of course I love you. It's just that I am older now. I want more out of life than to simply ride on your achievements, your wants, your visions. You have shown me the world, and I am grateful for that, but there are things I want to accomplish on my own as well."

What things? The question repeats.

"But we have accomplished so much together," I say.

Emilie shakes her head.

"No, you have accomplished, and I have celebrated at your side. I cannot continue to only see the world through you."

I try to absorb what she is saying. My life has been a scripted play, each move planned and achieved. Emilie has been a part of that script, until now. This was never planned for. This was never scripted.

"I love you Giacomo, but things are different now. Not in my love for you, but in what I want out of life."

I am sullen at her words.

"Actually Giacomo," she adds, "it is because of you that I need to change. I never would have known the world in such abundance were it not for you. It is because of you that I want more out of life. Don't you see?"

Actually, I do see, but it is difficult to abandon my script. Why do I cling to the innocent, yet unfulfilled Emilie so? Why do I resist seeing in her what I take as a given for me.

"I am my own woman, Giacomo," she says, and I know that I must either accept this change, no, this realization or lose her forever.

With change comes uncertainty; with uncertainty comes decadence for some, revelation for others, and for some, perhaps, both. I try to view the world through her eyes and it is a different world I see.

Through the streets of Vienna we stroll, Emilie and I, often stopping to absorb the Art Nouveau world blossoming around us. Flowing organic forms compete with the rigid industrialization of new tools, new ideas, new Vienna. It is more than steel and smoke and invention, it is a new way of perceiving. We behold the inner workings of our creations. Gears and drives move the world, and we strive to keep pace. Even the interior of the mind unfolds in Vienna's new science. Human gears and human drives are explored. They are the new public preoccupation.

Emilie is my preoccupation. She is the arousal of the unconscious. Her awakening echoes the transforming world around us. She is the new religion.

I take her to a wildflower field at the edge of a precipice. The scent of new growth blossoms around us. I stand at the edge and am afraid. I, who has faced hardships of every vein, stood fast in battle, held onto hope in despair, am afraid. I am wrapped in medieval stasis, a relic of rigidity. My future lies below, in the dark chasm of the abyss, or beyond in a world anew, a world of change. In the distance we see Vienna, a bronze backdrop of distant lights, but we are alone, my new religion and I.

I am no fool, once I accept that I have been a fool. I realize am not losing a possession. I too will gain, if I can only let go and be unafraid. My script is not scripture.

It has taken me some time to get here, to this precipice with Emilie. Many times I have told her that I love her. Of this there is no doubt. Now I say the words that show her it is so."

"What is your dream?"

Emilie smiles at me and all fear vanishes.

"I thought you would never ask," she says with a tear in her eye.

We celebrate the primal urges of our new faith. She crowns me with a wreath of vines and I place a constellation of flowers in her hair. We kneel as in devotion, but our ceremony is to one another.

I nest her head in my hands, her fingers touching mine. Circles upon circles pattern her priestess gown, which I peel from her shoulders, revealing a sacrament of flesh. I wrap her in my robe and together we pattern a new icon. We are like a mosaic on Ravenna's walls. Byzantine physicality is made spirit under the flickering candle glow of a million tesserae. Emilie is the spirit of a new age, tangible beneath golden leaf and filigreed spirals of Viennese splendor.

Emilie is pliant to my touch. She curls her toes over the abyss, willing herself to trust my embrace. She tilts her head in abandon to the new faith. It is a time of change, the end of one century, the beginning of another. The modern awaits and in its celebration we return to the eternal. We kiss.

Chapter Three

$\mathcal{T}$he oversized book rested heavily on Zanetta's lap, as if the words themselves carried the weight of physicality.

"Shall we continue from where we left off," she had asked Giacomo after helping him with his breakfast and getting him situated in his bed, trying to alleviate the soreness that came with extended confinement.

In truth, she found the expansive poem by Dante to be difficult wading, but Giacomo reveled in it, often interrupting to explain some tidbit of Florentine history referenced or the story of this or that historical or mythological or literary figure that was being described. When she told Giacomo how difficult it was to understand without his verbal annotations, he laughed and told her not to worry, he would be her Virgil, taking great pleasure in the analogy. And so she would read, and he would interrupt, until he grew too tired to listen. At such times they would sit in silence, he resting, sometimes sleeping, she losing herself in her own thoughts, or as she so often craved of late, not thinking at all, merely drifting as she embroidered or sat watching her uncle.

"I am tired," she confessed to her uncle just days before. And she was. More tired than she could describe, and it was not a dissipation of energy that a nap or a week of naps could resolve. In some ways she nearly envied the old man shrunken in slumber in the bed by which she sat. Each time he drifted off she wondered if he would wake again. She longed to let her exhaustion overtake her, but there was too much yet to be done. Sleep was not the answer.

"Why Beatrice?" she asked Giacomo as she opened the book to the third section, *Paradiso*, to begin reading?

"How do you mean?" Giacomo asked.

"Why is she waiting for Dante's pilgrim in Paradise? I mean, I get why Dante could not allow the pagan Virgil into Paradise, but why Beatrice?"

"He was in love with her," Giacomo said, as if that explained it all.

"How can he be in love with her? She is his guide in Paradise, all glowing and heavenly yes, but to fall in love with her? Isn't it rather unseemly to be falling in love with an angel or heavenly guide or whatever she is?"

Giacomo was amused.

"For the fictional Dante, perhaps, but not for the real Dante. Beatrice was real. He knew her."

"Did he?" She was truly interested, now that the story had the aroma of gossip.

"Oh yes. It is a tale of deep and unrequited love. You see, the real Dante, the Dante of history, first laid eyes on the girl Beatrice when he was but nine years old, and she was one year younger."

"Nine years old?" she asked dismissively. "Isn't that a little young to be falling in love? Smitten, perhaps, but love?"

"You may be right. Nevertheless, there it is. Dante was but nine when he first saw Beatrice walking in a dress of soft crimson with a girdle about her waist."

"You seem to know a lot about it," she teased him. "I know you are old, Uncle, and your exploits took you to many fantastic places, but were you there as well?"

"I'm not quite that old, Niece," he said with a grin. "No, Dante wrote of Beatrice in his *La Vita Nuova*. He describes his encounter just as I give it to you. He was smitten, yes, very much so. Obsessed even. According to Dante, writing many years later, he would contrive ways to see the young love of his heart passing by, though he never spoke to her but once. That occurred nine years later, when he was eighteen years old. He saw her again walking with two older women. She was dressed in white and she turned to greet this young man of whom she could hardly be unaware. She greeted him and that was that."

"That's it," Zanetta asked. "After nine years of unrequited love, all he gets is a greeting?"

"Apparently so. Beatrice married a short time later. Things were arranged, you see, so for Dante it was either a matter of pursuing his affections or allowing his fantasy to continue its hold on his heart. Had he pursued the girl and succeeded, he would have dethroned the beatific Beatrice from his carefully constructed image of purity, or he might have been rejected which would do much the same, or he could continue to worship her from afar, a much more satisfactory conclusion for the inwardly poet.

"Beatrice died only a few years later, at the tender age of twenty-four. Dante was devastated. He retired to his writing and began his most creative period. He wrote of his love for Beatrice in *La Vita Nuova* and composed sonnets to her. In his mind she became the pinnacle of love. Who better than she, then, to guide him through Paradise?"

"If God is love, then love is God? Isn't that what you often say," she asked him.

"That is one way of looking at it," Giacomo agreed. "Dante certainly did.

"In Florence the local legend has it that Dante would sit upon a particular rock while watching the construction of the great cathedral, thinking of Beatrice and composing his sonnets and his story of the new life. Small wonder that he would come to associate the lovely Beatrice with his visions of the Church. She became his Madonna."

"While sitting on a rock?" she asked, somewhat amused by the tale.

"Oh yes. The rock is still there, in fact. Dante lived but a few streets from the piazza of the cathedral. To this day they refer to it as *Sasso di Dante*, the Rock of Dante. There is, by tradition, an eatery next to it by the same name."

"By tradition?" Zanetta asked.

"Just so. According to the legend, Dante had a flawless memory. One day he was seated upon his rock, thinking lofty thoughts no doubt, as only a poet could, when a passerby recognized him and asked, 'Dante, what is your favorite meal?' To which he replied, 'eggs.' Two years later the same man found the poet again seated on his rock and thinking to stump him said simply, 'With what?' And Dante replied without the slightest hesitation, 'With salt.'"

"You're making that up," Zanetta said.

"No, it's true. At least it is true that such a legend exists. The eatery faces the Duomo. I dined there many times. Best *pasta e fagioli* I have ever had."

"Now I know you are lying," Zanetta said with a smile. "You told me mine was the best you ever had."

"Yes, well, my memory is clearly not as good as Dante's. Your *pasta e fagioli* is the best, my dear. Not even the famous eatery of Florence can compare, though it too is exquisite."

"Now you are just trying to win favor. You are afraid to offend the only person still willing to cook for an old reprobate like you."

"Yes, but I do so with a great deal of charm," he said with a wide grin.

"Yes, Uncle, that you do."

The conversation went back and forth, interspersed with reading from the great volume, until her uncle drifted off once more. Zanetta now watched Giacomo sleeping and recalled his words of days before, suggesting that she had shut herself out of life. Time had sealed her away, that's what he said. Was it true? The words bothered her.

Maybe she was avoiding life. And why not? She had once embraced life just as Giacomo preached, and see where that left her. Alone, save for a son soon to leave and a dying uncle, also readying to leave.

"Do you think it is possible?" she asked Giacomo after his story of Dante.

"Do I think what is possible?" he asked.

"To fall in love with someone, so completely, as Dante did."

"Oh yes," Giacomo replied. "I know it is."

"The other day," Zanetta continued, "the things you said about me, about time sealing me away."

"Yes?"

"That isn't so bad, is it? I mean, life isn't always the way we would choose it to be, is it?"

"No, I suppose it is not. In fact, I would say that life is never the way we think it will turn out."

Zanetta sat in silence, chewing on her lip and thinking. Giacomo finally broke the silence.

"Zanetta?" he prompted.

She hesitated before answering.

"My husband. You said that I was his bliss, that he would have gone to the end of the world for me. That isn't true."

"But I thought..."

"It isn't true, Giacomo. My husband was a good man, like you said, at least at first. I was in love with him, deeply in love, and he gave me Lorenzo, who is the happiness of my life, but it wasn't all bliss. Before he died, he, well, he wasn't..."

"Faithful?" Giacomo asked.

Zanetta nodded her head. She was crying now, silent tears tracking down her cheeks. She grabbed a napkin from the tray with the remnants of Giacomo's breakfast and dabbed them away.

"I'm sorry, Zanetta. I didn't realize, though I suppose I always suspected."

"No, nobody realized. He was discrete in his affairs, but after Lorenzo I was never again the object of his desire. There was always someone younger, someone without a child I suppose. He was never mean to me, I mean, not in a physical way, but what he did seemed much crueler. He stopped loving me."

"And you?" Giacomo asked in a tender voice.

"I continued to love him, despite all the hurt. At least I thought I did, until he died. Once he was gone I realized I no longer really loved him. It was just that I had grown so dependent on him, and I was afraid that without him I would have nothing. No one would ever love me."

"Do you believe that still?"

"After he died I was relieved. I didn't have to pretend any more, though I don't think I was pretending at the time."

Zanetta straightened and sniffed as if bothered that she had revealed so much.

"I don't expect you to understand."

"Because you think my life choices were more like your husband's than not?" he asked. "I assure you, I understand more than you realize.

"Had I known this of your husband I would have, well… What would have been done? What could have been done? But you should not have borne this all by yourself for all of these years.

"And this is why you are so worried for Lorenzo? It isn't just my influence you are worried about. You fear that he may turn out like his father as well."

"It sounds so awful. I'm sorry."

"Don't be. It is I who should be apologizing. I thought all these years it was the loss of your husband that isolated you so, but it was the loss of love. And so, like Brynhildr, you sleep."

The two sat in silence, each absorbing what had been revealed.

"In answer to your question," Giacomo broke the silence, "yes, such love as Dante had for Beatrice is possible."

"I thought so, once."

"But no more?"

Zanetta stiffened.

"Not for me. I had my chance and I cast it upon someone who could not be faithful to his wife."

"But he did love you, even if he later foolishly allowed that love to disappear."

"Same difference. You say time has sealed me away, that I am sleepwalking through life. I'm not. I simply refuse to be so foolish as to place myself in that predicament again."

"It is a defiant eye that sees no hope."

"Another Casanova truism?"

"Another lesson learned. Happiness is out there, even for you."

"I doubt that. I had my chance."

"And you will have it again."

"To be struck like Dante?" Zanetta asked incredulously.

"To be struck by goodness," Giacomo replied. "Now let's read some more to see where Dante's guide takes him."

It was late afternoon when Giacomo awoke to the din of a clattering tray and muttered expletives outside of his door. It took a few moments for the old man to orient himself. His eyes began to focus as best they could, only to be confronted by the tortured expression of a thorn-crowned son suspended at the wall beyond the foot of his bed. His body responded to his renewed consciousness with heightened pain spasming throughout. In his mind he imagined stretching, as in days of his youth, and pushing off the aches that continually buffeted him, but his weakened limbs would not cooperate, and he sank deeper into the familiar and ever present misery that was now his constant companion.

Giacomo shifted as best he could to relieve the soreness of his limbs and back. He was not successful and so relapsed into the molded indentations of his mattress and pillows. Someone would be in soon, if the clamor outside his door was any indication. He strained to listen for signs of activity in the house, but other than the footsteps pounding down the stairs, which he might well have imagined in his waking shade, he could not make out anything. He instead turned his attention to the distant sounds of Venice that were both his joy and his frustration.

"This bed is my cross, eh?" he said to the walled dying god. The crucifix remained mute in response.

Giacomo wondered, as he had many times, if his niece placed the crucifix on the wall facing his bed to provide him comfort or condemnation. He suspected she wanted to give him the former while fearing he required the latter. He grimaced through the wracking pain and said to himself, "She's probably right."

He gauged the long shadows cast across the room by the burning yellow light streaming through the high window. Darkened pillars colored the wall opposite the window as the rays were met and blocked by the upright posts at the foot of Giacomo's bed. The tall shadows reminded him of the heavy timbers sunk deep into the bed of the lagoon canals, jutting high above the waters as mooring posts for a flotilla of gondolas and as supports for the opulent homes fronting the waterways. It was late afternoon.

Damn, he thought, most of the day gone and I slept through it. He struggled to recall the events of the morning. His niece was here, in his room, sitting in the chair next to him. She was reading to him, passages from Dante's *Divina Commedia,* one of his favorite books. It was something she did for him every day since his confinement, but he had fallen asleep and so passed the bulk of his day.

"I don't have many such days left Signore," he spoke aloud to the crucifix. "I cannot afford to see my time squandered in sleep. There is too much of my beautiful city to miss, even if it is only through the remoteness of distant sounds or shadow imaginings." The wooden figure was static in its refusal to alter from its own tortured impalement against the wall. "Or is that the condemnation you have come to dispense? Is my paradise now to be my Hell? Venice just beyond my reach and even that is to be denied me by the betrayal of my body?"

Giacomo folded his arms tightly across his chest and scowled.

"Yes Signore, this is the penance I must pay for my indulgence in the wonders and joys of this world. Perhaps I did savor more than my allotted portion of all this life has to offer, but Signore, was it not you who created this world along with all if its temptations?" He pointed an accusing finger at the crucifix. "Am I to be damned for accepting your gifts?"

The old man's voice cracked as it rose in timber. "I am guilty, yes Signore, but only of living more of this life you gave me than many of my fellow beings. Is that to be my damnation?"

Giacomo turned his head away in petulant indignation, before returning his gaze to the crucifix, like a lawyer forming his arguments.

"And what of those who rejected the abundance of your gifts? Is the farmer who toils by the sweat of his brow, but never tastes more than the small plot of your world to which he was born and into which he will return to be rewarded in your celestial hereafter for his lack of inquisitiveness, while I, a sinner yes, am to be tormented in my last days, and for all I know in the eons of what is to come for daring to experience more of your world?"

Giacomo was warming to the argument before the tormented judge.

"And what of those who cowered before the challenges of your gifts? Am I to be rewarded for picking up the sword in allegiance to my king, in defense of our God, or am I to be condemned for soldiering in the name of the wrong king, the wrong God? Will I receive a reward in your divine presence or will that reward be given to the man who sat out life and never fought for a cause?

"Or is it, Signore, the degree of adulation for which I am to be rewarded or condemned? In my youth I served you, an acolyte at the feet of the good Abbé Gozzi, only to become an abbé myself, though a short-lived vocation. Am I to be damned for leaving you? But I never left you, Signore! I saw your hand in every work.

"If I am guilty, Signore, it is guilt of recognition. Did you not create all who recognize you by different names and in different guises? Will you, who transcends all, damn me for seeing in many the inadequacies of their all too human attempts to articulate that transcendence? Am I to be damned for failing to concretize the evidence of your glory? Would it have been better for me had I knelt solely at a graven tree rather than see in all the transcendence of all?"

Giacomo caught his breath, his eye fixed on the crucifix as he set to articulate his final argument.

"Or am I to be found guilty, Signore, of an overabundance of love? Yes, that's it! But Signore, was it not in the Eve of this world that I saw your greatest masterpiece? Do I suffer now and in the hereafter for heralding in her your most exalted gift, the union of two that is the eternal moment?

"Humph," Giacomo snorted, "then so be it!

"I am guilty, Signore! I am guilty of living this life that now seems all too brief. I am guilty of serving you and leaving you, only to find you. And most of all Signore, I am guilty of love. Yes, love!

"Like Tristan condemned for loving Isolde after drinking the potion wine, I accept my fate. If you are to be my Brangäne, warning me that I have drunk my death, then what choice do I have? It is a draft I would gladly drink again.

"I accept your punishment, Signore, without remorse. I am guilty of touching transcendence. I am guilty of love."

Giacomo sank deeper into his pillows. He turned away from the wooden crucifix and back towards the window and out to the blue, white-clouded sky that hovered above his unseen city below. Wistfully he glanced back at the Christ image, his voice softened, his words pleading.

"Still, Signore, would that I could remain awake in what little time I have left. I will know my plight after this earthly surrender soon enough. If you are a benevolent god, let me have this time, I pray you."

A knock at the door was followed by a turn of the handle and the creaking of hinges as his grandnephew pushed it open while carrying a tray with food and drink.

"Uncle," his grandnephew called upon entering, "are you awake?"

"I am now. Was that you making all that clatter outside my door?"

"I'm sorry, Uncle. The tray slipped. I had to go back down to the kitchen for more."

Giacomo waved a feeble hand. "Never mind. I needed to wake."

Lorenzo set the tray upon the bedside table. "Here, Uncle, let me help you."

He assisted Giacomo into a sitting position and lifted a glass of wine to his lips. "Drink a little. You've scarcely had a thing all day."

"Ah, that's better." Giacomo licked his lips and ran his tongue over his few remaining teeth.

The two sat in silence as Lorenzo fed him spoonfuls of soup, interspersed with small pieces of bread which he had to hold in his mouth, usually with a sip of wine before it was dissolved enough to swallow.

Giacomo appreciated the matter of fact manner of his grandnephew as the younger man wiped his chin clean of escaping soup and wine, unlike Lorenzo's good mother who, though not intending to, made sounds and comments as she would to an infant who had not yet mastered the skills of keeping food in its mouth. Aging came with a slew of humiliations, not the least of which was the inclination of some to confuse the lessening mastery over one's body with a return to infancy. He was grateful for Lorenzo's accepting manner.

As he ate in the mutual silence, Giacomo observed his grandnephew who, though attentive, seemed elsewhere and withdrawn. Something troubled the young man. Was it to do with their recent conversations? Giacomo signaled when he had had enough and waited to allow Lorenzo to speak, if he so wanted.

"Uncle," Lorenzo said, breaking the silence between them, "when I arrived at your door I heard your voice. I could not discern, but you seemed agitated. To whom were you speaking?"

"Oh, that," he answered. "An ongoing negotiation. A closing of accounts, if you will."

"I'm sorry?" said Lorenzo, a perplexed expression crossing his face. His uncle had many years hence turned management of all his finances over to his niece, when she and young Lorenzo were invited to live here. They were Giacomo's only heirs and for the past two years Lorenzo learned the intricacies of finance under his mother's savvy guidance and occasional instruction from his uncle. One day he would manage the inherited estate and he had to be prepared.

"It is of no importance," Giacomo replied without explanation. "My affairs are in good hands."

His grandnephew smiled at the perceived compliment to his mother, and by extension to himself, and Giacomo made no attempt to explain further.

Silence resumed and Giacomo waited until Lorenzo arrived at what was troubling him. Lorenzo's increased fidgeting signaled that he was anxious to speak.

"Did you truly love them, Uncle, the women you told me about?" the young man asked at last.

Giacomo considered the question before answering. "Have I not said as much?" he countered.

"Well," the young man pressed, "you use the word love a great deal, but how could you really, I mean, all of them?"

"You find that so implausible?" Giacomo asked. "Love has many faces."

"But, true love?" Lorenzo said.

"Ah, I see," Giacomo replied, now comprehending the source of Lorenzo's angst. "So, what is her name?"

"What do you mean?" Lorenzo asked with unconvincing ignorance.

"What do you mean what do I mean? Her name. Certainly there is a her, and she must have a name." Giacomo was delighted at his grandnephew's widening eyes.

"How did you know?"

"Hah," he snorted and said with a flourish, "I am Giacomo Casanova. I think I have learned a thing or two in my three-score-and-ten plus years of the effects a woman can have on a young man. You show all the signs of a young man on fire from heart to loin. Have you known her long?" he asked.

Lorenzo exhaled an audible sigh of relief of one who no longer must contain a secret.

"For years," Lorenzo answered. "I've known her since we first came to live with you, but she was just a girl then."

"Ah, a local girl. And now?" Giacomo asked.

"She is no longer just a girl," Lorenzo said.

"She lives nearby then?"

"Her family lives but one avenue down, fronting the canal, as our home does."

"I see," Giacomo nodded. "What is her name?"

"Costanza," Lorenzo said with relish. "Costanza Foscarini."

"Costanza," Giacomo repeated. "It is a beautiful name."

Lorenzo was beaming at the new flow of secret knowledge that he had so long kept hidden.

Giacomo continued. "Costanza," he repeated. "It means the constant one. That is a good sign," he reasoned. "It was the name of Gianlorenzo Bernini's greatest lover," he said with a wink.

"Bernini, the sculptor of Rome?"

"Yes. He carved a magnificent marble bust of his Costanza. Absolute perfection." Giacomo closed his eyes remembering. "He portrayed her at the height of sensuosity, eyes wide and engaging, gentle curves defining her cheeks, neck and shoulders, full soft lips parted as if just about to speak, no doubt words of her amour, and her blouse open at the neck inviting one's imagination to the fullness of her breasts. It is the very expression of love."

"You have seen this sculpture?" Lorenzo asked.

Giacomo focused again on his grandnephew.

"Oh yes. It was purchased by a wealthy Florentine collector and has remained in his family. It is a work of exquisite beauty."

Giacomo did not feel compelled to reveal the sordid aftermath of the story, that the constant Costanza was neither constant nor was their love one of happily ever after. She was, indeed, the young wife of one of Bernini's assistants and the two were engaged in a not so private affair that publicly humiliated the long-suffering assistant. Events spun out of control once the spoiled, self-indulged artist learned that Costanza was simultaneously having an affair with his younger brother, Luigi Bernini. Catching the two of them in embrace late one night, the artist chased

Luigi through the streets of Rome and right into St. Peter's Cathedral where he proceeded to beat his younger brother nearly to death, and would have killed him had not others intervened. And that wasn't the end of his selfish rage. He later sent one of his servants to slash the beautiful young Costanza's face, disfiguring her for life. A cruel genius, Bernini.

No, Giacomo thought, best not to reveal the whole story to the love-smitten Lorenzo. A first love should never be jinxed by another's woeful tale.

"A work of exquisite beauty," he said again.

"This Costanza," Giacomo brought the conversation back to his grandnephew's revelation, "her father is Sebastian Foscarini, the wool merchant?"

"Yes, Uncle," Lorenzo nodded in rapid agreement.

"I know the family," Giacomo said, "though it has been many years since we have spoken. Even before you and your mother came to live with me, my travels throughout the city were increasingly limited," he said by way of explanation.

"I had several business dealings with Signore Foscarini, most of them quite profitable. We became good friends. He is a good man, Sebastian Foscarini."

"He is very successful," Lorenzo said in a rush. "His warehouses are the largest on the island."

"Successful, yes, but commercial success does not always indicate goodness of heart, as you will no doubt learn. Foscarini is one of the great exceptions. He is a good man. He is a man to be trusted. Remember that."

Giacomo shook his head slightly in wonderment at the returning circles of life. He remembered a time many years past when his life first crossed paths with the promising young Sebastian Foscarini, and now, here his name comes up again, this time in connection with a new generation.

Giacomo continued, "I recall he had a daughter, a charming girl of golden curls and singular beauty. Would this be your Costanza?"

"It is," Lorenzo said in a rush, "though she is quite grown up now."

"So I should think. And Costanza of the golden curls, does she love you?" he asked.

"I, I don't know," Lorenzo stammered. "I, no, I don't think so. I don't know."

"What's stopping you from finding out?"

"It isn't something you just blurt out and ask," Lorenzo explained, a touch of anguish in his voice.

"This is the passage into the forest, my boy."

"What?" Lorenzo asked.

Giacomo pointed up to the valance circling the crown of his bed.

"You have a choice to make. Are you going to enter the forest of dangers and wonders, or are you going to refuse the call? You stand at one of the hidden byways."

"Uncle! I don't even know if she knows I exist."

"Nonsense! You have spoken to her?"

"Well, yes, many times, but not like, you know…"

"Then we can safely assume she knows you exist," Giacomo said dryly.

"Uncle, it isn't that easy."

"Nobody ever said it was. Not even for the great Casanova!" he said with a flamboyant wave of his hand. "But if you back down now, you may never know."

Giacomo sat back, allowing his words to settle in.

"This girl Costanza, do you love her?"

Lorenzo averted his gaze. "I thought so, but now," his voice trailed off.

"Do you now question your own love?" Giacomo asked.

"I'm not sure. Your stories, Uncle, they confuse me."

"How so?" Giacomo was surprised by the comment.

"The women you have known. You say you loved them, but how can that be? Each one passed to another. I would die to think that Costanza was nothing more than a passing conquest."

Giacomo stared harshly at his grandnephew. "Is that what you think of me and the women of whom I speak?"

"I'm sorry, Uncle," Lorenzo exclaimed. "I do not mean to give offense. It's just that, oh, I'm not sure what I mean."

Giacomo felt a wave of compassion for his grandnephew. He was in love, it was clear. He would not see Lorenzo hurt by failing to follow his heart.

"Listen to me, my boy. Many a young man has mistaken eros for love. You are attracted to her?" he asked.

Lorenzo nodded.

"This is covetness," he explained. "If this is the extent of what compels you to her then in pursuing her you could be perpetrating the utmost harm on an otherwise noble young lady. Is this what you feel?" he inquired.

"No! I mean, yes I am deeply attracted to her, but not only that. She is the most beautiful girl in all of Venice, but that is not all I see in her."

"No?"

"No."

Giacomo assayed his grandnephew's fervor. "Well then, perhaps you truly love her after all."

"But how do I know."

Giacomo reached out to touch Lorenzo's hand. "Search your own heart. You will know."

"How?" the young man implored.

"You will know that when you have touched the transcendent."

"Uncle?"

"Love is a boon that can never be taken, only lost."

"I don't understand."

"You will," Giacomo assured him. "When you have found the love that carries you out of this world, you will know."

Lorenzo looked at his uncle quizzically. "Did you ever find such love, Uncle?"

Giacomo turned away from his grandnephew to confront again the wooden crucifix facing his bed.

"I am guilty, Signore. I am guilty of such love."

Women Who Teach

Gianlorenzo Bernini
Ecstasy of Saint Teresa
1645-52
marble
Cornaro Chapel, Santa Maria della Vittoria, Rome, Italy

Is love any less real because one is young? It feels real. It pains real. By day I sit at her side, instructed in letters and rote, while by night I imagine us to be more.

So many times I ached to know what softness lay beneath Teresa's obscuring Carmelite robe, a sensuality implied by the heavy fabric's sway at the movement of her legs as she passed, or the abundant web of folds that creased downward from the swell of her breasts. Our time together is nearly at an end, unless I can convince her of my heart. It is time to tell her how I feel.

"I yearn to be taught," I say to her.

"You have been a good student, Giacomo. Perhaps my best."

My face flushes at the compliment and I warm at the sudden rush of blood to my cheeks, and other extremities.

"I still have much to learn," I implore.

"Of course, Giacomo, you must never stop learning." Excitement turns to exquisite pain pressing me forward.

"Surely there is more for you to teach," I urge.

"No my child, I have imparted all to you that I can." A friendly expression counterpoints the slight shake of her head. Heavy lidded eyes look down, a melancholy expression of loss for what is past, or of regret for what may never come. My child. How can she think of me as a child when I feel for her the way I do?

"No more grammar lessons?" I press. "No more conjugations?"

She expresses delight at my earnestness.

"No, Giacomo."

"No more math or logic or rhetoric?"

"No, Giacomo. In these you have mastered all I have to give."

"No more lives of the Saints?"

Her hand reaches to mine and comes to rest on my lap. Her nearness drives my passion.

"The Saints live on and what they have yet to teach, you must learn of them and from them on your own."

"And what of love?" I ask, voice quivering at my brave audacity.

"Ah," she says with intonations of understanding.

I expect her to withdraw her hand from mine, but it remains, steady and warm. I look at it and her slender wrist that disappears in the voluminous sleeve. The vein at her wrist is distended and pulsing, its rhythm belying her calm demeanor and matching my own heightened senses.

"I have taught you of the love of the Lord," she says. She directs her gaze outwards, away from me.

"That's not what I mean."

"It is the greatest of loves, wondrous and pure."

"There are other loves," I add.

"Yes, fraternal love, sisterly love."

"And others still?"

"Platonic love, love of the mind," she explains, her eyes still away from mine.

"I know all of these, but is there not a greater love still?"

"Amour," she says, her voice like a distant wind, "the love between a man and a woman."

"The love between a woman and a man," I agree.

My heart swims at the words. It is the first time I have called myself, or been called, a man.

She looks at me with sympathetic eyes.

"You will know this love," she says. "In time you will know it well."

"I know it already," I confess in a rush.

Her fingers squeeze my hand sending a shiver up my arm and into my chest.

"You are young, Giacomo." Her words are gentle and kind.

"Too young to love a woman?" I ask.

She hesitates to consider, then answers, "No, not too young to love a woman."

Scarlet colors her cheeks, transforming her Carrara flesh from marble white to reveal fires barely contained by her soft features. Without words she reveals her feelings too.

"But even here there are degrees of the heart," she tries to explain in defiance of what her face reveals.

"I love you, Teresa, with all my heart."

"You confuse ardor with love, which is itself but another degree of amour."

"Teach me," I plead.

"Giacomo, this cannot be." Her eyes divert.

"Show me."

"This should not be."

Her words come in rapid pace. Her hand cinches mine and presses into my leg. I cannot steady the emotions that wrack me. I will myself to her.

Her body wilts and she lowers her head to my shoulder.

"It has to be," she resigns.

My face buries in the folds of her habit. I am intoxicated with the aromas surrounding her. She smells of honey from hives the sisters keep, and lemon peel, and sweet herbs gathered in, perfuming rooms and robes.

"Come," she whispers, and I follow.

She leads me to a chaise upon which she lies. It is an altar upon which she is offering, and offered.

I stand beside and above her, my shirt removed, I'm not sure when.

Her eyes flutter open and closed, her breathing heavy and punctuated with itinerate moans.

"You are an angel in bodily form," she says, her voice a passionate rasp.

I am cherubim in her sainted vision.

She swoons back and still seems to arc fore, her hips grinding upwards as if crests of stucco clouds were pushing her to me. She is mystical and mystic, caught in a Baroque divination.

A celestial light floods the vault in which she receives me. We are contained in the richness of veined marble walls, like players upon a stage, and I imagine a gallery of spectators to which she is oblivious in her ecstasy. Golden rays shine down on her.

I am no stranger to a girl's charms, but a woman's pleasure transports me to new worlds. Impishly I lift and peel the heavy fabric of her Carmelite robe from her breast. I know what will be revealed and I too am caught up in the excess of her quixotic splendor.

I pierce her as a heavenly messenger striking with a golden arrow into her heart, into her most sensual flesh and soul. Together we thrust in rhythmic surrender. We have become something new. She teaches amour and I am cherubim.

Women Who See

Michelangelo Buonarroti
Delphic Sibyl, from the *Sistine Ceiling*
1508-1512
fresco
Sistine Chapel, Vatican City, Rome, Italy

She reads me like a prophecy written on leaves and scattered to the winds and I am left to wonder at what she sees. She is Sibyl and though we have only met she knows me, knows my mind and my heart and I find myself unprepared for the depth of her insight. She knows me better than I know myself.

Scattered to the winds. It could describe me. Aimless. Lost. Alone. On a journey of undetermined time, yet feeling time run away as I stumble and lurch, trying to hold on.

Life has been a series of lines to cross, and in each crossing I found not the reward of success, but the hollowness of achievement alone. All has led me to this place and it is here I sense the answers, the fulfillment I seek.

"How came you to Rome? Are you from here?" I ask, knowing she is not, embarrassed at the paltriness of my questions. All this way I have come, all the knowledge and experience I have gained, and all I can think to ask is where she is from.

She smiles in placid understanding and I am comforted. She knows more about me than I know of myself. She knows my questions even if they are yet to be asked. I detect it in her wide eyes. She is not offended at my simplicity.

"No," she replies, "I am from Delphi, north of the wine dark Gulf of Corinth, on the slopes of Mount Parnassus."

"I know this place," I say, happy to know anything in the presence of such refined wisdom. "There is a temple there. Ancient. Some say it as old as the world."

"Some say," she agrees. "Have you been there?" she asks.

I suddenly feel awkward and adolescent as if my failure to have seen her birth land makes me less in her eyes. I have seen the world. I have traveled far, into the East and back, to cultures alien and fantastical, but all seems as nowhere compared to the land that gave her birth.

"No," I stammer, "but I have read of it, in Sophocles and the oracles." Her parted lips encourage me and I go on. "It was there that Oedipus learned his fate." I am like a schoolboy delivering his lessons.

"Yes, Oedipus. He was a traveler too," she says without further comment.

"A traveler fated to tragedy," I say.

"As some travelers are, but not all."

"It is said he murdered his father and married his mother." I repeat from memory.

"It all seems very complex," she says with wry humor, "but that is the ancient tale."

I hear her voice as through the mouths of a hundred caves, as if from all places at all times. She is the eternal principle made flesh. I never want the echoes to stop their rumble through my soul.

"He blinded himself for his crimes, Oedipus did."

Sibyl nods.

"You know your history well, but in truth Oedipus was blind long before. He journeyed blind."

"Is this so?" I ask.

"The Oracle at Delphi warned him, but he could not see what he was given to see. This was his greatest tragedy.

"It needn't be that way," she continues. "The oracles speak to all who ask. It is up to the hearer to hear."

She doesn't need me, but I need her to need me. Poised in beauty she is contained, wrapped in red and cerulean blues. I can envision her sitting among architectural splendor across a vaulted sky, unreachable, unfathomable. Popes and priests kneel below. I, too, would kneel at her Sistine throne.

"And what would the oracles say today?" I ask, wanting only to continue hearing her voice.

A sad expression crosses her brow. "Today, the oracles are dumb. But if they could speak they would speak of what is past, passing, and to come."

I tremble beneath her. No woman has ever affected me so.

"But that is not what you asked, is it?" she astutes.

"No."

"You wish to know what they would say to you."

I nod my head, afraid she will not tell me. She glances away, and my pulse quickens. She is wisdom and sublime.

"You travel blind, like Oedipus."

"I am alone."

"This is your blindness. You seek in another your completion, but this is what blinds you."

"I am not alone?"

She shakes her head and looks away.

"There was a man once, much like you. His fame was such that he was renown throughout the world. He was a maestro, a creator, each new accomplishment was honor gained, every creation, prophets and pietas, was a masterpiece."

"Was he a traveler too?" I ask.

"Of a sort," she says. "From Florence to Rome, but his real journeys were not abroad. They were ever inward."

"He must have been the luckiest of men."

"His was a difficult nature, not of your charm."

I am embarrassed at the designation.

"He was, in life, a lonely man, but with every creation he heard the oracles' song. His was a journey of sight. He was never blind."

"He was a teacher?"

"He was an oracle," she says.

"I would like to see his creation."

Sibyl smiles. "You are seeing it now."

"You?"

"Do not journey for completion, Giacomo. In this you will find yourself ever alone. Journey for the experience of finding others traveling your way, and know that they, like you, are whole, and you are one. This is the way of one who sees."

"I am whole."

"Yes."

"I am one with all."

"Yes."

"I am one with you?" I ask with hope in my voice.

Sibyl gazes out again across the chapel expanse.

She breaks the silence with the words I longed to hear.

"Thou art that."

She says no more. She doesn't have to. I yearn to kiss her lips, to be held in arms made to hold, to be enclosed in her warmth. Centuries of men have desired her. Have they seen beyond her Quattrocento beauty? Have they seen her set against the sky?

To touch her mind is to touch eternity. I will never know a greater love than this.

Forgiving Women

Annibale Carracci
Jupiter and Juno, from *The Loves of the Gods*
1597
fresco
Ceiling of the Farnese Gallery, Rome, Italy

After all these years, am I still the man of her Olympian dreams? Can I still call down thunder as when we were young? Have I aged beyond my ageless bride?

"Wife, come bed with me," I suggest, with the promise of pleasures ahead.

Juno's eyes narrow in suspicious mischief as she chides me from afar.

"Husband, you have bedded enough," she says dismissively. "I am still mad at you."

I pretend to be hurt, though her barb is well placed, a lightning bolt of my own fashion turned against me.

"Things will look better with a mattress on your back. They always do."

"Is this your solution for everything?" she asks.

"Well, not everything. But it often helps."

"Not this time."

"Perhaps you are right," I say, contrition in my voice.

"Humph," she sniffs and turns away. She is not ready for such an easy capitulation.

"Of course I am right," she says. "By now you should know that even when I am wrong, I am right, though you are always late in thinking so. You are only pretending to be contrite so that you can lure me back into bed, old rake that you are. It won't work. I am not some young flit that you can dazzle with half an apology and then have your way."

"But I am not pretending. I truly am sorry."

"Sorry for what?" she asks, an accusation in her voice.

"Well, I'm sorry, sorry, for, I'm sorry for whatever it is I am supposed to be sorry for," I say, hoping it is enough, knowing it is not.

"You don't even know!"

"Of course I know. It's just that I am not entirely sure."

"Typical!"

"Consistent," I return with a smile.

"Yes, I'll give you that."

"Perhaps if you were to remind me what it is this old Saturn's son has done to incur your wrath?"

Juno folds her arms across her chest.

"That thing you were supposed to do," she states without elucidation.

"That thing?"

"That thing!"

"Ohhh. That thing."

"Now do you remember?" she asks.

"With crystal clarity." I don't.

"And?"

"And, I will take care of it immediately." I am firm in my pronouncement.

"Truly?"

"I am committed to the task," I say with bravado.

"Sometime soon?"

"You can rest assured, it will be done. Once you ask me to do something, you don't need to remind me every six months!"

"It has been eight."

"Juno, don't be angry with me."

"Angry? With you? Why on earth or in Heaven's vault would I be angry with you?"

Sarcasm becomes her.

"I deserve that," I admit.

"Do you?"

"Juno, love, we both know that I am undeserving of you. Must I grovel at your feet?"

She turns to me, a slight smile on her lips.

"A little, perhaps," she replies.

"Then this is me, prostrating myself like a mortal supplicant begging your indulgence."

Juno rolls her eyes at my theatrics.

"Maybe that works on some river nymph or dewy-eyed princess succumbing to you as a bull or you as a swan or you as a lusting cloud, but I'll have none of it. Only an eagle for this peahen," she announces with hands on her hips.

"You know me all too well," I say.

"I should, after eons."

"Better than I know myself."

"We are, after all, both born of devouring time."

"Time," I repeat, "so much time has passed."

Our eyes meet and share the understanding of eternities. It is the understanding couples share with the passing of years together. It is an understanding of virtues and vices, accomplishments and shames. It is the knowing of one's mate as well as oneself. It is comfort and familiarity and compassion profound.

"Do you remember our marriage day?" I ask. "It was in your month, the month to wed."

She beams at the recollection.

"How could I forget? You were like an eager cub, nuzzling at my breasts. It was either wed or bed. Fortunately, we chose both, though not necessarily in that order."

"We were so young," I muse.

"Young, yes, but I have no regrets on that account. You were the only one for me. I dare say you still are."

"A little older, perhaps," I bemoan.

"Hah! Look at you. You still appear the ruler of titans and men."

"A little more forgetful."

"I would agree with that," she says.

"But one thing has never diminished. I love you more now than I ever dreamt possible."

"Husband, you are very close to being forgiven."

"Such is the wisdom of age, knowing when to tell the truth."

"Aged yes, but you are the wisest of men, forgetful though you may be."

"But look at you," I say. "Age would never dare touch Juno Lumina, the heavenly light."

"Is that how you see me, still?"

"And Juno Regina, and Caprotina, my Juno of erotic love."

"Oh, we're back to that, are we?"

"We never left," I explain.

"What then was all that talk of passing time?" she asks.

"It is of no account," I say. "Times change."

"They do, but what is between us does not."

"I sometimes think we are throwbacks to a classical past, enshrined frescos of another era."

She flicks her hand in a dismissive manner.

"We seem to be in fashion once again," she says.

"Yes," I agree, "for a while, but fashions change. A tenebristic revolution is taking place. The Caravaggisti will claim the day."

"Perhaps they will," she says, "but I prefer the now, here, with my undeserving husband."

"Who loves you dearly."

"Who loves me dearly," she repeats.

"Now, about that thing. Perhaps if you were to give me a clue."

Juno gives me a look which softens as she lowers her draping stola, exposing shoulders and breasts, beckoning and exciting.

"We will discuss it later," she says.

I see in her the bride of wedded youth, made perfect with the passing of time.

"Wife, come bed with me," I say, and this time she does.

Asserting Women

Thutmose
Nefertiti
c. 1345 BCE
painted limestone

She is the beauty of the Nile. Across the lands, upper and lower, east and west, there is no one to match her grace, or her cunning way. The costume of her beliefs is different than mine, different histories, different manifestations, but the values we embrace are the same. For some this is not enough.

Ours are nuptials not favored by the priests. They have a vested interest in preserving the hierarchy of their ruling spirits in which they, as functionaries, benefit greatly. Nothing can be allowed to trump their influence. They couch their disapproval in the language of care, but there is little caring in the dismissal of one's traditions and beliefs in order to assert your own. There is more to their concern than the saving of my soul. Religious sanction is power and wealth. These are not easily abandoned once possessed. The priests do not approve of our marriage. They do not approve of Nefertiti. She will be my undoing, they say, but it is their own undoing they fear most.

Still, the priests have the ear of others who are eager to voice their disapproval in their stead.

"Your family despises me," Nefertiti says.

"They just don't know you the way I do," I say, trying to deflect her concerns, but I know she is right.

"They do not want to know me. I am not one of them."

"They just don't understand."

"What's to understand? I love you and you love me. We are both good people. Isn't that enough?"

I shake my head.

"It should be," I say weakly.

"Why can't they just accept me for who I am? Why do they hate me so?"

"Give them time," I say. "They will learn to love you as I do." It is not a satisfying response.

She is regal in her bearing. Like a finely painted bust she is placed on a pedestal for all to admire. Ebony eyes peer out beneath charcoal-lined lids in a flawless high-cheeked face. Her pomegranate tinted lips are yearning to be kissed. I long to press my own lips to hers as she extends herself, her graceful swan neck stretching towards me.

"They want me to convert," she sniffs.

"Convert?"

"To their beliefs, as if that would make me a better person and acceptable in their eyes."

I can feel my own anger rising. This is not the message I embraced in my own beliefs. This is not the truth of one with the other. This is tribal and excluding. This is chosen arrogance. Am I so insecure, are they, that we cannot accept the goodness in another, regardless of cultural inflection?

But ours is more than mere dalliance or the submission of a wife to her husband, which would satisfy the priests' need to maintain their domination over all things feminine, mortal or divine. Nefertiti is no chattel. She is co-regent in all that defines us.

Such things cannot be, say the priests. They will deride and abuse us, but they will lose. They have already lost. I will not bow to any idols whose jealousy excludes my bride. Only equals can truly love.

I banish all who deny the underlying truth of marriage, that no priest can join or divide what was never separate. Nefertiti came to our wedding bed not as a supplicant to become my consort of lesser standing, but to celebrate what always was, the awareness of one's self in one's bride. This is revolution in the eyes of jealous gods and their fearful priests.

Together we travel the great river and turmoil follows. Prideful tribes. We journey east, thinking to start anew and avoid the disappointments of family and faiths. It is not to be so. Like a cauldron in the burning desert, tensions boil. Ancient modes give way to new beliefs, new tribes. From one book are born three, but little unity can be found. And within each book, splinters form, each competing with the other for the right to claim one's soul. It is no longer the message of the book that matters, it is who can claim ownership of the volume. Wars are fought. False martyrs act. Lives are lost.

I have journeyed far to be here today. I will not abandon the goodness I have found for the comfort of tribe.

In poetic metaphor all religions speak to the universal, the realization that we are all part of a greater whole. Conflicts rise when metaphor becomes history, when tribe replaces humanity. Tribes forget.

Just as Nefertiti's beauty cannot be denied, neither can the abandonment of system for truth be ignored. The priests plot their revenge.

They will regain the day, but we will outlive them all. Theirs is an impotent rage that will find voice through the ages, but never will they completely subdue the truth, that we are all united in the net of eternity.

"It doesn't matter what my family says," I tell her, "or the priests. You are my wife. I chose to be with you in all of your complexities and differences and in the values we share. Nothing can take that away from us unless we allow it."

"You would leave your family for me?" she asks. "You would deny your faith?"

"I would deny small minds. My faith includes you and all."

Gracefully she leans into me and my lips touch the fullness of hers.

Others will find themselves in our place. Some will find unity in all, while others will bend to tribal wills, and the priests will rejoice. They will reassert their own favor as easily as counselors manipulating a boy king, but such renewed arrogance will die young and all of the gold and treasure they ascribe to their oppressive faith will remain hidden, buried in a forgotten waste.

One day it will be found and admired for its rarity and abundance, but it will never match the beauty of Nefertiti.

Women Enthroned

Fra Filippo Lippi
Madonna and Child with Scenes of the Life of St. Anne
1452
tempera on wood panel

"I had to escape out of a palace window to see you," I expel in a breathless rush. "Lord Cosimo had me locked away!"

"Locked away? Why?" she asks as if my tale is the most natural thing in the world to hear. Given that it is me reporting it, perhaps it is.

"I truly do not know."

"Truly?"

"Who knows the ways of powerful men? What can I tell you? I was a captive, and now I am not!" I add with a flourish.

"He must have locked you away for some reason."

"None that I can think of." I shuffle on my feet, feeling slightly uncomfortable under Lucretia's knowing gaze.

"I find that hard to believe."

"Nevertheless, it is true! I was treated no better than a common criminal, banished from all, left to rot in solitude. It was a hellish morning!"

"You were in prison?" she asks, a disbelieving tone in her voice. "For one morning? And you escaped?"

"I, er, not exactly a prison." She doesn't seem to be appreciating the spirit of my heroic tale, which is far grander than mere facts.

"Didn't you say you escaped from Lord Cosimo?

"Um, I believe so, yes."

"Lord Cosimo's palace?"

"That would be the one, yes."

"So you were locked away in the most luxurious building in Florence for an entire morning? How terrible for you!"

Her mocking dismissal of my ordeal does little to enhance the excitement of my story.

"I can assure you, my love, it was much more harrowing than it sounds."

"I'm sure it was. Now why would Lord Cosimo lock you away?" she wondered out loud. "Did he not hire you to do a job? A commission?"

"He did," I admit.

"And did he not pay you quite well, in advance?"

"He did," I agree.

"I see. And did you complete, no, let me rephrase that, did you even begin the work?" she inquires amusedly.

"Err, there may be some dispute as to that fine point," I confess.

"And so, Lord Cosimo locked you away until you fulfilled your obligation," she reasons.

"That may have been the order of things, yes." I shuffle my feet more than usual.

"Why didn't you just return his money, if you did not want to complete the job?"

"Ah, clarity of thinking! It is one of your commendable traits. I, too considered this, but alas, such a thing was impossible."

"Impossible? Why?"

"Because you are wearing all that I earned."

"Am I?" Lucretia is surprised to hear this.

"So you are. The day I was paid, I bought you the beautiful robe you now wear. I saw you admire it many times in the shop, ultramarine of the softest weave, fit for a Madonna of royal blood, and I simply had to get it for you." I shrug my shoulders as if that explains everything.

Lucretia laughs and angels seem to sing at the sound.

"Oh, Giacomo, you silly, impetuous fool. I don't need such opulence."

"Need?" I repeat, as if the concept is something new to sample and savor. "No, not need. But the mother of this spotless child deserves the finest robe and much, much more."

"And what of Lord Cosimo?" she asks.

"He'll be fine. I nearly finished my work for him, and I will return shortly to add the finishing touches. I just had to see you first. He will be quite satisfied. Though he may be none too pleased to find his upper room's bed sheets tied in knots and dangling from his window."

Lucretia laughs again and my heart fills with joy. Young Filippino stirs, his infant hands plucking at pomegranate seeds.

"You accede to me far too much honor, sir," she says. "You enthrone me. You look at me as if I was a child of immaculate birth myself, a daughter of Anne and Joachim, rather than the poor girl with whom you fell in love"

I imagine this imagined birth.

I see the woman facing me and in my mind's eye she is indeed enthroned. She holds our child at her lap and she has become the mother of all. She is perfection ascending. Her smooth, high brow slenderly crowns a flawless complexion, set with lilting eyes and tender lips that I long to kiss.

I shrug again, as if to say, I can't help it. You are as I see you.

"Honestly, Giacomo," she says in good-natured exasperation, "I am no Madonna."

"You once wore the cloth of a lady of the Church," I remind her. "That is close."

"Shh," she hisses, as if appalled, while glancing around to see if anyone overheard. "You are not to speak of that!"

"Why not?" I counter. "It is a noble calling."

"That's not what I mean, and you know it."

"What then?" I ask in all innocence.

"Need I remind you that you, too, once wore the cowl?"

I nod my head at her remonstration.

"A misguided profession for a time, I admit, at least in my case."

"You never were much cut out for a cloistered life, I suppose," she says.

"Not with nuns that look like you placed in my charge!"

"Hush. You're a devil!" I think she might throw the child's pomegranate at me, but she doesn't.

"Another fine reason for abandoning the cloth," I say. "But look at what we have to show for it."

She cradles our child closer to her and is again beatific in my eyes.

"Oh, Giacomo," she shakes her head contentedly, "what am I going to do with you?"

"That's what I came to show you," I say with a wink.

"You're a devil."

"And you are a saint. Now let's away before Lord Cosimo or his men come calling for me."

"I thought you said he would be satisfied, that you were nearly finished with his job."

"I did. I am," I say, "but they were his best sheets!"

Chapter Four

*Z*anetta felt like running, or, better yet, flying. But from what? To what? She wasn't sure. Only days before she spoke to Giacomo of how tired she was, as if that was her defense against his claims that she had sealed herself away from the world. And so what if she had? It was her life. Who was he to make such claims against her when he was the very example of someone who never stopped long enough to allow the pain of a failed relationship to hurt and halt? That's the problem with Casanova, she thought, he spent so much time in the shallows that he never experienced the sorrows of the deep.

No, that's not fair, and she knew it. Her uncle seemed to understand better than anyone what she was going through, though how such a lothario as her charming sinful uncle could know such things was beyond her. And yet everything he said about her was true. She had sealed herself away, deliberately so, but not without purpose. She was needed here, she reasoned. Lorenzo needed her, now perhaps, more than ever. And Giacomo needed her, but things change. In this too, she knew Giacomo was correct. Things always change.

Zanetta sat at her dresser in the bedroom she occupied across from Giacomo's. She moved to this room shortly after Giacomo's first bout with serious illness in order to hear him and be closer should he need her. It didn't face the Grand Canal as Giacomo's bedchamber did and so did not have a high window, as so obsessed her uncle, but it was warm and comfortable. She enjoyed the solitude it offered. Sealed away, she thought. But now, for some reason, she rather wished her room had a window.

Zanetta picked up the silver handled mirror that rested next to a matching brush on her dresser. They were a wedding gift from her husband, Lorenzo's father. She cherished them. Even after her husband drifted away from her and into the arms and beds of younger, childless women, she held this gift dear. Each night and following morning as she brushed her hair she admired the beauty of the ornate filigree design, but this morning she was more interested in the reflective glass and the visage gazing back at her.

Giacomo said she was beautiful. Well, perhaps, in her younger years, though not the beauty her mother was, but comely enough. At least so others told her once upon a time. Such thoughts had long since ceased to matter to her. Or had they? Giacomo's comments caused her to wonder.

She held the mirror up to catch the light of her lamp, angling it this way and that to view different facets of her face and to capture an overall appearance that she assembled in her mind. She stared into eyes that stared back at her. Turning her face slightly she inspected the tiny web of wrinkles that fanned out from the corners of her eyes. Old, she thought. Then she remembered Giacomo's words. How was it he described them? Rewards of years of laughter. She smiled broadly and watched the wrinkles deepen into accents pressed above cheekbones flush with rose hue at the gesture. Not old at all. The woman looking back seemed happy, though Zanetta wasn't quite sure who this woman was. It was not how she pictured herself. At least not for a very long time. The pleasant courteous smiles of a public encounter came easy to her, but how long has it been since she really smiled and laughed? Other than with Giacomo, of course, who could make a gargoyle laugh with his outrageous stories. Too long, she knew.

She arced the mirror over her head, catching view of her hair. It was indeed tinged with strands of gray. Filaments of moonlight, Giacomo called them, though she saw none of the halo or crown of which he spoke. She gathered a bunch of hair and held it aloft at the top of her head. She had grown accustomed to pinning it up simply for day wear, perhaps with some fine combs or lace overlay for Sunday mass, but this hardly constituted a halo. She let her hair fall back into place. A question was now nagging at her. Fortunately, she knew someone who would have the answer.

Zanetta stood and gathered her dressing gown around her, tying the sash at her waist. She pressed her feet into her slippers and stepped out of her room and across the hallway into her uncle's room.

Giacomo looked up at her as she entered. Zanetta did not bother knocking. That was an amenity they mutually agreed was to be ignored. He was partially propped up on his pillows, the best he could muster on his own.

"Zanetta, dear. You're early this morning. Why, you aren't even dressed for the day yet."

"I thought I heard you stirring. I just came to check on you."

It wasn't true, but it was an acceptable lie as an excuse for just barging in.

"Yes, well, my body and the stations of the day are not as in synch as they once were. I was listening."

Zanetta nodded. Giacomo often commented on things he heard, or thought he heard through his ever-open window. Zanetta traversed the room and sat in her accustomed chair beside Giacomo's bed. She casually crossed her legs and absently bit at her nail, still lost in thought.

"Something on your mind this morning?" Giacomo asked.

"Hmm? Oh. I was just wondering, what is beautiful?" she asked without a hint of irony.

"Oh my," he responded. "That is a very large question."

"Is it?" she asked in return.

"I think so," he said. "What prompted this?"

"I don't know. I was just thinking about some of the things you've said, about Beatrice and such."

She did not elaborate further.

"Surely you know beauty when you encounter it?" Giacomo prodded her.

Zanetta shrugged and remained silent.

Giacomo considered the question for a moment then said, "Tell me something that you think is beautiful."

"That's not fair," she replied. "I asked you."

"So you did. So you did. Just the same, humor me."

Zanetta let out her breath and raised her hands.

"Flowers," she said. "Flowers are beautiful."

"Oh that's too easy," Giacomo came back. "Everyone would say flowers are beautiful. And they smell good too! Come on then, give me something better."

"Giacomo!" she said in slight exasperation.

"Very well then, try this. What is your favorite painting?"

Giacomo watched her cock her head to one side and was pleased to see he caught her somewhat by surprise.

"Oh, let's see. I suppose it is Venus. Yes, Botticelli's *Birth of Venus.* I remember I nearly swooned when I saw it."

"Yes, I thought as much. And why is it one of your favorites?"

"Because it is beautiful. But this is a circular argument. What I really want to know is what makes something beautiful."

"Yes, that is a much better question. So what makes Botticelli's Venus beautiful?"

Zanetta gave him a doleful look.

Giacomo encouraged her. "You asked me, now play along."

"It is Venus. She's pretty."

"A variance of beautiful? Why is she pretty?"

Giacomo remained silent as Zanetta considered this.

"Very well, she has wide eyes and full lips. She has smooth skin and curves the way we expect a woman to have. She's young," Zanetta added with a touch of venom.

Giacomo folded his hands over his abdomen and smiled in a satisfied way, as a professor would after making a brilliant illumination.

"What?!" Zanetta asked. "You haven't explained anything."

"You just told me the hallmarks of what you think makes Botticelli's Venus beautiful, but are they?"

"Giacomo," Zanetta scowled, "if it going to be one of those days where everything you say is couched like a riddle of the Sphinx, I am going to walk right out of here and probably forget to bring you your breakfast!"

Giacomo laughed.

"All right, all right. It seems to be earlier in the morning for some than for others," he teased.

She raised an eyebrow at him.

"Everything you said is true. These qualities are all present in the painting, but they are not what make it beautiful. They are, more precisely, what makes the woman depicted attractive, at least to us."

"What's the difference?" she asked.

"The differences are many. What we may find attractive here may not be quite so attractive elsewhere. I have heard tell that people from different cultures sometimes have very different ideas of what makes a person attractive. What is attractive to you or me may be quite unattractive to someone from another place or another time."

"I am still not sure I see the difference," she said.

"When I first asked you to name something beautiful, you said a flower. Why?"

"I like them. I like their colors."

"Indeed. A bee also likes flowers, but for quite different reasons. They are attracted to a flower's nectar, which will become honey. They need it to live. To be sure, the flower is equally beautiful to the bee, but the nature of attractiveness is something altogether different. Do you see?"

"Maybe. Not really."

"Attractiveness is a value judgment. It is how we place our perceptions and desires onto another object or person. I once knew a man who only liked redheads. His own hair was black as coal and growing up he never saw a redhead, until he left his home as a young man. So why was this his attraction? I certainly don't know, but it is what he was drawn to. Styles change, fashions change, attractions change. So where does that leave beauty?" he asked.

Zanetta threw up her hands, a confession that she was no more enlightened than when she first sat down beside his bed.

"It leaves it," he explained, "right where it has always been, beyond the value judgments of attractive and unattractive, pretty and ugly, or even good and evil. Beautiful is beyond such deceiving dualities. True beauty can be pretty and attractive, but it can also be found in the unattractive, the difficult, or the challenging. And the reverse is true as well. I have known many attractive people, both according to my own preferences and the standards of a youth obsessed city, who turned out to be quite devoid of beauty. The truly beautiful, however, that which is beyond value judgments, is sublime."

Zanetta's head snapped up at this.

"You said," she hesitated before continuing in a small voice, "you said I was sublime."

"Yes."

"But I'm no longer beautiful."

Tears welled up in her eyes.

"Oh, my dear, that is where you are wrong. You are mistaking youthful attraction for beauty, and they are not the same thing at all. What we may find attractive in our youth is fine, but it is not the end. We place those qualities so high when we first come of age that we forget that just as our possession of those specific attributes will certainly change with time or location or popular fashions, so does our sense of attraction. And none of this has anything to do with beautiful."

Zanetta wiped at a tear that threatened to escape.

"I want you to close your eyes," Giacomo said.

Reluctantly Zanetta did as she was asked.

"Now, think of the most beautiful person you have ever known."

He waited for several moments.

"Now tell me who that is."

"Mother," she said.

"Yes, your mother.

"You know, she had you quite well beyond most women's childbearing years. It is something of a miracle you were even born. By the time my dear sister gave birth to you, she was no longer the youthful ingénue. Her hair had far more grey in it than your lovely silver threads. The girlish figure had given way to a more mature curve and her skin was no longer the flawless porcelain of Botticelli's Venus. But none of that mattered. To everyone who knew her she was the most beautiful of women. And to your father she remained, in addition, the most attractive woman in the world."

"Did she?" Zanetta asked through her pent tears.

Giacomo nodded.

"She was sublime, as you are, and that my child, is the most attractive feature of all."

Zanetta collected herself and stood. She started to say something, but, Giacomo supposed, there was really nothing more to say, as she turned and exited the room.

Zanetta reentered her bedroom and sat again at her dresser. She dabbed at her eyes, now swollen and red. *Giacomo Casanova*, she thought, *what a wonderful, sinful, and utterly romantic old fool you are. What will I do without you when you are gone?* The question stung at her.

The ornate silver hand mirror lay where she left it. She picked it up and stared again at her reflection. She was no longer the girl of sixteen who fist caught the eye of a handsome young man, who, it turned out, was not so beautiful of soul after all. But Giacomo said she was sublime, and if she could claim even a portion of the true beauty her mother possessed…

Zanetta opened a drawer at the side of the dresser and dug deeply. She withdrew a metal rod with a bone handle. It was a curling iron, tarnished with disuse. She could not recall the last time she held it over a lamp flame to heat it, as she now found herself doing. She propped the mirror against a jewelry chest and grabbing a clump of hair began winding it around the hot metal rod. Today Zanetta wanted to feel better about herself, and maybe this was the first step to seeing what Giacomo claimed to see in her. Today Zanetta felt like flying, and a crowning halo of silver threaded curls seemed, sublime.

The division of days became a hazy succession of impressions for Giacomo Casanova. Any sense of regularity was lost in the confusing arhythms of his fading body. Sleep gave way to periods of semi-consciousness, often punctuated by fractured dreams and fleeting images of a once vital life. Fictions became reality as passages from his written exploits waded through his muddied awareness. True memories swam in fantastical currents as the fevers that wracked him, robbed him of his surety.

Only in those moments of interaction with his niece or his grandnephew did he seem his old self. It was as if the gentle sparring with Zanetta focused his faculties in the same way a fencing duel or an impending battle or making love can sharpen one's observance of the world around him. Giacomo welcomed the companionship of his niece as the exchanges always left him clear-headed, just as his grandnephew's frequent chats did.

He and Lorenzo talked every day. Had Giacomo's lucidity been more constant he would have known that Lorenzo actually visited several times every day, even if just to sit and wipe the perspiration from his uncle's face.

Of late, it was the interaction with Lorenzo that Giacomo cherished most. Each time Lorenzo would provide his uncle with the latest update on his burgeoning romance with Costanza.

"Did you see her today?" Giacomo would ask.

"Yes Uncle. I walked past her home on the way to the market square and she smiled at me from her window."

"Ah, like Juliet on her balcony!"

"Who?"

"Romeo and Juliet. Shakespeare! Good God boy, didn't they teach you anything in that school you were in?"

"I know who Romeo and Juliet are, Uncle," Lorenzo said in good natured exasperation.

"So then, it is the east and she is the sun and what have you? Did she throw open her window and profess her undying love to you?"

Lorenzo cocked his head to one side before answering.

"Didn't Romeo and Juliet both end up dead?"

"You are missing the point boy. How am I ever going to guide you through this labyrinth if you keep walking into walls?"

Giacomo continued.

"How fortunate for you she happened to be looking out her window at the very moment you passed."

To which Lorenzo sheepishly replied, "I walk past at the same time every day. I think she knows when to see me."

Giacomo looked incredulously at his grandnephew.

"Do you mean to tell me that the two of you have a schedule and still you don't speak your heart? I would have better luck teaching a monkey to talk than I have getting you to do more than nod as you pass a pretty girl."

"I'll speak with her! I'm just waiting for the right opportunity," Lorenzo said.

"And when is that? At her wedding to some other man who could say more than 'Hello' or 'Excuse me Signorina, I didn't mean to get caught staring at your window?'"

"Uncle!" Lorenzo exclaimed.

"Well, at least she knows when she can see you passing by. That's something."

And on another visit, "You spoke with her? In person? This is news!"

"I have spoken with her before, Uncle," Lorenzo explained as if expounding common knowledge.

"So you have, so you have, but since you have come to feel as you have towards one another?"

Lorenzo didn't answer, but recounted instead the exchange between himself and the beautiful Costanza.

"She was passing through the market, with her father it so happened. They were on their way home from Signore Foscarini's warehouse when we just happened to meet."

"And did you prostrate yourself at her feet and proclaim your undying devotion to her?" Giacomo joked.

Lorenzo beamed. "We exchanged pleasantries. It was all quite proper, I assure you. But her father did suggest that I might call on them on Sunday afternoon. Signore Foscarini said he recently acquired an edition of Ariosto's *Orlando Furioso* and knowing that I am the grandnephew of a famous writer, he thought I might be interested in seeing it."

"Wonderful. At last, my notoriety may prove useful."

"Do you think I should go, Uncle?" Lorenzo asked.

Giacomo registered an expression of surprise. "You are the grandnephew of Casanova!" he said with grand exaggeration. "Of course you should go!"

Giacomo sat back bemused and satisfied as Lorenzo talked on about Costanza, how she looked, what she wore, the way she cast her eyes down when Signore Foscarini invited him to Sunday meal, and every other detail, real or imagined, he could recall.

Sunday came, and Giacomo waited eagerly for his grandnephew's promised visit. The weather was changing, the cold chill of fall finally gripping Venice in its gray clouded grip, but even the changing weather that robbed Giacomo of any comfort he had left could not dampen his pleasure at witnessing Lorenzo's quest.

For all the good humor, he knew that the invitation to the home of Costanza Foscarini was of great import to his grandnephew's happiness, and perhaps his future as well. It was late in the day when Lorenzo knocked at Giacomo's door and entered without waiting for a response.

One look told Giacomo all he needed to know. Lorenzo's countenance matched the grayness of the weather outside. The afternoon had not gone well.

Lorenzo sat heavily on the chair next to Giacomo's bed. After recounting the events that led up to his visit to the Foscarini home, Lorenzo revealed the reason for his dismay.

"I wasn't the only one invited," he said.

"Ah," Giacomo said immediately understanding, "a rival."

"A distant cousin," Lorenzo explained, "staying with the family for a spell. But it was clear he was interested in more than sharing old family news. He was fawning over Costanza at every turn."

"And what of Costanza?" Giacomo asked.

"That's the problem. She paid more attention to him than to me. We barely had a chance to speak. Every time I tried, he was there bringing up some cousin they both knew or someplace he had been or bragging about some exciting exploit in which he was always the victor."

"I know the type. It surprises me that Sebastian Foscarini would allow such a bore into his home, but then again, he is family, you said."

"Actually, Signore Foscarini was exceedingly nice to me. He asked about me quite a lot. And about Mother. He was particularly interested in my education and how I was learning to manage your estate. He seemed quite impressed with what mother was teaching me. And of course, he asked about you. He said he knows you quite well. He asked me to convey his well wishes for your speedy recovery and said he will visit soon, that it has been too long."

Giacomo nodded without comment, inwardly pleased at the prospect of seeing his old friend once more.

"And all this time, Costanza had little to say?" he asked.

Lorenzo shook his head.

"Once, when Signore Foscarini invited me to his study to see the Ariosto, Costanza did tell her cousin that I was the grandnephew of the famous Casanova."

"Ah! And what did the young braggart say to that?"

Lorenzo looked away before answering.

"He said he never heard of you."

"What! Now I am outraged! It is bad enough he inserts himself between you and your Juliet! Now he has insulted Casanova! He is worse than a braggart. He is a liar. Of course he has heard of me. He is an ignorant unlettered fool! He probably thinks an Ariosto is something he wipes after fouling himself. You have my permission to take my rusted sword from behind the door and run him through."

Lorenzo smiled slightly at his uncle's attempt to lighten his mood.

"I was a fool to have gone."

"You would have been a fool not to. Listen to me Lorenzo, love is full of obstacles. Heartbreak is the twin of heartsong. Every romance encounters bumps along the way. Sometimes you stumble and sometimes you fall. That doesn't matter. What matters is how you deal with it. Will the stumble and fall defeat you or will the adversity strengthen you. Your response will determine the man who survives."

"You think there is hope then?" Lorenzo was grasping at any sign of promise in what seemed a disastrous situation.

Giacomo shook his head. "One never truly knows until one knows, but if you don't persevere you will never know."

"Uncle?"

Giacomo looked directly into Lorenzo's eyes.

"Is she worth the risk of further pain to learn where her heart resides?"

Lorenzo answered his question with a question. "Do you think she feels the same as I do?"

"I can't answer that, my boy. Only she can, but you will never have peace until you know."

Lorenzo remained silent for a while as he absorbed this advice.

"Uncle, what if she doesn't love me? What if I lose her for good?"

Giacomo reached across and placed his hand over his grandnephew's, giving it a gentle squeeze.

"Loss and hardship are also aspects of love, Lorenzo. Loss too, is a part of love."

Women Who Long

Queen Uta
1249-1255
painted stone
Naumburg Cathedral, Naumburg, Germany

"Are you cold?"

Uta presses her wimpled cloak artfully to her cheek against the chill of the low river valley air.

"Yes, cold."

Her voice is barely above a whisper, yet it echoes its hushed tone throughout the cavern nave, giving her voice a distant quality.

I daren't touch her, though I know her hands would betray the iciness she feels.

"I could warm you."

"No, I fear not."

Even this small exchange is more than we have spoken in some time. A chasm grows and I fear it has become so large it cannot be traversed. When did it begin, this end that looms?

She stares away, past me, a faraway vision gripping her. Her face is serene, detached, a fairy-tale reminder of Teutonic romance. She is stately and regal in her loneliness. I see her without me, on the other side of our life together.

I shift uneasily, not certain what to say. The scrapings of my feet echo in the hollow of the cathedral. We are alone, save for the carved presence of ancestors and saints looking down from a remote past. I think to change the subject, if only to turn her attention back to me. If she speaks, perhaps I will hear what I need to hear.

"You come here often." I do not pose it as a question.

She does not answer.

"Do you find comfort here?" I ask.

"Somewhat, I suppose."

"What is it about this place?"

"Mass," she says simply.

"I don't understand." She has never professed a strong belief before.

Her head turns from door to altar so smoothly that the draping folds of her robes are fluted still, the worn heraldic colors placing her in a different time. She begins to explain, her face maintaining the same distant gaze.

"There is a church, very old, at least more so than this one, erected in the next town."

"I know it," I gently encourage her to continue.

"I have been there many times, but I always come back here."

"What is here that compels you so?" I ask.

A slight shiver and her pretty face shrinks a little more into her tightly held cloak.

"The words are the same, you know? Here or there, they are the same," she says in a small, detached voice.

"Are you speaking of the Mass?"

She nods almost imperceptibly.

"The words are the same, but the message is different." Her voice is nearly lost in the grand basilica.

"I'm not sure I understand. If the words are the same, how is it different?"

She nods again with a faint quiver, as if my response is to be expected.

"In many ways it is a grander church, in the next town over, larger, richer. Did you know they have the relics of a martyr? A local girl who died for her faith," she explains. "They say she can heal the sick," she says with a curious shake of her head. "Anyway, that's what they say." Her voice drifts off along with her focus.

After a pause she continues, "Many pilgrims visit her reliquary. The church thrives from the traffic, but I prefer it here."

"Why?" I am genuinely curious now, as if the explanation will balm our break.

"The carvings in the other cathedral, they were done in the Roman manner. Romanesque, that is what the Father told me. They are full of," her voice trails off again.

"Full of what?"

"Pain."

I try to recall the sculptures of which she speaks. Madonnas and saints, ancient clergymen memorialized. Memories falter, but I do not recall the sculptures as she describes. "I never realized."

A small turn of her head and I feel less for my failure to have recognized the full depths of her sorrow before now. Our drifting apart is more than apathy. Uta is in pain, for reasons I cannot begin to fathom. It colors her. It devours her. She tries to flee rather than face. She seeks escape in drink, but each night of loss merely dulls. Infidelities she thinks to conceal push us even further apart.

Uta explains. "It was a time of pain, I suppose, when they were carved. Plague, hardship, sorrow, it is what they knew. It is what they carved."

"And what has that got to do with the Mass?" I ask.

She looks directly at me for the first time, as if only now noticing my presence. For so long I have wanted her to pay attention, to talk to me, to banish the darkness that has surrounded us. Now I wish she would look away.

"So much difficulty. It was all around them. The Mass in that place is a warning. A fearful thing."

"Do you really think so?" I ask.

Her head moves in slow assent.

"And here?" I pursue.

"The Gothic soars. Look around you, the carvings seem almost real. They stand in perpetual attendance. They do not cry the pain of the now. They look to the hope of tomorrow. That is my craving. I long for the promise this place brings."

"You hope for tomorrow?"

"Yes."

"Why?

"Because today, for me, lives in that other church whose carvings are so full of pain."

I begin to plead. "I will give you that hope today. Together we can find it."

She shakes her head no and sadness permeates all around her.

"Will you let me try?" I ask.

A tear escapes the corner of her eye and rolls down her cheek unimpeded.

"Uta, where are we going? What is to become of us?"

She withdraws a little further.

"I don't think there is an us anymore."

"That's it then? We can still try."

It is a hollow plea. It takes two to try and save a relationship.

"I live for another life." Her voice is almost a whisper.

"And our life?" My words choke in the asking.

She looks away and I am no longer in her sphere.

"I am cold," she says, and pulls her cloak more tightly to her.

Women Who Challenge

Édouard Manet
Olympia
1863
oil on canvas

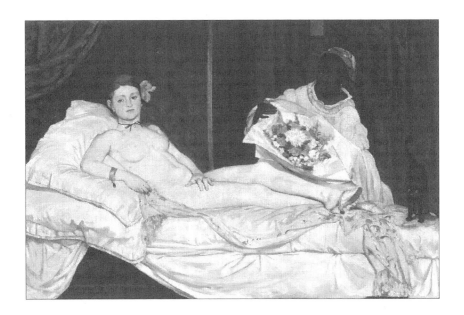

She ignores with studied disdain the extravagant spray of flowers her maid displays, a gift from a client or lover or one who unrealistically wishes to be both. I linger in her doorway, leaning against the jamb, one foot crossed casually in front of my weight-bearing leg, arms folded across my chest. She returns my gaze, level, challenging, unwavering, as if to ask, "What do you want?" Instead she says, "I thought you might show up."

"We did arrange for it," I say.

"I wasn't sure you would come."

"Why not?"

"You're different."

"Is that a good thing?"

Her shoulders raise a bit.

"Do I shock you? Here, like this?" she asks.

"Not particularly."

"You don't look at me like the others do."

"How do I look at you?"

"Like I'm a person."

"You are a person."

"Why are you here?" she asks.

"I thought we covered that."

"Not really. Are you a customer then?"

"No."

"So you want something. Something I would normally sell?"

"Not as you would think."

"Time is money."

"Then I will leave."

"Without what you came for?"

"You mistake me."

She studies me. "Like I said, different."

"Someone sent you flowers," I state the obvious.

She flicks her hand dismissively, her eyes never leaving mine.

"Someone," she says flatly. "I'm not sure who."

"Aren't you curious?" I ask.

"No."

"Why not?" I am intrigued by her disinterest.

"They are not for me."

"I believe they must be," I counter with some certainty. "It is unlikely they are for anyone else."

I look at her maid, still holding them for her mistress's approval, who gives a slight shrug in my direction.

Olympia shakes her head without a change of expression.

"No, not really."

"Then for whom are they intended?" I inquire, trying to sound casual.

She sighs deeply. "Me, I suppose."

One side of her mouth curves up in a half-hearted smirk and she rolls her eyes.

"Is this a game of wordplay?" I ask.

She glances at me, one eyebrow cocked in assessment of my mental faculties.

"They're from a man," she says. "They are always from a man."

"I guessed as much," I reply.

She registers a sardonic smirk.

"This one probably thinks he's in love with me."

"If he thinks he is in love, then isn't he?"

Her look is withering.

"He is in love with a commodity, this body, nothing more."

"Maybe he believes it is more? Maybe he is in love with you."

I scan the entirety of her form lounging on the bed before me. Olympia is starkly unclad. She is unabashed in her confrontative stare.

Her glowing white flesh resembles that of a Titian model. An Urbino Venus made real. A black ribbon adorns her throat. A sumptuous flower is at her ear, with pink petals and orange-red veins that catch the coppery redness of her hair.

"He is merely in lust then?" I counter.

"Perhaps. Probably. I give men with they need, an exchange of touch and release. That isn't love."

"And what about you?" I ask. "What do you need?"

"What makes you think I need?"

"Want, then."

"What I want is of little matter. Life is what it is. This is my lot."

How did Olympia come to this place? How is it that she does not see herself as I see her? In moments away from this chambered store of flesh, she is full of life. Her wit is the challenge of any man. Intelligence radiates in an endless stream of questions and observations. She is quick to laugh and even quicker to feel what others can only see from afar.

She flips a Turkish slipper, letting it thump against the sole of her foot. Its twin has fallen off to land unrecovered on the crumpled sheets of her bed.

"Does love not touch you then?"

Her hand clamps firmly over her sex. She is no Susanna startled at her bath, or Aphrodite on a foamy bed of waves. She rebels against her time. I see her in bold, simple, painterly impressions of light and dark.

"This way is more practical," she mutters.

Her maid shoots a disapproving look, unseen by her mistress. She carries the flowers away to secure them in a vase. I shift my weight from one foot to the other trying to find some balance in myself that seems missing in this courtesan model.

"Practical, yes, but surely you want more?"

"What?" It was not a question so much as a dismissive snort. "More? Shall I fall prey to the palpitating want of my clients who mistake port for palace?"

"Would that be so bad?" I ask.

"It is not for me. The damage is done."

"It does not have to define you."

"What we have, you and me, it isn't real. Oh, you think that is who we are, who I am, but it isn't so. I am not that carefree girl you meet in the cafes or stroll with hand in hand through the Champs-Élysées. Those are illusions. That is a make-believe realm. We deceive ourselves. I hear the jeers and disdain I invoke. Do you really think your Academicians would ever accept me?"

I ponder her question. "In time, they will. You are too great to ignore."

"Too raw?"

"Too new," I amend.

Her small black cat, Baudelaire, jumps to the foot of her bed, intrigued by the thump, thump, thump of Olympia's slippered beat. His back arches and his tail stands erect in imitation of her scheduled visitors. I can't help but be amused by the little Sphinx *chatte*, promiscuous and dangerous to those who would succumb.

"New," she says, "a new commodity."

"A new way of seeing."

Baudelaire mews and pounces at the beating shoe.

"Do you really think they will ever accept me?" she asks again.

"I have."

"The flowers, they're from you?"

I nod and turn away as Baudelaire jumps off the bed.

Bewitching Women

John William Waterhouse
Circe Offering the Cup to Ulysses
1891
oil on canvas

She is the Daughter of the Sun, an enchantress, a seductress.

Enthroned on tamed golden beasts she presides, mistress and empress of Nighttown, goddess of the wild beneath Monte Circeo, *Grota della Maga*, cave of the sorceress.

Circe. I first heard about her from friends, young men in a glorious drunk, having tasted the wine of forgetfulness from her proffered chalice.

The chimes strike twelve. Midnight. Dublin sleeps while Circe's palace comes alive. It is a brothel night. My day's odyssey has brought me here. Better here than home, I think, a cuckold's lair.

"Welcome," she chants from her regal perch.

She raises a wand above her head as if casting a spell and I am transfixed, less by her sorcery than by her flawless beauty. Cream smooth flesh displays beneath a shear blue chiton, her barely covered breasts delightfully tormenting me. Bewitching lips are parted, ready to weave an incantation, or escape a wispy moan, or to kiss and be kissed.

"I don't know why I am here," I say by way of an introduction.

"Men and women come for many reasons. For many reasons they come," she muses.

"I should leave."

I think of my duty.

"For home?" she asks.

I think of Molly's bed, shared with another.

I shake my head. "No. Not yet."

"For her," she says. It is not a question.

"Swine before pearls," I mutter.

"Molly's pearl?"

"You know her?" I ask astonished.

"I know you, that is, I know of you." She indicates my fallen friend, bloated and slouched at her side, a beast for her sexual appetite. "He told me you would come, but you are not like him. You are no swine."

"Like him?"

"Him and those like him who come, but flounder without a guide."

"A guide to what?" I ask.

"The left hand path."

"I see no path."

"It is before you. I am before you."

"You are the path?"

She seems pleased, but does not answer.

"Why do you wander?" she asks instead.

"What makes you think I wander?"

"Ulysses wanders while Penelope gives roof to her suitors."

"The roof of my once home. Hearth fires burn while I am away. Still, it is a blaze that will soon flicker and die," I say, not believing my own words.

"And you?"

"Dogsbody. I am more like him than you realize." I nod in my swine-friend's direction.

"No," she shakes her head, "you are not like him, merely blown off course."

"And you will guide me back?"

She shrugs. "I know the way."

"I have my own way."

"Not theirs," she says, indicating the sotted beasts.

"They drank your wine. The wine of forgetfulness. I don't want to forget."

"They did not come to forget," she corrects. "They came to pretend to live. They came, perhaps, not knowing that they would never know. You do not pretend."

"She doesn't know that," I say, thinking of Molly.

"She is as they, a slave to wanton lust. She does not know the way."

"I have a different way."

"Show me."

I withdraw from my pocket a vial and hold it high, a drawn sword.

"Hermes's gift," I pronounce, "a talisman, a moly."

"A flower like to milk," she says with disdain. "That is not the way."

"It is an easier way than to a cuckold's bed."

"Pride!" she snarls. "You let her fall you. Learn the true way and you cannot be felled."

"I do not want to become a beast like them."

"Then learn."

Circe rises from her golden seat and approaches. Her ruby lips touch mine and I am carried away. I become intoxicated with her.

My thoughts become a play within a play within a play...

CIRCE: You will not forget.

GIACOMO: I have forgotten how to forget.

CIRCE: It is a kiss.

GIACOMO: An opium kiss.

The Poet appears.

DANTE: She is your guide.

GIACOMO: My Virgil?

DANTE: Your Virgil. Your Virgin.

GIACOMO: Is it Mariolatry in Nighttown?

DANTE: She is but one guide along the way.

GIACOMO: It is a black mass.

CIRCE: *Schorach ani wenowach, benoith Hierushaloim.* I am black but comely, O ye daughters of Jerusalem.

GIACOMO: You are Mary then?

CIRCE: I am Mary. I am Solomon's concubine. I am Lilith and Demeter and Cybele and Pistis Sophia and Shakti all.

A dark presence makes itself known.

PRIEST: Beware the left, the cult of Shakti!

CIRCE: I am Shakti.

Dante has become Shiva in the play within a play within a play...

SHIVA: She is my initiation. She is female power incarnate. She is the left hand path. She is my bride.

PRIEST: Blasphemy! Abomination! You are become the darkhidden Father. You are dyad. It is an evil way!

SHIVA: She is the emanation of my dream. She is the emanation of the image of the universe. We are Shakti Shiva.

GIACOMO: (*Raising my hand*) Unman me not!

CIRCE: To be merely a man is to be unmanned.

PRIEST: Evil witch, the father of my fathers severed you long ago!

CIRCE: He cannot sever that which lies within.

GIACOMO: What lies within?

CIRCE: I am in you as you are in me.

GIACOMO: The female power in man?

CIRCE: Yes.

GIACOMO: The male power in woman?

CIRCE: Yes.

GIACOMO: And what of Molly?

CIRCE: She doesn't know what you know. She seeks in dalliance what she does not recognize in herself. She is as they (*she indicates the swine*). Only in recognizing that true love is found in the discovery of self in another can you truly be whole.

GIACOMO: Male female. Shakti Shiva.

CIRCE: Yes.

GIACOMO: What do you call this esoteric wisdom?

CIRCE: God.

GIACOMO: In me?

CIRCE: Yes.

GIACOMO: In you?

CIRCE: In all. The face of God is the face before you. See. (*She indicates the mirror behind her*).

GIACOMO: (*My image transforms to that of father Shakespeare*) God of my fathers.

CIRCE: What do you see?

GIACOMO: Will Shakti. Shakti Will.

The reflection speaks.

WILL: I was once as you are now.

GIACOMO: And what of Ann Hathaway, your Molly, your wife?

WILL: She did not know the way. In my will I left her my second best bed.

GIACOMO: A cuckoldress's reward.

WILL: If others have their will, Ann hath a way.

GIACOMO: It is much ado about nothing then?

WILL: When one knows.

CIRCE: The way is love. See.

GIACOMO: (*The image in the mirror transforms*) Will Shakti. Shiva Shakti. Circe Shakti. Dante Shakti. Giacomo Shakti.

CIRCE: You are the way.

Circe's lips part from mine. It was a hallucinatory kiss, all of a play in but a moment of time.

My sotted comrade snorts jealously and tries to nuzzle her sex.

"A pig's whisper," she says while batting him away.

"Do you bestow Godhood in a kiss?" I ask.

"Truth in joining," she replies. "I am whole. You are whole. I and the other are one."

"God is in the face before me."

"Yes."

I stay with her twelvemonth whole. Even when she is not there, I feel her within. Who can see the comings and goings of a goddess, if the goddess does not wish to be seen?

Women Who Advise

Theodora and Her Attendants
c. 547
mosaic
From the south wall of the apse, San Vitale, Ravenna, Italy

In the flickering light of a hundred candles and more she conveys a sense of the divine. Quite an accomplishment considering her origins.

There is nothing of the actress she once was in her now. Or, perhaps, she has become the consummate actress and only the stage has changed.

How different Theodora was then, so young, so exuberant in plying her craft, both onstage and off. It was not the most respectable profession for a young woman, but respectability wasn't her goal, living life was, and life had a greater destiny in store for her.

She is staged in regal splendor. Like a character in one of the plays of her youth, Theodora has a new persona, a new image. The clouds of her past give way to the perception of a greater reality. The physicality of the girl breaks apart. Planes shatter and lines dissolve. The spirituality of an empress shines like a thousand glittering tesserae.

"What will you do?" she asks.

Tension permeates the room. All eyes turn to her as she breaks the silence as one might shatter the ice of a newly frozen pond, endangering all who stand nearby.

The question is put to me, but it is as much for the advisors around me as for anyone. As always, she is keenly aware of her audience.

"You heard their advice," I say with more than a little disdain in my voice, indicating the assembled council. Advisors! Each with their own agendas. It is times like this, when all seems lost that you measure the true character of a man or woman. Who will advocate to run? Who will wish to capitulate? And who will stand?

These are dangerous times. The world seems bent on self-destruction, one faction eager to feed on another. A mob sees weakness and will act, even in defiance of the greater good.

"I heard them," she says, her level wide-eyed response not letting me off so easily. The disdain in her voice speaks louder than any condemnation of words.

"They say we should flee," I send it back to her.

"That is what I heard them say," she says with a wry expression.

"There are riots. People are killing one another. The city is in turmoil," I explain, but she knows all of this. The extremes would have our state fall over a cliff rather than compromise their fanaticism, as if they pledged a child's pledge. Intransigence is a dangerous quality in statesmen.

"Narrowness of thought," she says darkly. "Is He one? Is He three? Is His nature solitary divine or is His nature man and more? It is a Monophysite dilemma, and for these dogmas they kill each other. They expect their religion to dictate the actions of all. Metaphor becomes history and difference becomes evil in their eyes."

She sees more clearly than all of the advisors combined.

I nod my agreement. "East, west, man, God, and for these they kill each other."

She considers me and tilts her head, indicating the others.

"And if we leave, where would we go?"

"Rome?" I posit, knowing already that is not an option.

"The puppeteer to seek refuge among the marionettes?" she asks sardonically. "No. Running is not the answer."

She places her hand on my arm, a reassuring touch.

"Then we stay," I reply matter-of-factly.

Her Byzantine mind considers all the permutations, all the intricacies as a fine weaver surveys a tapestry for the most hidden of flaws. She sees none.

"We stay," she says.

The advisors shrink back. It is not an exchange in their favor. There is advantage for some of them in retreat. Back alley deals made that now will not be honored. It is just as well. There was no honor in the cowards' deals to begin with. They would sacrifice the state if it meant their own continuance.

"It will be dangerous, and brutal," I explain, though this, too, she knows.

"You have been tolerant," she says, "but tolerance is never an option for fanatics. You have bargained in good faith, but they will not stop until their way is the only way. You know this."

I nod my head gravely. It is the way of the small minded.

In the distance I hear the maddening clamor of the mobs. The Hippodrome rumbles with discontent.

I turn to my advisors. "Call for Bellasarius."

Theodora shivers slightly at the name. She does not like the General, but she understands his usefulness.

"Yes," she says, "he will succeed."

"It will not be clean."

Theodora's brilliant, piercing eyes follow my aide as he departs to call Bellasarius. I watch as the others begin to calculate the new decision, determining how they will turn it to their advantage. They will claim they were with me all along, for the good of the state. It is of little import. They serve a purpose, but I serve the state, and that means everyone, even the unrestful.

Theodora is lost in her own thoughts.

"My father used to work at the Hippodrome," she says, almost absentmindedly. "When I was a girl he was the keeper of the bears. I watched them baited and I was afraid of them, but my father told me I had nothing to fear, nothing, he would say, unless one should get loose in the Hippodrome."

She faces me, eyes wide.

"Bellasarius is a bear," she says with finality.

"He will be turned loose in the Hippodrome. It has to be done."

"It has to be done," she echoes.

Theodora pulls herself up to her full height, chin held high, adorned with pearls and fine raiment. There is none of the actress about her now.

This is real, as real as it gets, and she made her choice. She stands with me. She stands with the State. She stands, even when doing so is not to her personal advantage, but is for the greater good. This is how she will be remembered, the actress who became an empress, the ruler who would not run, the offering bride of state in Ravenna's court.

Women Who Leave

Edgar Degas
Glass of Absinthe
1876
oil on canvas

It used to be a pretty hat. I bought it for her in happier days, sober days. She donned it to her finely curled tresses, carefully arranged to frame a delicate, youth imbued face. She tilted her head with delight as we passed through crowds of admiring onlookers, admiring her for her beauty and me for my good fortune.

She wears it now, though tattered, twice crushed, and faded out of habit, or perhaps out of tattered, crushed, and faded memories of what once was. It is a shambled symbol of Laurel's decline into an oblivion she seems determined to find.

I often look for the seeds of her discontent. She once embraced life, though over the years she sought escape. The responsibilities of life became a burden too large for her to bear. Even the children in whom she found such joy are left behind in her downward spiral of drink and decadence. My quest to help her is a fruitless effort. You cannot help one who does not want to be helped. She seeks an alternate life that I can't provide. Her escape will destroy her.

I wander through the bracing night in search of her. The early morning mist dampens my face like tears I am afraid to shed. I know where I will find her, in the den of those already lost, but I cannot bring myself to seek there first.

The Moulin Rouge is alive with merriment. It is where we once played, she and I, dancing and dining and loving. We don't go there anymore. It is a world we left when family and responsibility came of age. She still sometimes went there with friends, before. I hope to see her there, as she once was, laughing and singing, but there are no more friends. They have all left, or have been driven away.

Each former haunt is explored. The faces are new to me. I see none that we once knew. Like Laurel and me, our former friends outgrew the frivolity of the clubs as we embraced other, more satisfying calls in life, but with change comes demands that for some are too difficult to live. Laurel could not endure.

I do not find her in the dens of carefree abandon, and so I continue on to those that cater to another clientele. I walk from club to club, each worse than its predecessor, knowing she will not be at any of them.

At the outer rim of decency is a bar, filthy, seedy, a repository of lost selves. The approach is not one of welcome, but lined with fallen bodies, from either drink or narcotic or violence rendered. Desperate whores cower in the shadows, emerging to offer the only thing they have left to barter before slipping back into the darkened alleys in which they ply their trade. I brace myself for what I know I will find inside and enter.

She sits at a bare plank table on a hard wooden bench. Sawdust on the floor retains the stench of spilled drinks, tobacco and opium, urine, vomit, and sweat. This is not an establishment of comfort or amusement. It serves only one purpose. This is the final stop. There is little repeat business, but never a shortage of the lost as they make their final farewells. Gas lamps emit an eerie glow that cannot hide the pallor of her face. Her vacant face.

She does not see me. She does not see anything.

A glass of absinthe sits on the table. It is not her first. Or second. Or third.

A disheveled, grimy sponge is seated next to her. He notices me and casually turns away. He knows why I am here. He can read the concern and disappointment on my face. He pretends not to know her, and he doesn't, but that does not conceal his intent, or his opportunism. He moves his hand away from her, from where it eagerly plunged before I arrived. Her dress is creased between her thighs where he groped with her absent compliance.

Bile sours my throat. I am moved to violence, but she is my concern now. He moves off, drunk, but not so drunk as to forget his own safety. It is a wise move.

I approach her. Her shadow projects behind her, unmoving, flat, and dark. It is as alive as she. She doesn't look up.

Her eyes gloss and stare at nothing. They are devoid of the beauty they once held. Her face is lined and old beyond her years. At the corner of her mouth and down her chin remain dried traces of another man, another absent compliance, another drink paid for. She will not remember.

"Laurel," I say softly, "I am here to take you home."

She looks up finally, but without recognition. I am just another patron of this den, another user, another drink.

"Laurel," I repeat, "let's go home."

A faint glimmer of recognition sparks in her eyes.

"Hey you," she slurs, then wavers, almost falling at the scant movement of her head.

No one pays attention to us. They are in their own decaying worlds and have no interest in some fool's hopeless attempt to recover one of their own.

I take Laurel's hand and help her to unsteady feet. I hold her tightly to me as I guide her out the door. It is as far as she can manage. I lift her in my arms and carry her. She does not know I am bringing her home. She no longer thinks of it as home. She does not remember her children sleeping there. She has gone where we cannot.

I manage her to her bed, our bed. I slump into a chair and watch over her. I think I will sleep there, but I will not sleep. I cannot leave her, yet I know she will leave me, soon, for good. She will leave her children. She will leave her better self. She already has. One night I will not find her to bring her home, or she will not want to be found.

Will she ever return? I already know the answer.

I will care for her children. They deserve better than just me. They deserve her, as she once was. So does she.

She turns on the bed and her once pretty hat falls to the floor. I pick it up and set it gently on the bedside table. I wonder if I will ever pick it up again.

Chapter Five

"*G*iacomo!"

Zanetta's scream reverberated down the hallway and throughout the palazzo. The glass of wine she was bringing to her uncle and the embroidery she carried with her to occupy her as she sat by her uncle's bedside crashed to the floor, the glass shattering at her feet.

The unconscious body of Giacomo Casanova lay sprawled on the floor near his bed. His face was turned away from Zanetta, though a widening pool of blood spread on the floor from beneath his head.

"Giacomo!" she yelled again as she ran to kneel at his side. "Giacomo, can you hear me?!"

She hastily turned his body to try and assess the wound, or to determine if he was even still alive. The side of Giacomo's face was covered in red-black blood, which seemed to be streaming from a gash on his forehead. Zanetta quickly pressed her hand to the spot. She could not discern if he was breathing and had no way of knowing if Giacomo was still alive.

"Lorenzo!" she yelled at the top of her lungs. "Lorenzo, come quickly!"

She heard the rapid stomp of her son's footsteps as he raced up the stairs, taking two at a time. She turned as he burst through the door.

"Uncle!" she heard him exclaim.

"Lorenzo! The doctor! Fast son. Fetch him as fast as you can!"

Lorenzo hesitated only the briefest of moments to register the sight of his fallen uncle and then was off again, descending the stairs even faster than he had come. Zanetta heard the front door slam as Lorenzo ran to find the doctor.

"Giacomo, oh Giacomo!" she kept repeating, while frantically yet constantly pressing on the open wound that pulsed beneath her hand. She realized with a start that the pulsing blood that seemed to defy her pressuring hand indicated that Giacomo was still alive, but for how long? She had no idea how long her uncle had been there, unconscious, bleeding, nor did she know if the gash on his head was the extent of his injuries. All she could do was continue pressing on the wound and wait for the doctor to arrive. The seconds and minutes seemed an eternity as she strained to hear any sound that would indicate help was on its way.

"Don't you die on me old man! Don't you dare die on me, you sinful old fool! Can you hear me Giacomo? Please hear me. Please!"

Zanetta's head jerked upwards with the bang of the front door being thrown open and footsteps racing up the stairs. A man entered at a run. It took Zanetta a moment to realize it was not the doctor or Lorenzo. It was her neighbor, Sebastian Foscarini.

"My God," he exclaimed, quickly taking in the scene before him. "Is he alive?" he asked in a rush as he grabbed a napkin off of the bedside table that held a tray with the remains of Giacomo's meal.

"I don't know. I, I think so." she replied.

"Here, let me," Foscarini said, removing her hand from Giacomo's forehead and pressing the folded cloth napkin to the wound. The exchange of hands had an immediate effect on stemming the flow of blood, the napkin and the broader expanse of Foscarini's palm successfully covering the wound.

"What happened?" he asked in a firm but calming voice.

"I don't know. He was like this when I came up here. It looks like he was trying to get out of bed. He's too weak," she explained. "Why would he do that? He's been far too sick to walk on his own. What was he thinking?"

She looked up to see Foscarini looking back at her, before returning his gaze to the man whose head he held firmly beneath his hands. There were questions neither of them could answer.

"Here, hold his head steady while I continue to press."

Foscarini released the hand not pressing on the wound and guided her hands to either side of Giacomo's head.

"Help hold him still," he said.

She did as he instructed, grateful to have someone else present who seemed to know what to do. She watched as Foscarini pressed his fingers against Giacomo's neck.

"He's still alive," he said, "but barely. The doctor should be here any minute."

Zanetta did not ask how he knew, nor did she even stop to wonder how her neighbor came to be here. She was just grateful for his arrival and his presence.

Foscarini moved his eyes over Giacomo's prone body, as if examining it for further injuries. Zanetta followed his gaze. Apparently satisfied that there was nothing more that visibly required his immediate attention he removed his fingers from the side of Giacomo's neck and, without removing his hand from her uncle's head he stretched his arm to grab the hem of the unconscious Giacomo's nightshirt which in the fall had risen to expose his emaciated legs, and pulled it down as best he could to cover his thighs.

The gesture seemed to awaken Zanetta from her shock at finding her uncle collapsed and injured. Foscarini, her neighbor, he was here, helping her. He was trying to stop the bleeding from her uncle's head. And even with all of this, he managed to think about covering her uncle's naked crotch and thighs. Not that any of this was unknown to Zanetta, who had long ago grown accustomed to helping her uncle bathe and, during his latest illness assisting him with his bodily functions, but still, the gesture comforted her. This man, who seemed to arrive out of nowhere was not only trying to help save her uncle's life, but with a small action he protected her uncle from the indignity of exposure. Not that Giacomo would ever know, nor would she ever tell him, but it was a thoughtfulness she knew he would appreciate nonetheless.

Neither of them heard the ascent of others up the stairs and both heads turned at once as Lorenzo burst into the room followed closely by the doctor who went immediately to the injured man.

"What happened?" the doctor, a man of fifty years or so asked to anyone. He was Giacomo's regular physician and had been treating him for years. He was well familiar with Giacomo and knew his way through his home.

"He fell," Zanetta heard herself explaining. "He was like this when I got here."

"Quite a nasty gash on his head," Foscarini added.

"Has he been unconscious the whole time?" the doctor asked.

"Since I found him, yes," Zanetta replied.

She felt the doctor take her by the shoulders and gently guide her back from the body.

"Let me in here," he said.

Zanetta rose and backed away. The doctor knelt opposite Foscarini who was still applying pressure to Giacomo's forehead.

"A pulse?" the doctor queried.

Foscarini replied, "Yes, but barely."

The doctor nodded, taking in the information.

"Let me see here."

He indicated for Foscarini to release his hold on the blood-soaked cloth and he lifted it to expose the wound beneath. Blood continued to trickle from the cut.

"The bleeding has slowed," the doctor said. "Here," he drew a thick clean bandage from his bag with his free hand and placed it over the wound. "Continue pressing down, like so." Foscarini followed his instructions.

"Boy," the doctor called to Lorenzo. "I'll need water, preferably hot. We need to clean the wound, so I can see what we are dealing with."

"Will he be alright?" Zanetta asked.

The doctor ignored her question.

"Young man, the water, now," he ordered. Lorenzo, still breathing heavily from his run to call the doctor hastily exited to do as he was told.

"Signora," he addressed Zanetta, "We will need towels. Can you bring me some?" He was more gentle in addressing the clearly distressed yet controlled woman.

"Yes. Yes, of course."

It took Zanetta only a minute to locate and grab an armful of folded towels and return with them to her uncle's bedroom. As she brought them to the doctor she realized her hands and arms were covered in blood, Giacomo's blood. She pulled the top towel from the stack as she set them beside the doctor as he indicated and began rubbing vigorously to clean herself as best she could while never averting her eyes from her uncle and the others. The doctor immediately began grabbing towels and placing them around her uncle soaking up the blood on the surrounding floor.

Lorenzo arrived with a basin of water and delivered it to the doctor, who immediately tested it with his finger.

"It's only warm," Lorenzo explained. "I only had a teapot of hot water to add. I'll bring some more."

The doctor nodded. "This will do for now. Go and put some more water on to boil. We will need it later."

Lorenzo left again, following the doctor's instructions.

"Shall we move him to the bed?" Foscarini asked as the doctor went about soaking one of the clean towels in the warm water and began wiping down Giacomo's face.

"No. It is best we leave him here until I can assess the extent of his injuries."

The two men continued in their actions, the doctor wiping and cleaning, and Foscarini alternately applying pressure and moving his hand aside whenever the doctor wished to examine the cut. Zanetta did not like her inactivity, and so began collecting the towels on the floor, mopping up the blood as she did so, and laying new towels in their place.

The act of cleaning up the horrific site steadied her, as did the calm and efficient manner of the doctor as he set about treating her uncle's wound.

"In my bag, she heard the doctor saying to her, "there is thread, and a needle. I need to suture the wound."

Zanetta crouched down and searched the bag until she found what she was looking for, a ball of thread and a long curved needle.

The doctor's hands moved swiftly as he took the items from Zanetta. He quickly had a length of thread strung through the needle and, as Foscarini gradually exposed the wound, he made a series of sutures, pulling the sides of the wound together before tying each one off and clipping the thread, nearly stemming completely the continuing trickle of blood. Little by little he proceeded until the entire cut was closed.

The doctor rummaged again in his bag and retrieved another roll of bandages, which he proceeded to wrap around Giacomo's head. He turned to address Zanetta.

"Is there something you wish to place on the bed, a blanket or such? I think we can move him now, but there is still much to clean."

"Don't worry about that," Zanetta replied, grateful that she now felt they were discussing matters over which she had some control. I can change the linens later. Let's just get him up there so I can tend to him better."

Lorenzo reentered the room carrying a second basin of steaming water. He set it on the chair beside the bed.

"Help us," the doctor said, and together the three men lifted Giacomo's limp body and placed him on the bed. Once they had him situated, they backed away.

The doctor noticed the basin of water sitting on the chair and dipped his hands into it, scrubbing them free of the blood. Zanetta handed him one of the last clean towels to dry his hands.

As she handed him the towel she asked, "Will he be alright doctor?"

The doctor accepted the towel and sucked in his breath.

"It is hard to say. The wound, in and of itself is not too severe. There is a lot of blood due to it being a head wound, but he lost so much. Your uncle was very frail to begin with, and now to be concussed... Infection is the real concern. I just don't know. The next twenty-four hours will tell. If he makes it through the night his chances are better, but even then, well, like I said, he is very frail."

The doctor gave her instructions on applying fresh bandages and monitoring Giacomo's temperature in case a fever set in. If so, she is to call for the doctor immediately, otherwise, just watch him and pray for the best.

Zanetta thanked him and watched him leave.

She turned her attention back to her uncle's unconscious body on the bed. His face, still streaked and stained with blood, was otherwise swollen and ghastly white, even paler than he had been of late during his most recent illness. His stringy white hair was colored by a thick mass of crimson. He looked tiny, as if the fall robbed him of what little physical stature he still possessed. She could barely see the rise of his chest, so shallow was his breathing.

"I'll need fresh water, and more clean towels," she said to no one in particular.

"You go, Mother. I'll stay here and watch, Uncle."

"Yes, yes, of course," she said, gathering her wits.

"Signore Foscarini," she said, as if noticing her rescuing neighbor for the first time. He was still standing near the bed from which he had not moved since helping move her uncle. His graying hair was disheveled, as if his rush upstairs and the activity of administering to her uncle had taken its toll, but he otherwise stood there, tall and protective like an aging soldier or athlete who, though time had made its mark, had not lessened his confident bearing. "Thank you. Your presence was a godsend. How is it you came to be here?"

"I was on the walkway just outside when young Lorenzo here ran into me. Literally. He told me what had happened, and I ran and let myself in to see if I could help," he explained.

"How fortunate then for us that you happened to be there to come to our aid. My uncle's life may turn on it. Thank you."

Foscarini picked up the basin of water, now tinted pink with blood, from the chair beside the bed and said, "Perhaps you will allow me to be a bit more of service. Let me carry this down for you."

"Thank you, Signore, but Lorenzo and I can manage."

"I am sure you can," he replied, "but please allow me nevertheless."

Zanetta nodded her head in assent, somewhat uncomfortable and unaccustomed at accepting the help.

"Thank you," she said again.

Zanetta retrieved the other water basin and moved to the door. Once there she noticed something on the floor and nudged it with her foot.

"Please be careful here, Signore Foscarini. I am afraid I dropped a glass when I first arrived."

"I will take care of it Mother," Lorenzo offered. I'll start cleaning in here until you return to take care of Uncle."

Zanetta nodded and exited, followed by Foscarini.

She led him down the stairs and to the kitchen at the back of the first floor.

"I've always admired this palazzo," Foscarini said as they wound their way to the kitchen. "From canal side it is a jewel, but the interior is equally exquisite. Casanova always had a way of mixing opulence with comfort."

"You have been here before?" she asked.

"Years ago," he replied. "I had occasion to visit on numerous occasions, for both business and pleasure."

Zanetta stopped and turned to Foscarini, an eyebrow decidedly arched.

"Pleasure?" she asked rather pointedly.

Despite his earlier confident behavior, Foscarini actually blushed slightly.

"I uh, I assure you Signora, I mean nothing of a lascivious nature. Your uncle is a great raconteur to be sure, and there was more than one evening that we, I and others, enjoyed the amusement of his stories over drinks and a game of cards. That was before he first became ill, of course, and had to cut back on his social outings. Before you and your son joined his household, Signora.

Zanetta started again towards the kitchen.

"Yes, my uncle is quite the storyteller," she said flatly.

Together they entered the kitchen and emptied the stained water down the large stone sink set against the wall. Two tea kettles and a pot filled with water were boiling on the wood burning stove. Lorenzo had set them to heat before bringing the second basin of water. She grabbed a rag and set them aside from the fire to cool a bit before she could pour them into the basin to bring back upstairs. She glanced around and saw that all six buckets of water that Lorenzo carried from the well in the piazza early that morning were now empty, save one that was still half full. She would ask him to refill them as soon as she had the chance. Zanetta emptied the last remaining water from the partially filled bucket into one of the basins and added some of the hot water from a teapot to warm it up. She moved aside, indicating the basin to Foscarini.

"Your hands. Please," she said.

Without a word, Foscarini went to the basin and washed his hands of the blood that covered them. Though she had earlier tried to clean with one of the towels she had retrieved, Zanetta followed his example when he was done and more thoroughly washed away the remaining blood from her own hands. Her dress was well stained, but she would tend to that after she finished washing her uncle.

"Thank you again, Signore Foscarini. I don't know what we would have done without you."

She felt flustered at his continued presence, though it was not unwelcome.

"I, um, I have more hot water. Can I offer you some tea?"

"Thank you, no," he answered. "After the events of today, I think I will retire to something a little stronger."

"Ah!" she said. "I think I can help with that." She opened a cupboard and withdrew a bottle. "Uncle Giacomo's brandy. Under the circumstances, I don't think he would mind."

She reached back into the cupboard and set two glasses on the counter. "And I hope you don't mind if I have one myself," she said.

"Well earned and well deserved, I should think," Foscarini replied.

Zanetta poured a measure into each glass and handed one to Foscarini.

"Your uncle's health," he said, tipping his glass slightly in her direction.

"To Giacomo's health," she replied, taking a sip, then a second larger sip, allowing the warmth of the brandy to steady her.

"He's a sturdy old bird," Foscarini encouraged. "I am sure he will pull through this."

"I don't know, Signore Foscarini. I hope you are right. I just don't know." She sipped at her brandy.

The two stood in awkward silence, each drinking their drink. Foscarini finally broke the silence.

"Your son, Lorenzo, he's grown into a fine young man."

"Thank you, yes he has."

"I can't help but notice that he has a bit of your uncle's charm in him."

Zanetta rolled her eyes slightly.

"Lorenzo will be thrilled to hear that, not to mention Giacomo."

"I meant it as a compliment. It seems to me you have raised him well. You know, he visited us this past week, for a Sunday."

"He talked of nothing but," she replied. You had a new volume of Ariosto he wanted to see, as I recall."

Foscarini emitted a little laugh.

"I don't think it was the appeal of an ancient book that drew your son's attention. Just the same, it is a credit to you that he maintained enough generosity to an old merchant to at least feign polite interest. As I said, he is a fine young man."

Foscarini finished his drink and set the empty glass on the counter.

"Thank you for the brandy. I won't keep you any longer," he said.

"I need to get back to Giacomo," Zanetta replied. "Thank you again, Signore Foscarini."

"Please Signora, do not hesitate to send for me if I can be of any further assistance. I owe much to that man upstairs."

"Signore?"

"I owe him my life."

"Giacomo saved your life?" she asked.

"So to speak," he replied. "Not physically, but he made the things I have cherished most possible. Did your uncle never tell you?" he asked. "No, I don't suppose he would. He is indeed a great spinner of yarns, but he keeps the goodness of his heart private."

Foscarini went on to explain.

"It was many years ago. Long before you and your son moved here. I was much younger then, of course," he said, somewhat chagrinned at stating such an obvious fact. "I was just starting out in my new business and not having much success. You know how things are in Venice. Merchants guard their territories jealously. I was in love with the girl that would become Costanza's mother and hoping to marry. It was make or break for me. My future, my ability to marry and provide for a family depended on it. Just when I thought my entire business venture was a failure, and I along with it, your uncle, Casanova came to me with an offer to invest. It was a tremendous gamble on his part, but he told me that no man should ever be denied the hand of the one he loves because of a few selfish businessmen. How do you like that? Casanova! A lover of lovers, eh?"

"That sounds like Giacomo," she said with her first genuine smile of the day.

"We did quite well too. Oh, there were other business dealings that followed over the years. Not after he, well, not for many years, since he has been ill off and on, but I will always remember him as the man who helped me find my dream."

"That is a wonderful story," she said.

"I was young and lost and your uncle was there to help me out. He told me, Signora, that sometimes we all need a helping hand, someone to deliver us back into the world. Please Signora, Zanetta, remember that."

Foscarini nodded his head in a slight bow and exited the kitchen. Zanetta remained still, listening until the front door shut, and then she set about pouring water and finding more clean towels.

"You old fool! What were you thinking?"

Zanetta was rowing full and it was all Giacomo could do to keep from being consumed in her wake. Best to let her get it out of her system, as there was no stopping it anyway.

"I, er, I don't know," Giacomo muttered, barely comprehensible.

"Look at you! It's a wonder you didn't split that empty head of yours wide open. And it would have served you right too."

Giacomo gingerly touched the still swollen mound that stretched taught his forehead. It was covered in bandages and throbbed continually as if straining to burst the stitches that now crossed his flesh.

"Any chance you can bring me that mirror?" he asked when she was changing his bandages.

"Certainly not. It will only make you feel worse."

"I'm not sure I can feel much worse," he said, gently touching the swollen bump again.

Lorenzo had been a bit more forthcoming, describing the injury in an effort to satisfy some of his uncle's curiosity. The cut, he was told, was deep, but not life threatening, although in his state that was no guaranty. His forehead was vastly swollen, like an egg, and the bruising extended from his crown down past his eye and onto his cheekbone. His eye was blackened, giving his face an even more sunken appearance.

"Not the first black eye in my life," he tossed off to Zanetta when asking again for the mirror, as if making light of the whole matter.

"No? Well, it was nearly your last." She was not going to let him off easily.

"Zanetta, dear, I am sorry I made things so difficult for you."

Zanetta merely grunted and continued tucking in sheets and straightening covers as if his body wasn't even there, lying in the middle of them.

"Was it really so important for you to look out the window? Was it really worth risking your life?"

Giacomo shrugged, though she paid no notice.

"I wanted to see Venice," he said simply.

"All this just so you could look out a window," she practically growled.

"I wanted to see Venice," he repeated.

"Zanetta, please, sit. All your fluttering about is making my head throb even more. I promise I won't try to get up again. Not until I am stronger, eh?"

It was a hollow promise they both knew.

Zanetta relented and took the chair beside the bed.

"Three days, eh? I was out for three days?"

"We nearly gave you up for dead." Zanetta's voice was somber now, devoid of anger and recrimination.

Giacomo wanted to say that it would take more than a bump on the head to kill Casanova but decided it best not to make another dismissal of the situation in light of all he just put his niece through.

"I am sorry," he said again, this time truly meaning it.

A silence birthed between them and lingered while each was lost for a time in their own thoughts. It was Giacomo who finally breeched the silence.

"And you? How are you doing?"

Zanetta made a dismissive gesture with her hand.

"Fine. I'm fine," she said.

Giacomo did not believe her.

"Three days," he repeated, almost to himself. "Do you think there is a significance to that?" he asked.

"To what?"

"Three days in the tomb, so to speak."

Zanetta's eyes widened with incredulity.

"Why, you sinful old devil! Has the great Casanova now become Christ risen! Is this to be the next volume in your memoirs? The Gospel of Giacomo!"

He chuckled. "Hardly. I was actually thinking about you?"

"Me?!"

Giacomo nodded, even though the motion increased the intense throbbing in his head.

"What were you doing during those three days?" he asked.

"I was taking care of you, what do you think?"

"Yes. And I thank you for that, and for all you have sacrificed on my behalf, but what about later?"

"What do you mean what about later?"

Giacomo fixed her with a steady, knowing gaze. Zanetta stiffened.

"I am not going to have this conversation again," she said sharply.

"You can't run away from it," Giacomo said.

"I am not running away from anything. It is just pointless to discuss."

"It is true. You are not running away from anything, and that is what concerns me."

"You're talking nonsense. That bump on your head addled what brains you have left."

"I have been selfish, Zanetta. I have allowed myself to be the instrument of your entombment."

"What are you talking about?"

"You can't stay locked away from the world forever, my dear."

"I'm not locked away from anything. And when did this become about me?"

Giacomo laughed. "It always has been."

"Hmph!" she sniffed. "And so what if I am locked away, as you put it. It is nobody's business but my own."

"Society is jealous of those who remain away from it."

"What do I care of society?"

"You have a role to play."

"The only role I have to play is to take care of you and Lorenzo. Anything else is none of society's business."

"Perhaps. Perhaps. But consider this, I am in the tomb, three days notwithstanding. You can deny it all you wish, but we both know it is so. And Lorenzo? While you may want it to be that he is still in the womb of hearth and home, his departure too is set. Your role is changing, and you need to change with it. You cannot follow me. Not for a long, long time. And you cannot prevent Lorenzo from his own fate, if such a thing exists. It is time you looked beyond the confines of your self-devised underworld. Inanna must return," he said. "She only needs to find the way."

Silence resumed for a time, neither wishing to press their point.

Giacomo tried to relax into his pillows, but fell into a coughing fit, instinctively raising his hand to his bandaged head as if the gesture would relieve the shooting pains.

Zanetta held a glass of wine to his lips from which he gratefully sipped. After regaining his composure, he spoke again.

"Lorenzo tells me that Signore Foscarini has been back, since my fall that is."

Zanetta's head snapped up at the mention of Signore Foscarini's name, then she quickly looked away.

"He has been here, a few times, yes," she replied, a little too nonchalantly. "He wanted to know how you were faring."

Giacomo slightly nodded his head at the information. "Ah, that was nice of him. Sebastian Foscarini is a good man."

"Yes, so he seems."

"I knew him quite well, you know, when he was first starting out in his business."

"He told me." She did not offer more.

Giacomo decided to try another tack.

"How go things for Lorenzo with his daughter, Costanza?"

Zanetta immediately perked up at the change of subject.

"She is a lovely girl," she admitted, "but Lorenzo is distraught. Another suitor, I gather."

"Yes, he indicated as much to me. A distant cousin or some such. It is not an easy thing, this love for which we all strive. Not an easy thing at all."

Zanetta nodded, for once in complete agreement with her uncle.

The days were growing shorter. Giacomo Casanova knew he would not last to see them lengthen again. There would be no renewal of light. He was on a voyage into darkness that began many years before, though now the pace was quickened and there was still much to do, but not for himself, Giacomo mused. He lived his life and now it was time to let it go, but not before he accomplished his one final task. Not before the mantle he wore had been transferred.

He mulled his task. Through the chaotic waters of the abyss he had learned to swim, to navigate their torrential pulls, and to survive. More than survive, he had defied their annihilation and became a guide to others lest they drown or become devoured by the leviathan waiting to consume the unprepared, or the unwilling. Giacomo knew he was about to exit those depths, a watery wasteland to most, a lifespring to some, and he was not ready to see his wake disappear with the onrush of the numbing void. If he was to be displaced, as he was surely soon to be, he would see his role refilled, but in order to do that he must show another how to swim and survive those dangerous currents. The journeyer must find return. And if, in the process, he saw his grandnephew on a path that would bring the young man a measure of the same fullness of life he had experienced, so much the better.

More than once Giacomo beat death, disappointment, and sorrow to find redemption on the other side. As he knew only too well, one can only find the redemption of the other side if one is willing to cross the threshold to life, and subsequently, as he learned more than once, the threshold to the way back.

Time is running out, Giacomo thought. And what little time was left he nearly threw away with his recent fall. Priorities, he thought. As much as he longed to see his beloved Venice once more, if only through a high window from his entombing room, it was not to be. Not if he would see his task fulfilled.

"Lorenzo, my boy," Giacomo called as the younger man entered his room, interrupting his thoughts. "I was wondering when you would visit your old uncle today."

"I came earlier. You were asleep," Lorenzo explained.

"Ah, yes, well, I am afraid this old body does not conform to my willed schedule as it once did.

"How do I look today?" Giacomo asked, as he did every time Lorenzo visited since his fall.

"You look good, Uncle. The swelling is down, and the black eye is barely noticeable," Lorenzo said with a smile.

"You are a poor liar, Lorenzo," Giacomo said, not unkindly. "I am a mess, and we both know it."

Lorenzo shrugged and sat heavily in the chair next to the bed.

"It's cold in here," he said. "Shall I shut the window?" he asked.

"Bah!" Giacomo waved away the suggestion. "You sound like your mother. Leave it. I'm fine."

In truth, he was frigid cold, but he dare not ask for another blanket as the weight of those covering him was already such that it made his breathing difficult. He may not be able to traverse the room to see his Venice, but sure as hell he would not deny all of his senses. Priorities.

The two sat in silence for a while, each enjoying the comfort of mutual quietude. It was Giacomo who finally spoke.

"You haven't asked to hear any more stories lately. Have you lost interest?"

"No," Lorenzo said a little too quickly. "I mean, I want to hear more. I just thought that since your accident," he left the thought unfinished.

"I see. And does your consideration for my convalescence also, perhaps, have anything to do with the lovely Costanza Foscarini?"

Lorenzo's head turned up at this.

"What? No. No, I haven't really seen her lately."

"Why not?"

"I've just been busy. Mother has me working on some of your accounts. She is thinking of investing in a wool trade venture and is guiding me through some of the research. You know mother. She does not enter into anything without checking it out first."

"A wool trade venture," Giacomo repeated with a raised eyebrow. "Interesting."

And what wool merchant comes to mind?

You are a sly and surprising woman, Zanetta, Giacomo thought to himself. He turned his attention once again to his grandnephew.

"Is this the only reason you have not seen her?" he asked.

Lorenzo jerked his head to the side but said nothing.

"The cousin, he is still in the picture?"

Lorenzo looked down at his hands.

"I suppose."

It was clear that Lorenzo was torn over what to do about Costanza.

"Why don't you just ask her?" Giacomo finally said in some exasperation.

"I can't do that," Lorenzo replied.

"Why not? What do you think will happen?"

Lorenzo remained silent at this, and then changed the subject.

"Uncle, you told me before that sometimes things, you know, don't work out. Is that always the case?"

Giacomo chuckled slightly. "No, not always. Sometimes though, it just happens. People drift apart, events occur, you find out the one beside you is not the same person you fell in love with. Things change."

"Did it ever bother you?"

"You mean did it hurt? Yes, of course it did. It always does."

"But then there were others," the young man said hopefully.

"Others," Giacomo repeated without inflection. "Is this me we are talking about, or you?"

"Uncle?"

"Costanza. You are so wrought over not knowing whether or not she feels the same about you as you do of her that you are already looking for a replacement in your heart. It seems a little premature to me."

Lorenzo sulked at this.

"Uncle," he asked after several silent moments, "is it always so difficult?"

Giacomo regarded the young man tenderly.

"Yes, I suppose it is, but not impossible. The sharpest pangs of love are those we inflict upon ourselves."

"What do you mean?"

"By not asking, for instance," Giacomo said. "You are at a fork in the road my boy, one of many that you will encounter. The easy path is tempting, but unsatisfying. The wasteland is filled with sheep benignly waiting for life to come to them. If love strikes, wonderful. If not, then perhaps they will settle for whatever substitute they can convince themselves is the real thing. The more difficult path requires the most difficult risk of all, the risk of the heart. My advice to you, take that path and never look back."

"But what if I take that path only to find she doesn't love me after all?"

Giacomo exhaled deeply. "Then you will still be on the right path and ready for your next discovery."

"And what is that?"

"Redemption, Lorenzo. Redemption."

Bathing Women

Rembrandt van Rijn
Woman Bathing in a Stream
1654
oil on canvas

She is an old man's solace. She is this man's salvation. I never thought to love again. Broken hearts do not mend, or so I thought, only to learn that while loves lost may never fully heal, the heart expands, and new loves are born.

"It's cool to the touch," she giggles, hiking her shift higher to keep it from getting wet. She has no idea how her carefree ways defy the ever-calculating hesitations of one who has lost, only to find again.

I watch intently. I have seen her before, in my bed, in my studio, with far less than the linen slip that covers her now, but she has never been more enticing. The plunging, open neck and the ever-climbing hem conceals more than it reveals and I am moved to imagine the recesses of the deepest shadows between her legs and the abundance to be displayed with the slightest parting of her neckline. My anticipation goes unfulfilled and with it my yearning increases.

Hendrickje is her name, a northern girl.

Amsterdam, our home is a city of wealth. Ships arrive, and goods come and go. Sponsors line their pockets and prosperity flourishes. Merchants are the new princes in this kingdom of coin, and each new prince wishes to proclaim his importance.

I have benefited from their affluence. The new princes must be validated, so I validate. Sitters sit, corporate bodies align, always in order of importance, by which, of course, I mean in order of wealth. I don't mind, I paint them all. It is a means to an end.

My own fortunes increased with each new commission. The Baroque has become personal under my hand. Once the theatre of the Church, it became the statement of the State, but these are new princes so I apply my chiaroscuro brush to their likenesses, their personal theatre of worth. I was in favor, more than any other artist of my day. They liked my style. They liked that I portrayed their individuality, they liked the tightness of my brush. They liked that they were seen as saints and kings.

But styles change, mine, not theirs. I am in fashion one day, out the next. That is the way of things. That is the way of commerce. Young merchant princes take place of the old. They mistake inheritance for accomplishment. The more I see, the less they approve.

Individuality is good for business, to a point. It was my job to observe, and to paint what I saw. I saw too much. The new princes did not wish to be seen so well. The deeper I peered the less in favor I became. It was me who changed, not them. Portraits, corporate commissions, even scenes of myth and faith, all changed the more I gazed into the depths. Tightness flees with an awareness of the spirit. It was too much for some.

"He's mad," some exclaimed. "He paints with frenzy. Look, it isn't even finished!" But they were finished in my estimation. The spirit is not so confined as surface flesh.

Styles alter. Fortunes shift. Lives are not the same.

Before Hendrickje was Saskia, my flowered girl. She was my life and then she was gone. Is this what altered me, my style? Was it the loss of love, or was the loss of Saskia the catalyst for a deeper search of love? Deeper I searched, and deeper I saw. The new princes wished to be presented. They did not wish to be seen. Styles and fortunes change.

I managed to survive, but just barely. A minor commission from an old friend to buy food, collections and treasured items from a past I no longer lived sold off, a home left behind, but once one learns to see the soul it cannot be unseen. I cannot go back to my old brush. And then Hendrickje came and I was renewed. A heart, never fully healed, expands.

"It's cool to the touch," she repeats, "and the stones are slippery."

She wades carefully into the water. I glance past her, at her gold brocade dress strewn on the shoreline rocks, chastity discarded. She is bold in her night foray. She is Bathsheba and I am her David, her voyeur, her audience, the seducer seduced. Will she be spied by me alone, or caught, perhaps by Captain Cocq's night watch on patrol? How would I explain to these merchant guards such a titillating sight? The thought amuses me. It would not be so difficult. I am thought mad, after all.

Torchlight illuminates her tentative dip, adding to the illusiveness of line. I discern her in earthy hues, her ever higher shift an impasto of loose white strokes. Beneath her, in the mirrored surface of the ringlet waving water she reflects, a sketch of a sketch. I render her as no one else can.

She is no tightly brushed merchant prince, my Hendrickje. She is passion and sensuality and tantalizing nymph. She is the reflection of my mind.

The princes have given me another chance, a commission for the new town hall. Amsterdam's founding myth to be made history viewed. It is glory they seek, not truth. I will give them truth. How can I do else? There will be no corporate portrait like merchants around a disciples' table, despite their expectations. I will give them the brutality of the Batavians' oath, broad, painterly, and deep. I will give them the essence of spirit rather than the civil Civilis they expect.

It will be rejected, but how can I compromise to a former style once I have seen into the soul? This is not madness. It is truth.

"Come Hendrickje. I will dry you and take you home." She is an old man's solace and satisfaction.

"Just a little longer," she pleads.

"We risk being seen," I say, not really caring if we are. I see more than a passing guard could ever imagine.

"My legs are very wet," she says as she steps further into the deepening pool.

Women of Ritual

Snake Goddess
From the *Palace at Knossos*, Crete
c. 1600 BCE
faïence

Beyond good and evil they writhe, intertwined as the one that becomes two that become one. With her arms extended she commands them, as if the world generating force that flows through all opposites flows through her as well. She is Pasiphaë, the shining daughter of Crete.

"I thought to never find you again," I say upon my arrival.

"Was it so difficult?" she asks.

"Like all good quests, it had its challenges. The journey was labyrinthine, like meandering through a palace built upon a palace, and you are its treasury."

"But you did find me."

"I had to."

"Why?" she asks, and I can hear the delight in her question.

"I think you know."

"There was an emptiness when we parted, even though it was only for a time," she says.

"Yes."

"You wish to fill that emptiness."

"I wish to understand its source. I think you possess the answer. It is why I came."

"What I hold then is of value," she says, her eyes wide in anticipation.

I hesitate before answering.

"It is not what I expected." My words do not convey disappointment. "Why did you bring me here, to this house of double axes?" I ask.

"This was the home of my mother before mothers, my namesake, even she who tamed the moon's creature, though such a truth is terrible for mortals to behold. Not so for gods."

"Then how shall I learn the truth? We are not gods," I say.

"Indeed?" she says without surprise.

I consider her and the difficulty of finding my way suddenly seems less than only moments before. She stands unabashed, bare-breasted, her fitted dress dancing in a blaze of color and calling to mind a priestess of the archaic Aegean. Mystic royalty is poised upon her in feline grace. She offers herself to me, body and spirit. It is a body I have known, a spirit I seek to know.

"What did you expect to find?" she asks with a touch of mischievousness.

"Not vipers," I say.

She shakes her head. "No, I would think not."

I am entranced by her every move as she places the two small reptiles in a faïence vessel on the ground. When she stands again she looks more like the lover I sought than the priestess I found.

"Why did you come to me?" she asks. "Not that your presence is unwelcome," she adds.

"You know why I came."

"To love me," she says.

"Yes."

"To know me?" she adds.

"I thought I did know you, but now…"

"Am I now so different?"

"Yes, different, and no. You seem older, somehow."

Her response is quick and playful.

"Is that any way to talk to a lady?" she asks.

I blunder through an apology.

"I didn't mean…"

"It's alright." She lifts her hands again, this time in a reassuring manner. "I think I know what you meant. Age only matters to the youthful blind. Upon me rests the mantle of my ancestors, the same as those of the three divines, Demeter, Artemis, and Athena."

"That seems a heavy mantle to wear, yet you shoulder it effortlessly. You are more than I realized," I say.

"How so?"

"When we became lovers, I saw little more. Now, here, I see you more as you are."

"And how is that?"

I ponder the question.

"I am not sure. Lover, yet more. You seem to hold the secret of life over death."

"It is no secret."

"Then tell me."

"I showed you on your arrival."

"The vipers?" I ask. "I do not understand."

"That is because you see with eyes of duality, afflicted by the sunlit world in which all pairs of opposites appear to be distinct. The ophidians are but a symbol, a writhing metaphor. They are the self-consuming, self-renewing principle. The phallic female, the vaginal male."

"You speak of things I don't comprehend."

"I speak as he who was blinded and in such blindness gained sight."

I search my memory for lessons of my youth, recalling legends of a distant past.

"The prophet blinded by Hera, gifted by Zeus?" I ask.

"The same. He saw the serpents as the metaphors they are, not as some diabolical garden tempter to be vilified in book and belief, the genesis of misunderstanding. To see elements of unity in oneself and in the lover, one seeks is to know what she, he, the seer knew. It is to possess the caduceus of the Lord of Knowledges beyond death.

"These are mysteries far beyond my understanding." I shake my head in bewilderment.

"Only to those who do not seek. The serpents I held are seraphim, spirits, angels on high. Know their mystery and you will become as the prime mover, knowing all opposites in one."

"I think I am beginning to understand. Despite perceptions, they are the same? The serpents? Male and female?"

"As they mate, so they are," she answers.

"But their genders?"

"Images of the dual. We see them as opposites, but the male inhabits the female, as the female the male. We unite in body, but in spirit we were never divided. This is the truth you seek. It is what you have always known when not looking with your eyes upon a divided world."

"What you speak of," I say, "is a view of the divine."

"Yes."

"And the division then, between mortals and gods?" I ask.

"Divinity is in mortality," she says.

"Between male and female?"

"*Hieros gamos*, the sacred marriage reveals that there is no division."

"Between you and me?" I ask at last.

"I can only show you the way. What knowledge you glean is yours alone."

Walls fall as I search her eyes, staring beyond the beauty of flesh and curve. In her I perceive the beginning. In her I see me.

"We are not apart," I say, "and never were. Now I understand."

"Then we have become as gods. Now love me."

Watching Women

Bartholomeus Spranger
Vulcan and Maia
c. 1585
oil on copper

She is young and bright, like an early May star in the first hours of life's night. Too young for me. So why do I entertain such thoughts? And why does she?

"I am surprised to see you," I say. "Not many come here unless they need something." I motion around the expansive smith's shop. "It isn't an easy journey, after all. Not many willingly venture beneath Etna."

Maia smiles her dimpled smile but says nothing. In another woman such an expression would appear coy, in her it is natural. She is in no apparent hurry to tell me why she has come. She seems comfortable here, and I am out of comfort with her presence.

"Do you need something? Have you come to request a service? Is there a job you need me to do?"

"No, not really. I just came to see you."

Does she know how I feel about her? How she makes me feel? She is young, but not so young that she does not understand the effects of a charming woman on a man. Is this but a game of flirtation? It is not a game I wish to play.

She wanders around the forge tracing her fingers along the spiraling filigree of a recently completed shield, a gift fit for Aphrodite's lover.

"This is nice," she says.

"You are a fancier of armor?" I ask with some amusement.

Her giggle betrays her youth.

"No, it's pretty, that's all."

Maia drifts along, content in her silence. I resume my work, happy for her unexpected presence. After a time she stops meandering and takes a seat opposite my forge. I am aware of her, but she is poised in patience, content to observe without the need of drawing attention to herself or filling the silence between us with self-centered chat.

I complete the task at hand and break for a rest. Maia is still there, sitting, watching. I set down my tools and lean against a post, now giving her at last my full attention.

"How is your family?" I ask just to make conversation.

"My sisters? Oh, you know, the same as ever." She is less than enamored with her sisters' frivolous ways. "Seems like every other day one of them is in love with this boy or that, and every other day after that they are just as quickly out of love and on to their next crush. They live for the chase, and being chased."

I do know. Maia is the eldest of seven sisters, seven shining Pleiades, brilliant stars in the firmament, and though she is by far the prettiest she is also the most sensible, and the most shy. The other six sparkle and shine, drawing attention wherever they go, but it is Maia who merits real observation. There is much more to her than surface gild.

"But not you?"

She lets out a deep breath.

"It's all so tiring, isn't it?"

"Is it?" I ask. "Why so?"

She doesn't answer. Instead she toys with a small silver figurine of Mercury, messenger of the gods on the table near her chair.

"Did you know that Mercury was the conveyor of souls to the underworld?" she asks, an apparent non sequitur, but I follow along with her. Maia is not one for idle conversation. There is usually meaning behind her words.

"That is the legend," I respond.

"And," she continues, "he is sometimes credited with the invention of the civilized arts." She toys with the little figurine. "You as an artisan should appreciate that."

"I do," I reply. "So, is there a connection, between the two roles he played?"

Maia scrunches her nose as if laboring in thought.

"Well, the invention of the civilized arts was through the feminine wisdom, which Mercury well understood. Everybody knows that," she explains, as though this is an indisputable fact. "And the conveyance of souls is a reference to death, but death isn't really death if it is just a metaphor for rebirth, so maybe the connection is that if you accept the wisdom of females you will be reborn a more gifted man." She flashes a radiant smile at her sophistry.

"Hmmm, the logic sounds a little forced to me."

"Really? That's just because you haven't been gifted with a female's wisdom yet."

"Perhaps you are right."

"Of course I am right." She says brightly.

"And your understanding of these truths would be because you possess the female wisdom?" I ask.

"I am female."

She is indeed.

"And you are wise," I add, meaning it. "Not at all like your sisters, if you don't mind my saying so."

"Thank you for saying so. I would loath to be thought as silly as any of them."

"You are many things, Maia. Silly is not one of them."

My conversation with Maia continues into the evening. Talk turns to events, but she is not one to talk solely about things. Always she turns to the underlying ideas. The range of her mind astounds me. An item of civic gossip is quickly dismissed in favor of examining the body politic and how it can be more effective in helping the greater good, rather than reinforcing greed and divisionism. News of a distant dispute becomes a plea for tolerance of other ideas, other beliefs. Reports of the poor prompt her observations on the need for charity, and gossip of an unfortunate leads to the need for compassion and understanding. Nothing in Maia is surface ease and I cannot help but be drawn into the depths of her. One of seven sisters, all beautiful and young, Maia is so much more. I once thought of her that she was too young, but I was wrong. Wisdom is ageless in the mature. She teaches me, and I am the one who has much to learn.

"I'm glad you came," I tell her.

"I wanted to come. I like being with you."

"You do?"

"You don't treat me like other men do. You listen to me. I feel good around you. And you actually think and create. You're smarter than those other fools."

"Because I don't chase your sisters?"

"Definitely a point in your favor," she laughs.

"And what if I chase you?" I ask.

"You don't need to chase me," she says.

"Why is that?"

"Because I'm already here." She flashes her tender look and leans up to give me a kiss.

Maia returns daily, each visit moving us closer. When we become lovers, it is complete. Her lithe body arches against mine in the giving. She is the female wisdom, the conveyor of souls.

Women of Position

Francisco José de Goya y Lucientes
The Clothed Maja and *The Naked Maja*
1808
oil on canvas

In the hollow silence, images form. She inhales, and I capture forever in my mind the rounding line of her breasts, arms raised with hands meeting above her head. It is an invitation, a surrender.

I read the open expression on María's face and understand the solace she allows. We have each been alone, she and I, separate in divided worlds, but no more. Where once I would not have been allowed into her class, forever on the outside looking in, circumstances now permit.

Her world is not mine. Hers is a duchess realm of privileged rank, filled with glittering wealth and fine clothes, leisured time, and sumptuous foods, never tasting of hunger. My world is that of one who observes from without, struggle and toil, knowing the difference between famine and feast, forever deaf to the music of her court, but understanding more than others can. On her chaise, however, our worlds blend like palette hues.

"Only for you," she says, her muted words a silent dance upon her lips. The divide that once separated us is now gone.

Her mantle parts, exposing the clinging tug of her translucent white gown, a pink sash at her waist, the only constraint against the liquid silk that washes the swell of her breasts, the curve of her hips and rounded thighs, and the languid fall into the valley between.

Another time, another place and we might not have found each other, but these are not usual times. Madrid burns and we are left to sift through the ashes. War touches the rich and poor alike. Perhaps in such times it is not so unusual for two distant souls to meet, and to love.

"I am afraid," she confesses in a moment of candor.

"You will be safe here, with me."

"It isn't my physical safety I worry about. I know you will protect me, if it comes to that."

"What then?"

Maria looks around her apartments with some dismay. Already they show the decay of neglect. Once an abode of polish and shine, tended by a small army of servants, each dedicated to the preservation of the patina that signaled her status and wealth, her home is now in decline. The servants are gone, run away in fear, conscripted to a rebel cause, or fleeing in opportunity, taking pieces of her wealth, silver, jewels, money, with them as they fled. The polish is off the finely crafted furniture, small damages in want of repair.

"Just look around you. Everything is falling apart."

I can only nod in sympathy. I have never possessed such wealth. I do not fully understand how she must feel to see her world slipping away, but I do understand loss. I know what it means to be hungry. I know desolation and despair. She is not there, but the loss of the familiar is always painful.

"These things, Maria, they are not you. They do not define you."

"Don't they?" she asks, the timber of her voice rising. "I was Doña María del Pilar Teresa Cayetana de Silva-Álvarez de Toledo y Silva, 13th Duchess of Alba de Tormes, Grandee of Spain! This home, these titles, this is who I was. Now who am I?" she demands.

"You are María," I reply simply.

"That is nothing," she says.

"That is everything," I respond.

Her world is in danger of disappearing. The Corsican's brother is seeing to that. She has too many ties to a deposed king to go unnoticed, but she will survive. It is in her nature to do so, and I am fortunate to be a vehicle of her survival.

"I love you María."

Her visage softens.

"Even without all of this?" She gestures about the room.

"This, María, *this* is nothing. It is worse than nothing. Because of all this we were once held apart. Our worlds would never be allowed to join."

María sighs deeply. It is a cathartic sigh, exorcising and accepting.

"You are right, of course, though how I ever could have lived without you is beyond me.

"How is it you perceive so much," she asks. "You see what others do not. You hear when your own ears would deny you sound." I ponder her silent query.

How is it that others perceive so little, I sometimes wonder in turn? To render sight into truth is a dangerous pursuit. That is what I tell her. She courted more danger in bedding a common man who pierces the twin veneers of self-importance and political opportunism than I do in succumbing to the charms of an aristocratic Maja.

Spain darkens. A pretender king kills all who would defend the old realm. A May slaughter of innocents is but one of the atrocities of war. I watched in horror as the parade of the condemned stepped forward. A peasant stretches out his arms, catching the light of torch flame, casting him in a mandorla glow. Behind him men and women tremble and fear, yet he meets his end as a savior god, unable to save himself. There are too many atrocities to paint them all. I cannot hear the cries, but they ring through my soul nonetheless. There are greater losses than silver and coin and polished wood.

I need not fear for María. She will learn the difference between what she had and who she is. She opens herself to me, seeking salvation. I am no savior, but I will do what I can to save her.

Stripped of her gown, she resumes her pose on the lace trimmed bedding. Now she is simply María, lover of a visionary who cannot hear, but sees all. I am not of the world she once occupied. I am no aristocrat and certainly no savior, but I have María and that makes me the wealthiest of men. She is my naked Maja.

Patient Women

The Birth of Siddhartha
2nd–3rd Century CE
stone
Zen You Mitsu Temple, Tokyo, Japan

I hunger.

I am like a sleeping cobra, inert, gripping, holding on to a life that is no life.

Maya awaits. In her I see the life that can be.

"We can be together," I suggest.

"You are not ready." Maya closes her eyes meditatively, her presence a soothing calm to me.

"I long to make love to you," I implore.

She opens her dark probing eyes and I see the bemusement of one who is awake towards one who is not.

"No," she quietly explains, "to long is not to share one's soul."

"But I don't merely long for you," I say in an attempt to convince.

"Perhaps, but you are not ready nonetheless. You exist without animation. You possess, but only to hold. You live without life."

She is not to be persuaded.

"When will I be ready?" I ask, hoping to keep the disappointment and frustration from my voice.

"When you know," she says.

"I don't understand."

"When you know, you will." Her calm demeanor disarms me.

"Who are you?" I ask, no longer certain.

"You know me," she says, but I am left to wonder.

I retreat to my coiled self and an alimentary existence. I slumber through life not knowing what I do not know.

I yearn.

Seasons come and go, but Maya is never far from my thoughts. Life becomes pleasure. Pleasure is life. How foolish I was those many years past. I did not understand. Now I know the fulfillment of carnal joy. I am ready for the woman who has been my single dream. Now I shall seek her out.

I find Maya at her favorite resort. Reunion is sweet and many years of non-existence evaporate upon seeing her once more.

"I have returned," I announce with devilish confidence.

"So I see," she says, clearly pleased to do so.

"You were right," I say. "I was not ready when last we were together. Not for one such as you."

"And now you are?" she asks, challenging my bold assertion.

"Let me show you." My heart pounds, its rhythmic urge reaching deep into my loins. "I am not the man I was."

"You are more than you were," she says, with some admiration.

I lean in close to her, my lips to her ear. So close, I can smell the magnolia fragrance on her hair. I swim in her sensual pool. I whisper to her what I wish to give, and receive.

Maya brightens and turns her head.

"Yes," she says, "that would be a great pleasure."

I press my case.

"Come, bed with me."

Fingers touch my cheek and I feel the fiery warmth of Maya's caress.

"When you are ready, I will be here."

"I am ready now."

She begins to walk away.

"No," she says, her voice fading, "you have found pleasure in life, but not life itself."

She stops and looks back. "When you are ready," she says again, and then she is gone.

I strive.

How empty those conquests become. Pleasure without purpose is what she saw in me. How foolish I have been. I will accomplish. Now I will achieve purpose.

Will to power drives me. When Maya views the city of the shining jewel my life's work builds, she will be impressed. I will succeed, and she will bear witness.

Rewards come my way. I won them. I earned them. Recognition is the greatest reward, the greatest save one, Maya. There is nothing I cannot achieve, should I put my mind to it. This, surely is what Maya was telling me. Now, I have mastered my world and she will come to me. I have but to wait and she, too, will be mine.

Accomplishment is hollow without her.

I touch.

To Sakya I am compelled.

I live without life. That is what she said when I first met her these twenty years past. I was not ready. No.

From existence to satisfaction, from satisfaction to achievement, it was all emptiness. I thought to seek a meaning to life and missed the experience of being alive.

The blackness of Maya's eyes pulls me deeper into the eternal chasm than I have ever been before. She is different now. She is large with child, ripe with life itself, even as I am devoid of it.

"You have returned," she says, her voice like the soft echo of rolling thunder.

"In my heart I never left."

"That is true," she nods.

"Who are you?" I ask.

"You know me. You have always known me."

"You are an illusion."

"I am a dream of a dream."

"How can such a thing be?" I ask with a touch of desperation.

"I dreamed of you." Maya's hand absently strokes her life-filled belly.

"Of me?" I ask with surprise.

"A dream, an intuition, call it what you will. A bodhisattva came to me, riding a magnificent white elephant. Ganesha's touch told me you would come."

"You speak of things beyond me, but I had to come."

"Yes."

"You are a dream?"

"Yes."

"And my life?"

Maya does not answer, but leads me to a tree.

"When we first met you thought only to survive," she says.

"Yes."

"And what did you learn?"

"That survival is not enough," I respond.

"Pleasure, pain, and everything in between?" she prods.

I contemplate before answering. "These are but empty sensations without something more."

"Something more?"

"I, I thought if only I could accomplish great things, then maybe, but, here I am."

"Here you are," she agrees.

"I want to understand."

"Listen," she whispers.

I strive to hear, but all has fallen silent, greater than any silence I can describe.

"That is the sound of everything," she says at last.

I am lost.

Maya continues, "I ask again, what did you learn?"

I think for some time before answering. "That survival without purpose is vain solitude. That physical love without connection is selfish and cold. That achieving for oneself is a community devoid."

Maya nods in satisfied agreement.

"You describe aloneness," she says.

"Aloneness, yes" I agree.

"And you wish for more?" she asks.

"With all my heart," I choke, as the anguish of a life unfulfilled crushes upon me.

"Then listen."

I labor against the deafening silence, the sound not heard, and as I listen Maya becomes my dream. In my dream she radiates warmth, as from her right side a child is born, a birth of the heart, a miraculous nativity.

I call out in my dream, "Who are you?" and she answers.

"You know who I am. I am Maya, mother of the enlightened one, but I am known by many names, always giving birth to the virgin born."

"The mother of deities?" I ask in my amazement.

"No," she corrects, "the mother of illumination. See," she commands and indicates the child.

The infant child walks, seven steps of spiritual awakening, and points, first upwards, then downwards. He speaks, "Worlds above, worlds below, all things are Buddha things."

I watch in wonder as the child transforms into every person I have seen in my life, lovers I have known, friends, enemies, strangers I have passed. My eyes fill with tears as the child becomes those whom I have hurt, or used, or damaged, or ignored, and my heart wrenches as each of those whom I cherished or reviled, valued or dismissed becomes a personification of me.

Maya gestures with a wave of her hand and the dream ends. The child is gone and Maya is here as she ever was, beautiful, primordial, and maternal.

"I am not alone," I say through my tears.

"You never have been," she says.

"The others?" I ask.

"*Tat tvam asi.* Thou art that. This is the birth of compassion. This is the opening of the heart. This is the virgin birth."

"Thou art that," I repeat.

"Listen," she says, and this time I need not labor to hear. The silence is filled with the song of everything, the voices of all, the sound of *aum.*

Chapter Six

*Z*anetta took one last appraising look in her mirror before setting it firmly on her dressing table. It seemed a different woman looking back at her, but it was a woman she once knew and wanted to know once more. It was a woman with whom she was enjoying a renewal over the past days. She smiled inwardly, the way one does when a long-overdue determination is made and the tranquility of decisiveness blankets the uncertainty of the past.

Standing, she smoothed the wrinkles from her dress. It had been a long time since she pulled it out of her armoire. She was pleased that it still fit. Not her finest that she wore to Mass or on holidays, it was, nevertheless, her favorite.

She allowed her hand to caress the silken green brocade. Accents of cream lace fanned at the sleeves and trimmed the split at the front of her dress. Lacy pleats repeated in cascades down the front. The dress flared at the hips as it fell over the underlying supports as was the fashion of the day, though only slightly, not in the ridiculous exaggerated expanse that many social climbing women affected in an effort to be at the forefront of the latest trends. Above the hip accented flare, the dress hugged Zanetta at her still slender waist, though slightly more snug than in previous years. Nothing a slight alteration couldn't address, and she was pleased with the result. The bodice pressed at her breasts, pushing them upwards. Well, she thought laughing to herself as she arched her gaze downward, gaining a little weight wasn't such a bad thing after all.

The dress was richly embroidered with cream and emerald florals, reminding her of a romantic garden in a Rococo painting by Watteau or Fragonard or one of the other French masters her uncle introduced her to by way of his collection of color-tinted prints and reproductions. One in particular, of a woman on a swing had caught her fancy and it was to this painting she directed her thoughts. How free the girl in the painting appeared to be. A happy idyll, perhaps the purview of a young girl not yet familiar with the ways of the world, but surely some of that happiness remains to be discovered once more. She moved about the room and imagined the leaves and flowers of her embroidered dress fluttering in a breeze as she kicked higher on a velveted swing.

Giving a final pat to the ringlet curls at the side of her hair, she checked to catch any stray strands, but all was to her satisfaction. She wore her hair up, as usual, but now with a flourish of ribbons and curls that captured it at her crown. She had fleetingly considered wearing the powdered wig that sat in a box on top of her armoire, but the thought was quickly dismissed. She was not, after all, being received in the Doge's Palace, she was just taking a promenade through the city on an unseasonably warm late fall day.

As she left, Zanetta opened Giacomo's door and peeked in. He was asleep, as she expected he would be. Earlier she told him she would be out for a time so that he would not be concerned should he wake and not see or hear her nearby.

Zanetta made her way downstairs and to the front door. Something halted her. She held to the doorknob as if frozen. She exited and entered this door many times each day, going to the market, to the piazza well for water, to commune with neighbors and exchange news, or to church, or for any number of reasons, yet this time it felt different. It wasn't the dress, certainly, she thought. It is true she usually wore simple workaday dresses other than for church, but this isn't what halted her. It was the crossing. She felt, as she never felt before, that she was about to reenter a world she had all but abandoned, even though it was a world through which she moved daily.

"Martyrdom is for saints," Giacomo told her the night previous, during one of their conversations.

"I'm no martyr," she protested.

"Then why do you fight the world so?" he asked in a pointed return.

"Why do you say that? I am not fighting the world."

"Perhaps, perhaps," Giacomo allowed, "but you are not living in it."

"What? Honestly Giacomo, I think the fall you took addled your brain more than we realized. I do plenty of living in this world, in case you hadn't noticed."

"Existing in the world and living in the world are not the same thing."

"Another Casanova truism?" Zanetta asked.

"The world is a wasteland, full of opposites from which we think to choose. Good and evil, light and dark, love and apathy."

"Don't you mean hate?" Zanetta asked.

"No. The opposing duality of love is not hate, it is apathy. Love is the finding of one in two. Apathy is the loss of the desire to find and hold that oneness."

"And this applies to me how?" she asked.

Giacomo shrugged.

"We walk the face of this earth confronted by the dualities it offers. We think to choose one or another, often never realizing it is but an illusion. A wasteland of false choices. All the while the real world waits."

"The real world? Something more real than this?" Zanetta waved her hand to indicate her surroundings.

"You found it once, when you found love."

"Now that was an illusion!" Zanetta scoffed.

Giacomo sighed. "Yes, it is true it was not to prove lasting, but for a time you touched the transcendent. You existed beyond the dualities that separate us, and you were one with another. You were truly living in the world."

"Maybe love doesn't last. Did you ever consider that?" She was not about to give in.

"Love is," he said simply.

"You are so exasperating Giacomo. Fine. The world is a wasteland and love is. And maybe I have chosen apathy over risking another broken heart, but I am no martyr!"

"Then return."

"Return? To what?" she demanded.

"You have been to the real world, where all is one, my dear. It is time you realized that you have never really lost this, or left it, you have merely forgotten how to see it."

"Why? Why should I care to do such a thing, even if it is true?"

"Because," Giacomo quietly explained, "because I am dying."

Zanetta choked on her response, not knowing how to respond anyway.

Giacomo continued.

"Many if not most of us find love. For some it holds in a state of happily ever after. For some it disappears in the selfishness of others, or ourselves. For some it never comes and those are the poor souls destined to wander in eternal blindness.

"It is a heroic thing, this love. It strikes at times most unexpected, and it demands much if we are to lay claim to hold it. Sometimes this is beyond our control, but such is the power of the transcendent. What we become is determined by how we deal with that awesome power.

"For some, love never dissipates, though they may lose the object of their unity through death or some other circumstance beyond their control. There are those who find the transcendent without ever realizing they are walking upon sacred ground. They are blessed idiots never fully appreciating the godhood they have touched.

"Others, like you, may love and lose, tasting for a time of the sublime only to have it disappear. It is the poor soul who returns to the wasteland of the dual, thinking if they cannot hold love, that they then must choose its apathetic opposite. They wander in despair, sometimes without knowing they are doing so. They sleep as you have slept, but my dear, you can sleep no more. I am dying and I need you to find and hold the transcendent once more."

Zanetta sat silent at this for a while, considering his words.

"I can't just go out and find love, Giacomo. It doesn't work that way."

"I am not asking you to. I am asking you to realize again what you once knew, that true love is the awareness that we are, all of us and all things, connected. We are one. Marriage and romance is but one manifestation of this. I am not asking you to find something new. I am asking you to return to the knowledge you already possess. Anyone can find love," he continued. "More often than not it finds us, but this is only half the journey. We are all heroes in our birth, born of waters and wonder and set upon a journey to find again the oneness we once knew. But we need not make this journey alone. There are of necessity, guides to help us along our way. There must be those who see and remember, to help others find their bliss, and to help them again should they forget."

Zanetta stared at Giacomo with a sudden realization.

"This is why you have been telling Lorenzo all those stories of love, isn't it?" she said. "You are his guide."

"Somewhat," Giacomo said, "but that can no longer be. As we both know, I am dying, and I intend for you to take my place."

"Me? What makes you think a young man will listen to his mother when it comes to love? It isn't quite the same as hearing tales told by the great Casanova."

"You are quite right. Lorenzo is on his own path. He will find his own guides. But you, my dear, you must complete your journey. Your destiny is not to wander in the wasteland. It is time for you to awake. It is time for you to return. And who knows? Once you do, another manifestation of the transcendent may find you once more."

Sleep did not find her for many hours that night. Her mind turned Giacomo's ideas over and over. Was he right? She couldn't say, but by the time her eyes fell heavy with sleep, she had determined to take a day for herself. She would even dress for the occasion, she thought, and then she drifted off feeling quite pleased.

Now, here she was at the door. In her mind, turning the handle was an admission that Giacomo was right and that she had been avoiding life.

This is my day, she thought, and without any further hesitation she opened the door and stepped across the return threshold.

The savor of the saltwater flowing in the Grand Canal hit her, as it always did when exiting her house, though so accustomed was she to the sounds and smells that it usually went unnoticed. Today, however, it seemed to reach her anew and she relished the bracing sensation. With only a general sense of destination, Zanetta turned away from the waterfront and struck out across the greater San Marco neighborhood towards the magnificent Cathedral. Neighbors greeted her as she passed, some remarking on her beautiful dress.

"Oh my! Are you on your way to a ball?" an elderly woman who maintained a small stall of herbs for medicinal purposes called out as Zanetta passed. The old woman cackled and Zanetta smiled back in return. The aged merchant stall keeper was a neighborhood fixture. Most of the residents in the area frequented her stall to obtain the mild remedies that were more easily and affordably available from her than from the local apothecary, though she was only the first option in taking care of the ill. Fine for minor needs, but nothing more.

"No," Zanetta waved. "Just out for a stroll."

After a short distance, Zanetta no longer wanted to explain her sudden appearance in her secular finery, so she turned aside, making her way through some of the side streets to avoid her usual course to the market or to San Marco Square, and thus avoid most of her immediate acquaintances.

Her promenade was leisurely which was, for Zanetta, unusual. She was accustomed to walking with intention, only to get from here to there, so this slow meander allowed her to look around and see more of her beautiful city. She was used to Giacomo's waxing on about his beloved Venice, but to be truthful it never seemed so to her. True, it did have its picturesque sights, more than most cities she imagined, but she rarely took the time to really appreciate its wonders. Today she was taking the time.

Turning again she crossed over a small bridge spanning one of the inner canal tributaries that webbed the island that was the social and religious and political focal point of the multi-island lagoon, and onto a wide avenue that passed directly behind Teatro La Fenice, the new Opera House, the most recent architectural pride of the city. She recalled the dilapidated buildings that once stood at the site and how they were razed to the ground to make way for the massive new structure. Like a phoenix rising from the ashes, Zanetta mused.

As she walked past the wide open back doors, left ajar no doubt to catch a breeze to air the cavernous interior, she heard the lively strains of a violin concerto. Rehearsal, she thought. Zanetta stopped to listen, as several others out and about appeared to do.

Zanetta tried to place the music, but she could not. Vivaldi? She was familiar with the famed Venetian Red Priest, known so for his striking shock of red hair. Though no longer living, he was still the musical pride of Venice and his compositions were played frequently. Zanetta was familiar with one of his works, something about the seasons, but this composition filtering out the open door, if indeed it was his, was unfamiliar to her. It didn't really matter. It was lively and upbeat and it suited her mood perfectly. Zanetta lingered until the music stopped mid-tune and she could hear the raised voice of someone, possibly the conductor or the composer, followed by the scraping and shuffling of chairs. It must be time for their break, she thought, and so she and the small crowd that had gathered at the back doors of the Opera House moved on.

Over the tops of buildings Zanetta could see the massive dome of San Marco Cathedral and the towering campanile. She continued her zigzagging meander, stopping occasionally to inspect the foods of a vendor's stall or to peer inside shops, vowing to return to enjoy their goods at some later date, until she reached the expansive Piazza San Marco.

The massive square was filled with people milling about. Workers making deliveries, vendors selling wares, casual strollers and those engaged in business traversing beneath the shadow of the majestic cathedral were joined by throngs of tourists pointing in awe at each new marvel. Artists at their easels were surrounded by interested onlookers as they rendered the picturesque sites as their master, Canaletto had taught them. They would be purchased and brought back to their homes as remembrances of the city she was only now beginning to appreciate.

Zanetta walked to one of the outdoor cafes that lined the interior of the piazza and took a chair at one of the outer tables. From here she watched the people pass and point and laugh and chat.

"Signora?" a solicitous waiter caught her attention.

She quickly turned.

"Oh, yes. May I have a tea?" she asked. "No, wait," she reconsidered. "Do you have a... a *limoncello?*" Zanetta was nearly embarrassed to ask. It was still mid-morning, but she remembered coming here with Giacomo just days after she and Lorenzo arrived in the city to live with him, well before the series of illnesses that would eventually confine him, and he ordered for her one of the fruit liqueurs. She had delighted in the taste and though it seemed decadent, she wanted one now.

"As a matter of fact we do, Signora. We have a *limoncello* all the way from Sorrento."

Zanetta beamed.

"Fine. That is what I would like."

The waiter nodded his approval and disappeared into the cafe.

After a time he returned with a small glass of the bright yellow liquid and placed it on the table in front of her. She handed him a few coins and thanked him.

Zanetta gazed out again across the piazza. From where she sat she could take in the entirety of the facade of San Marco, and the running colonnade of the Doge's Palace next to it.

She wondered, as she had wondered before, if the legend of the cathedral was true. It was said that Venetian merchants in the ninth century stole the bones of the long-martyred Saint Mark and spirited them out of Alexandria and back to Venice. They succeeded in passing the relics under the noses of Alexandria's ruling Muslims, so Giacomo told her, by covering them with slabs of pork which, they explained, they were taking to another market. The Muslims, who would not touch pork, let them pass unquestioned and unmolested. The great cathedral of Venice grew up around these holy relics, and more specifically around the legend. It seems doubtful, Zanetta thought, that a bunch of merchants would know where to find the bones of someone who died nearly eight hundred years earlier, but it was a good story nonetheless. Venetians took great pride in the legends of their patron saint.

Zanetta picked up her glass and lifted it slightly towards San Marco. A toast seemed in order. She considered what it should be.

"To patron saints," she said, then smiling to herself. "To you, Uncle Giacomo."

She sipped her drink, savoring the fruit laden sweetness that warmed her through.

Giacomo sat staring at the crucifix suspended beyond the foot of his bed. He awoke earlier and managed to push himself up to a semi-sitting position, taking small sips of the wine Zanetta left him earlier. It had taken him some time to remember that she had told him she would be out for a good part of the day. It must be important, Giacomo thought. Zanetta rarely left for more than a half hour or so these days. But this was not what troubled him. He scowled at the small sculpture as if demanding it acknowledge his presence.

"I am beginning to understand you, Signore," Giacomo said to the ever-suffering god on the dull and flaking whitewashed wall. "Your final gift torments me! I thought to die by now, Signore, but you have yet to release me. Instead you stretch my days and fill them with visions of life lived and life yet to come. Memories wax and wane like the phases of a primal moon, my consciousness narrowing to a bull-horned sliver, only to die into blackness before resurrecting as an opposing arc and the tangible reality of impending death. I am become a seer, as you have been before me, Signore.

"This world closes and restrains. These, my prison walls to which age and decrepitude confine me, press in upon me as in a labyrinthine cave, depriving my senses save for the pound, pound, pound of the waters against the canal. I drift and swoon and become lost in a journey of echoes in time with the repeating refrain."

Giacomo lowered his voice to a conspiratorial whisper, though only he and the mute crucifix were in the room to hear.

"I leave death's bed, Signore. Yes, it's true, though I do not know how it is so, other than by some incomprehensible design of your deific grace. I would think it a trick upon an old man's fading reason, but you and I know otherwise, don't we? You punish me with loss of my beloved Venice and soften the sentence with journeys inward and out. You have a wicked sense of humor, Signore, or perhaps just a reckoning of fairness I do not comprehend.

"Out of this frail machine that dies by day, I fly. But to where, Signore? That is the question. What are these realms to which you send me?

"My walls press in and the dancing shadows disappear only to be replaced by designs of the eternal maths, lattice grids, punctuating spots, and spidering lines. I see them as surely as I see you before me now. They spiral and swirl about me as my worldly realm dissolves and I tunnel, upward in flight or through mystic rushing waters, where Alph the sacred river ran, through caverns measureless to man, traveling freely between your three tiers until I arrive. Is this your existence, Signore, this place of alternate reality?

"I see her there, you know of whom I speak, and I understand then that this place, too, is as real as the confining room I have left behind. I am Dante reaching the beatific vision of his beloved. I am Othin on his windy tree. I am St. Francis and Zarathustra and Odysseus, and I am you!

"But how can this be? Is this not blasphemy? Ah Signore, is this to be my final torment in this life, not knowing what you give me to know?

"I see and hear and feel this place. Yes, hear and feel, like the buzzing of a thousand bees that sting and prick, enlivening now malleable flesh. I transform. Your power, the power of this realm infuses my spine, standing me tall and straight as once when I was young. It surmounts and flares above my crown like the moon-arc horns of a cave bull or the confuit rays shining forth from the Deliverer as he descended Sinai, returning once again to a world of duality, pain and sorrow, as I inevitably do.

"I see those that have passed before me and I see the power of their love as their limbs stretch forth as if to touch me once again, and it is then that I know the meaning of this place to which you bring me. This is the realm of wholes, where all is indivisible."

Giacomo nodded his head, content that awareness was dawning.

"Thank you, Signore, I am, at my dusk, beginning to understand you," Giacomo repeated to the crucified man. "You bring me there that I might return to the boundaries of time, to share what you have shown. The winding journey is not for me as I will make that final descent soon enough. It is for another, is that not so? And perhaps it is for Lorenzo as well. Yes, Lorenzo.

"Thank you, Signore. I see now that what I thought a curse is but another of your gifts, a boon to be dispersed. We are not separate, Signore, that is your lesson to me, is it not? This is the lesson of my loves, of all loves. It is the lesson of the labyrinth.

"And so I return, as your will demands, to this body of age and pain to convey your boon. Ah, you are wise, Signore. Wise and wicked and wonderful. I die only to be shown the truth of life. I am reborn. It is the birth of compassion. I am virgin born."

Giacomo sank deeper into his pillows, at peace now with the constant pain he felt, knowing it was but a temporary necessity. He allowed his mind to drift, catching snippets of activity from the city

outside his window. His reverie was interrupted by a knock at the door
followed by his grandnephew's entry.

"Ah, Lorenzo, I was just thinking about you," he said in a weak
voice. "Is your mother still out?" he asked, already knowing the answer.

"She hasn't returned yet."

"Did she say where she was going?"

Lorenzo seemed distracted.

"No. She didn't say, but she was wearing one of her nicest dresses."

"Indeed," Giacomo said approvingly. "So, it begins."

"What begins?" Lorenzo asked.

"Never mind. Your mother is returning."

Lorenzo shot him a quizzical look, but Giacomo did not feel
compelled to explain that he was not referring to Zanetta's day outing.

"Do you need anything?" Lorenzo asked.

"No, nothing. I am quite fine now. Quite fine."

Giacomo read a troubled look on his grandnephew's face.

"What is it, Lorenzo? What's wrong?" he asked.

Lorenzo hesitated before answering.

"Your stories, Uncle, are they all true?"

Giacomo considered his grandnephew's query in light of his most
recent conversation with the deity hanging on the wall opposite his bed.
Had he not, in a sense, posed the same question? What is reality? What
is truth?

"Why do you ask?"

"I don't know," the young man deflected. "I just, I was just
wondering, that's all."

Giacomo indicated the volumes of his memoirs sitting atop the
chest of drawers at the side of his room.

"You are not the first to ask that question. I have been accused of,
shall we say exaggerating my exploits before."

"That's not what I mean," Lorenzo replied.

Giacomo waited, allowing Lorenzo time to compose his thoughts.

"Mother told me she thought you were prone to literary license, but that she thought your stories were true, for the most part."

"Hmmn, a generous if unenthusiastic endorsement."

"I'm not sure she meant it as a compliment," Lorenzo added.

Giacomo looked again at crucifix suspended on the wall.

"No, I rather doubt she did. What do you think?"

"Well, I wasn't really talking about your books. I was thinking more about the stories you have been telling me."

"Do you doubt them? Doubt me?"

Lorenzo was careful in answering.

"No, it's just that I haven't heard them before. You didn't write about them with the others."

"And their unfamiliarity causes you to question?"

Lorenzo shrugged.

Giacomo fell silent while thinking of how to answer.

"There are many truths," he said, "depending on one's vantage point."

"That is not a yes," Lorenzo said pointedly.

"There is truth behind all perceptions of truth," the old man explained.

"Uncle!" Lorenzo exclaimed.

"I see that does not satisfy you," Giacomo said. "Then let me set your mind to rest. Yes, my stories are true."

"All of them?"

"Yes. But, Lorenzo, don't you see? There is more to them than history."

Lorenzo was not hearing. His mind, Giacomo knew, was racing to thoughts of Costanza and weighing them against his uncle's tales.

"And what about your story, Lorenzo?"

"My story?"

"The story you have constructed of Costanza. Is it true?"

"I haven't constructed any story about her," Lorenzo protested.

"Haven't you? Not only have you fashioned a story, you are trapped by it."

"I'm not trapped!"

"Then why don't you call on her? Why do you bury yourself away? Why don't you talk to her? Ask her?"

"Ask her what?"

"About her damn cousin! Quit the unknown. Find out!"

"You don't understand."

"What do you think all of my stories are about? I understand perfectly. Do you think your trepidations are something new? Unique to you? I hate to break it to you, but you aren't the first person to be devoured by self-doubt. You have been swallowed by a whale alright, but it is a leviathan of your own making."

"I was just asking if your stories were true, that's all."

Lorenzo was desperate to get out of this uncomfortable conversation.

Giacomo, however, was not to be refused.

"Yes, my stories are true, in ways you cannot yet comprehend."

Before Lorenzo could respond, or leave, Giacomo girded himself and launched into more recollections. He had a boon to give his grandnephew and time was running out.

Women at Home

William Hogarth
Breakfast Scene
From *Marriage à la Mode*
1745
oil on canvas

Marriage à la mode.

"Good morning, my love." *Good God I am tired. I wonder if she suspects? I hope she doesn't suspect. I pray she doesn't ask about my night. Did I tell her I would be late? Can't remember. What did I tell her? It's not exactly a lie if I can't even remember, is it?*

"Good morning, my darling," she says airily.

Hmmn. Too easy. I wonder why she doesn't ask? She must suspect.

"Beautiful morning, what?" I say. *That's it, keep it simple. I'm exhausted.*

"Oh, it's a lovely day, yes."

She's yawning. Did she stay up waiting for me? She doesn't seem to be mad. I must have told her I would be late. That was thoughtful of me.

"Have you been up long?" I ask. *I've got to lie down.*

"Mmn, no, not long," she answers.

So why is she yawning? Is something afoot? Oh damn, now she is making me have to yawn. Ooh, ow, yawning makes my eyes hurt. I could use a drink. Hair of the dog.

"Have you breakfasted, my dear?" I inquire. *I hope she has. Lord knows if I will be able to stay awake while pretending to eat. As for myself, I ushered in the morning with eggs, ham, and Sally, or was her name Sherry?*

"Eaten, no, not yet, tea only," she says. "I am not very hungry this morning."

Not hungry? Good. Wait. Is she upset that I wasn't here?

I slump in my chair. She stifles another yawn. *It was just a night on the town, nothing to concern Jane about. It's not exactly a lie if I just keep my mouth shut. Hearth and home, after all, nothing will ever disturb this tranquility.*

Marriage à la mode.

"A late night of work, dear?" she asks.

Damn! I must have forgotten to send word. Work? Not exactly work, I would say. Sherry? Was that her name? No, it was Sharon, or was it Shelly?

"You know how it is, dear, late night dinner with clients, deadlines to be met, just not enough hours in the day to get all the work done. I would have sent word, more word, um, it was morning before I even realized." *It isn't exactly a lie if I am not contradicting some lie I told her previously.*

Better change the subject. "And you, my love, another quiet night?"

"Dreadfully dull," she says. "I did miss you so. Thank goodness I had a music lesson to break up the monotony."

"Oh, lovely," I say. *What? Wait. She takes music lessons? Well, good, better that than dwelling on my comings and goings.*

"And how are the lessons coming?"

"Splendid," she says. "Antoine is such a wonderful teacher."

Who the hell is Antoine? Antoine? Her music teacher is a he? Hmmm. He sounds foreign, or worse, French!

I wonder if she suspects I was with Sherry-Sharon last night? Shelly? No, it was definitely Sharon.

"Ah, yes, I see now. Your violin and music seem to have fallen off the chair." *I nearly stumbled over the damn thing coming in.*

"Oh, dear, yes, I, um, last night, Antoine, he, he tripped on his way out," she hastens to explain.

"Poor chap. I do hope he is alright." *Serves him right for being French!*

"He's fine," she says a little too quickly. "I mean," she slows, "he's fine. Truly, fine."

I wasn't that concerned. I wonder what she means by that? Nothing untoward, I'm sure. Now Sharon, she was truly fine.

How fortunate I am to have such a loving, faithful wife, who doesn't ask too many questions. A Frenchman? And Jane? How silly it would be of me to even entertain a thought.

I wonder if she suspects anything.

Marriage à la mode.

"Isn't that darling?" Jane says. "Fido is so happy to see you. Look, he is clamoring at your coat."

"My coat? What?" *Oh, damn! Sharon's hat. I forgot. Damn dog!* "Oh, yes, I, um, I must have inadvertently wiped my hand in my pocket after I ate last night. That's it, Fido smells last night's meal." *Damn dog! Quit shagging my coat! Go away!*

That was close. Better be more careful next time. Still, easier to explain Sharon's hat than her knickers. I'd better check my other pocket as soon as I get a chance.

Wait a minute, what's that? It looks as if the curtain covering my private painting of Aphrodite in the back room has been pulled aside. I only show it to the lads on occasion, and maybe to the maid when I want to tickle her fancy a bit. And she has a fancy worth tickling! Now who would have drawn that curtain back?

"Dear, the painting in the back room?"

Jane registers surprise.

"Oh, my, I, that is, Antoine never, I mean, it must have been James, the steward."

"James? Ah, well, in that case I suppose I must have a talk with him." *James? My God, unless Aphrodite is posing with a ledger, he wouldn't even notice her. Still, maybe there is some fire in his cold britches yet. Hah!*

As if on cue James walks through the room.

Uh oh, looks like he has the bills.

"Not now James," I head him off. "Late night at work, you know."

The steward gives me an assessing look, then a glance at Jane and rolls his eyes.

Hmm, I wonder what that means. Oh well, never mind. At least I don't have to talk about finances. Or Sharon.

"It's good to be home dear," I say. *Now if I can only make it to my bed before any more questions are asked. It isn't exactly a lie if I go to sleep without explaining, is it?*

"Yes," Jane says, "I am so, so pleased."

She's a good wife. Nothing to worry about there. Jane's a good girl. Now Sharon on the other hand...

Hearth and home. Nothing will ever disturb this tranquility.

Marriage à la mode.

Waiting Women

Jan Vermeer
The Letter
c. 1666
oil on canvas

"For your mistress's eyes only," I warn, as I hand the carefully folded and sealed letter into the maid's waiting hand. It is not the letter I would have preferred to write, but it is the letter that must be sent.

"I understand, sir," she replies with a conspirator's wink. Her eyes dart about the bustling market as if to make certain no one is watching before she tucks it into a pocket beneath her apron. She is a simple girl, but devoted. She will see the letter delivered in hand.

The maid can be trusted. Many times she has carried my words to her mistress and without doubt would keep watch while Catherina and I met for secret trysts, should the need arise. It is the way of things in Delft. One must always understand allegiances, if one is to survive. The maid was bound to Catherina's family long before the business of marriage was arranged.

I look after her as she wedges her way through the jostling customers, merchants, strollers, children pulling at their mothers' arms, soldiers and sailors watching the young girls, and hastening businessmen cutting through the square on their way to their next big appointment, all thronging the open marketplace until, at last, she disappears behind a wall of unidentifiable heads.

Catherina waits, hoping I will come if I can, send regrets if I must. To meet in consummation would be her wish. And mine, if the situation was different. The letter will be all and end.

We never meant to fall in love, if love it can truly be called. It eked its way into recognition at social dinners where a neglected wife found conversation with someone who valued her words. It steeled its conviction in the shared amusements and interests she was denied in marriage. It founded its union in the casual familiarity of two who understand one another, when sadly such familiarity was not to be had at home. Love was not intended. It grew.

Light floods the front room of Catherina's home as she sits near the lion-mantled hearth, a sun dappled interior, rich in color, soft in detailed harmony.

Music filters through the house and out onto the street below. A song of love unquenched, each strum of the lute evoking a harmony of sympathetic vibrations in the heart. She plays this plaintive tune alone, her duet now solo. My own complimentary score is unused, unfulfilled, and to remain so, untouched on an empty chair in a room apart.

The music stops as the maid enters. One glance tells Catherina I am not coming, and though I can imagine the disappointment that creases her face, an expression I have witnessed before, I see too, the anticipation in her eyes as the maid produces my letter from the folds of her dress. I picture her well, as if through a curtained portal, the heavy drape drawn to one side to illuminate my waiting love. Time ceases as I capture the likeness of my Catherina, like the halation image of a camera obscura, forever reflecting this scene of domestic purgatory. She is a body of luminous hue in ermine trimmed yellow, attracting to her the warming rays of the sun just as she attracts my yearning need.

"He sent this," the maid says, not daring to speak my name as if the utterance might somehow find its way to the absent master of the house, but he is gone on one of his many trips, business taking precedence in a life that leaves little room for Catherina. His is a solitary walk along a forlorn sandy path. He fails to recognize the love he leaves behind. His is the walk of the damned.

She takes the proffered letter. A knowing exchange and the maid leaves Catherina to the privacy of my words. Catherina touches the note to her lips before breaking the seal.

My words pour forth, expressing a love we can never share other than in stolen moments of passing time, never allowing our desires to be slaked. I tell her of my love for her and the pain I feel in the knowledge that we cannot be together, not just today, but for the days to come. I must walk away before damage is done. Her marriage, unhappy though it may be, cannot be denied. Not by me. I feel for her, would spare her the sorrow and loneliness of her sequestration, but she must determine the course she will take. I cannot be the man she believes me to be and at the same time be the cad that would place her in jeopardy for a raptured afternoon. She must decide.

Perhaps she will choose to leave him, the damned, but I think not. Catherina is a romantic, but she is practical to a fault. Security outweighs the heart, at least for now. She may yet change. The heart may win out. Will I be here when it does?

I can envision a day when our love will bloom, when I will take my place at her side. It may be years, but it will be worth the wait, once she is free. It is a dream most coveted, and should it ever come to pass I will wear her words like a wedding band, "What took you so long?"

Back through the market crowds of Delft I walk, away from the maid's blazing path. Like the master of the house, my walk is now a solitary walk, but I know all too well what I leave behind. I walk the walk of the damned.

Like a picture within a picture our love is destined, for a time, to reside enframed in her sad domestic tableau. We are as boats sailing fast before a chasing wind on a tumultuous sea, the depths of which are as unfathomable as the love we share and the passion we bear.

Catherina folds the letter and with a nod to the inevitable, she touches it again to her lips. Light fills the room and plaintive music once more wavers on the air.

Welcoming Women

Titian
Danaë
1554
oil on canvas

She welcomes me like a shower of gold, raining in abundance upon her. Danaë has been waiting, held captive by a little man who could never see her as the daughter of fulfillment, but merely as an extension of his own all too limited self.

It is the failure of little men with little eyes and little minds to see and comprehend only little things. It is the fate of such men to inflict their stunted sense of self onto others in their sphere. The malignant father infects his own, unless another can show the true value of one's soul.

How small Danaë's world must have seemed, ever restricted to her father's confinements. He cannot see beyond his own failures, so he tells her they belong to her. He cannot rise above his own sloth so he convinces her she can achieve no more. He cannot master his own selfishness, so he forces her to his gratification. He is a little man of little life and he would limit her to his own little hell. But she will not be held any more.

I see in Danaë all the potential of a woman free, a mind that races to realms even I can only glimpse from a distance. I feel in her the compassion so denied her in childhood. I desire in her the touch of her greatness, all waiting to be revealed.

Her father, little man that he is, would deny her all, but Danaë will not be denied.

"What am I going to do?" she asks, tears flooding her eyes. "My father will," her words trail off in despair.

"Your father will say nothing," I assure her. "He cannot stop what is between us."

She looks at me searchingly, strength shining through her tears.

"I used to think I would never have a child," she says. "How could anyone want to bring a little one into this world so filled with pain? But you made me realize it isn't so. I never really saw the world, only my father's own sickish view, but that view changes with you."

"You are no possession," I say.

Danaë smiles.

"No, I am not."

"And you will not be confined."

"No, I will not."

"And someday, should you so choose, you will decide with whom and how you will experience this world once denied."

"I have decided already."

She is a survivor. I can read it in her face, in her bearing. All she needed was time to come into her own, and someone to say, "I believe."

I believe.

Our joining is frantic and strong. She asserts herself in the giving. She is her own woman and she allows me to join her as she flees the confines of the small world imposed in her childhood. No more will she be captive to her father's fears.

Like an aged fool he closes his eyes to the future of his daughter's happiness, as he always has, selfishly seeing her as an extension of his own inadequacies. The failures of the father shall not be visited upon the daughter. Fathering is more than spawning, parenting more than dominance.

He fears the son she has yet to conceive. He knows Danaë is favored of the gods, despite his neglect of her welfare. He can never be the man her son is surely destined to be. He thinks to deprive Danaë of that blessing, but the goals of little men are easily thwarted.

No Venetian tower can shutter Danaë. Like the canal laced lagoons of the city, there are a myriad of avenues around and about, each leading away from her shuttered life, and with each new way comes a new view. Oppression breeds the need for liberation, and I am to be her liberator.

"I have decided already."

But little men do not give up their selfish realms so easily. He will manipulate as he can, but his is a broken power.

Her maid is the key. Set to guard, she is the constant gate beyond which none may pass, but hers is not a faithful service. She is greedy and avarice ridden. An apron full of coins and she abandons all loyalties. The goals of little men are easily and cheaply thwarted.

I go to Danaë.

She welcomes me to her bed, lined with silken sheets beneath a velvet awning.

Danaë looks at me wistfully, her casual recline is open and inviting. I cannot help but question my worthiness before such a self-made being. I speak well of love and strength and potentials fulfilled, but am I all she seems to believe. Can I truly be the partner she deserves? She leaves behind the hardness of her father's meager soul to become the mother of heroes. What place do I hold in such a constellation?

I am like Marsyas, the satyr, a Titian beast flayed by mighty Apollo. In my arrogance I imagine myself a victor, rightful heir to the spoils of a contest won, as Apollo, however unjustly, defeated the myth of mother earth. And like Marsyas, sheared of his flesh in payment for his loss, I too must be flayed. As in the Venetian master's work I see the child of my childhood portrayed, innocent of what is to come. I see me as a young man at the height of my prowess, confident and full, the artist of life. And I see the old man I am to be, yearning to know if I, like Marsyas have flayed myself enough? Have I bared my soul enough to be worthy of Danaë?

I go to her and in her I find my answers. Her world is not to be mine. Rather, my world will be expanded by hers. To her son I will be the father she was denied. It is a responsibility I readily accept. It is an expanded world I am eager to share.

Danaë welcomes me like a shower of gold, raining in abundance upon her, and Marsyas heals.

Hissing Women

Caravaggio
Medusa
c. 1590
oil on canvas mounted on wood

Should I meet her blackblood eyes, the more frightening will her Gorgoneum be.

A scream, a throaty hissing scream, as if spitting Medusa's curse, issues from her Libyan craw.

It is an old argument, well rehearsed and well worn.

"You always say that!" she says, fury in her voice.

She often says that, I think.

She paints a chiaroscuro scene of lightness and dark, leaps of extreme with no middle hues painting her from here to there.

"Always?" I ask, somewhat sarcastically.

"You know what I mean," she replies, pinning me with a withering look.

I am not inclined to surrender.

"I don't *always* say that."

"You are such a bastard!" she sneers.

"Because I am precise in what I say?" I ask.

"Like I said, a bastard. A precise bastard!"

"Typical. You can't discuss things in a logical fashion, so you resort to name calling." It is the last refuge of emotion's venom, the mythic gnosis turned dark, swallowed by black time.

"You're *so* logical." She embarks upon a new tack.

"It helps to be." I didn't need to say that. I am throwing fuel on the fire.

"You always have to be right," she snarls.

"Not always."

"See, there you go again. You are always correcting me."

"I am not correcting you," I reply. "I'm just trying to defend my position."

"So you can be right!"

"Isn't that rather the point of an argument?" I submit, knowing well that my response would not help matters any.

"I'm not arguing, you are!"

I was under a different impression. Round and round we go, and I, like Perseus donned with wings must circle and weave to avoid her circuitous strikes.

"Really?" I say. "The yelling and name calling fooled me."

"Bastard!" she yells again.

"Hmmn." There is much I want to say, but don't.

"You never let me have my own opinion," she says defiantly.

"We weren't talking about a matter of opinion. We were talking about a matter of interpretation. Your interpretation," I add.

"It was my opinion!"

"Does your opinion include making up words that I never said?"

"I didn't make up anything," she insists.

"Really? What do you call putting words in my mouth that I never said?"

I sit back waiting for her response. Her counter is less convincing.

"It was my *opinion*!"

I press my case. "Either I said those very words, or I didn't."

"That's *your* opinion," she says, barely above a whisper. It is a feeble argument.

"No," I reply, "that's a fact."

"You just like to argue."

"I like to be accurate." I force myself calm. "And no, I don't like to argue. I don't like it at all, but I like even less being accused of saying things I did not."

"I wasn't accusing," she sulks.

"You claimed I said things that I never did."

"It was my opinion." It is a very unconvincing retort.

"What did I say?" I prod.

"What?"

"You heard me. What did I say? Not what is your interpretation of what I said, but what did I really say? What were my actual words?"

She puts on an air of exasperation. "I don't remember your exact words."

"You don't remember what was spoken less than five minutes ago?"

"I don't remember every single word you said, though I am sure you do." She isn't going to make this easy.

"My exact words were..." I rehearse verbatim the phrase that initiated this mess.

She broods at my repeated statement.

I continue. "How you went from that simple statement to accusing me of meaning something completely different is beyond me."

"It was my opinion." She repeats her mantra without conviction.

"Sorry, but your opinions don't give you the right to change my words so you can assign them meanings I never said and never intended. That's not playing fair."

"I didn't do that."

"You do it often."

"I don't," she insists.

"Sure you do. I can make a simple statement of fact, even something trivial such as 'This beef is a little tough,' and you immediately conclude that what I really said was 'I hate your cooking, you are an incompetent wife, and I wish I had married your sister!'"

She sniffs at the absurdity, and familiarity of my example.

"It's not that bad," she says under her breath. "Besides, my sisters aren't your type."

"True enough." I shudder at the very thought of them. "They are Gorgon beasts, immortal in their spite."

"True enough," she agrees.

"Then why does it so often become such an argument?" I ask, not expecting an answer.

She replies, "So I respond emotionally. That's who I am. Why do you want to change me?" she says with a quivering lip. Sometimes tears prevail where venom fails.

"I don't want to change you, but I don't want you to change my words either." My tone is calm and, perhaps I should fear, logical.

"Fine," she says with a sniff.

"The solution is quite simple, you know?" I say.

"It is?" She is dubious.

"Yes." I spread my hands as if the explanation was self-evident. "Don't interpret."

"It's what I do," she says.

"I know. It isn't fair."

"Then next time why don't you just tell me?"

"That is precisely what I did," I explain, "but then you get upset even more and say I am not letting you have your opinion."

"How am I supposed to not interpret?" she asks, as if she had already concluded it was an impossible expectation.

I do my best to explain. "Listen to my words, my exact words. Don't assume I mean anything more than what I actually say. If you don't understand, or think I must mean more than the actual words imply, ask me. I will clarify. But here's the rub, once I clarify what I mean, or do not mean, you need to abandon your interpretation and accept what I say and intend. And should the tables be turned, and we find that I am interpreting your words to mean anything other than their actual intent, I will do the same. Anything else is false and unfair."

"I thought I did do that." She seems defeated, all argument severed, a trophy for wisdom's shield.

"No."

"I can't not interpret. It's who I am," as if that pronouncement justifies it all.

"I'm not asking you to change the nature of who you are. You read things more emotionally than me. You interpret. I don't think that will ever change, but please allow me the right to clarify what I actually mean and accept my clarification. I won't lie to you."

"Fine, I'll try," she murmurs.

I sit back, satisfied that perhaps this time we have come to some understanding.

At length I say, "That's all I ask. Good communication will spare us a lot of arguments."

"Ohhh! You always do that!" she yells, catching me off guard. Her circuitous fury scorches her face and fixes me with a stare as if to turn me into stone.

"Do what?" I see all of our progress fleeing from this Earth-heir queen.

"You just made all the arguments my fault!"

"What?!" I am incredulous.

"You are just as much to blame!"

"What are you talking about? I never said all the arguments were your fault. I never said any such thing," I protest.

"You just did," she says with poisonous finality.

I counter, "I said nothing of the sort. You are interpreting again. What were my actual words?"

"I'm not getting into that again," she evades. "This is just like the time you…" She recounts an argument long past, and I thought long ago resolved.

"What's that got to do with anything we were just talking about?"

"It has everything to do with it. You won't let me be me!"

Twenty hissing serpents, all of a head, and I never know which one will strike next.

Unfaithful Women

Henry Fuseli
The Nightmare
1781
oil on canvas

I stir at the approaching footfall, her bare feet scarcely sounding across the cold stone floor, but I am awake and attuned to her arrival. She hopes to slip in unnoticed. Her eyes, unaccustomed to the darkened room lit by a single flame do not see mine taking in her slightly disheveled dress, the result of an earlier hasty exit she now wishes to conceal. The hedonic smells of alcohol and sexual sate mingle with her perfume as she enters. She stumbles and catches herself, forcing herself upright in defiance of her state.

"You are late," I say in a voice devoid of surprise or recrimination as she enters the room.

She starts at the sound of my voice, fearing a confrontation she would rather avoid. It would not be the first.

"Mmn, yes," she says in a near whisper as if not to awaken me, though clearly such precaution is an unnecessary consideration. Her voice is slurred with drink. I am not surprised. There is never a night without it. Even those nights she is here, with me, she leaves us for the solitude of the glass, until even the glass is not enough. She says she doesn't need it, but she seeks it out from the hidden places.

"I was delayed. It was unavoidable. I'm sorry I didn't get word to you." Her voice trails off, her message, preconceived and delivered in too much of a rush. How many times I have heard this oft repeated excuse? Too many times to even question it anymore. We both know the story it conceals and conveys.

"I see." I try to sound neutral. I don't know if I succeed. My heart is filled with a now all too familiar disappointment. It is not the first such late-night return.

Her eyes quickly divert from mine, though I doubt she can make out their resignation in the night shades.

"I'm tired," she says. "I just want to go to sleep."

Tired, I think. Yes, tired.

She disrobes, turning her back to me in a modesty displayed in my presence only after all such modesty has been discarded elsewhere. Clothes are hastily set aside and where once I found private delight in my baring bride, I now find none.

"Anna," I begin as she dons a white sleeping gown, "I think we need to talk."

"Oh?"

She doesn't ask what I think we need to talk about. She knows.

She will repeat her story, with variation. It is never the same in the retelling, as if new details or excuses must be added in order to convince me with their mounting abundance. No matter if consistency fails.

She will defend her lateness. It will be a hollow defense, easily penetrated.

She will become upset, as if it is my fault for asking. I will not respond.

She will become distraught, profuse in her repentance. I will not believe.

She will accuse, where no accusation is merited.

She will seek to place me low. I am already there.

"I'm really tired," she says dismissively.

Perhaps it is just as well. There is little left to say. What new humiliation would I learn? A name? A place? These no longer matter. It is not me, not here. There was a time when these details were of great import, as if learning them would somehow lead to an end and to her return. So it seemed. It is not that she loves another as I once feared. In the multitude is an absence of feeling. She does not love another. She does not love me, though once she did. She does not love herself, and in this is the end.

She climbs into bed, her back to me, her body tense and away. It is far from the demon-spent recline I imagine of her earlier unspoken rendezvous.

I see her as in a dream, a nightmare only in the sharing, hers unwilling, and mine unbidden. I see her as I have seen her before, when she was convincing in her fidelity. I see her as others now see in absence of me.

The sight of her unfaithful incubation clarifies in my mind. Her body arches in abandon. White gossamer paints the fullness of her spreading thighs and gathers at the valley of her inviting sex. Arms and head loll back and down, blonde locks tumbling towards the carpeted floor, an ecstasy shuddering surrender to the rhythms driving her. Unrestrained. Wanton. Prodigal. Breasts heave against the thin bodice of her gown as she exposes her warm-veined neck. She is willing prey, an eager victim to the spirit of lust. It is a lascivious sight, devoid of romance. It leaves me cold.

He is but one in a succession of many, this demon lilim kin of my imagination. He presses on her like an incubus hovering at her breast. She is enraptured by the bestial taking of an intimacy that was once my sole domain. There is no discretion in her desires.

I am surveying it all, like a wide-eyed Völsi flaring from a shadow void, and the couplings of our past are but a distant ritual shrouded in memory. Anna, like a sky-riding Valkyrie or an Indus queen took me to herself, an equine sacrifice to her fecundity. But no more. Our once private rite is diabolized beneath her demon lover's perch. The sacred come profane.

The nightmare recedes and my thoughts return to the now and the tensetight wall of Anna's back. I no longer question why. Nothing is said tonight, and we will not revisit it tomorrow. I don't understand why she keeps coming home. Is there a comfort here that she needs despite her nightly escapes? Nothing remains but to say goodbye. The time to leave is long past. I have already left, just as she left me long ago. I cannot give what she wantonly craves. I am not forbidden, just wrongly devoted. I blow out the candle and stare into the dark.

Chapter Seven

"*I* see a change in you. I can't quite place my finger on it, but there is definitely something different about you these past few days."

"There is nothing different about me Giacomo," Zanetta replied, setting Giacomo's tray on the table next to his bed.

"No, it's there," he said, studying her expression. "Right there," he indicated her face.

Zanetta's eyes widened in mock exasperation as she shook her head. "There is *nothing* there!"

"Wait a minute, there it is again. Is that a smile?"

"Oh hush," she said while batting away an imagined pointing finger. "I frequently smile," she protested.

Giacomo nodded.

"Yes, that is true. You smile often, when I tell you a joke or when Lorenzo does something that pleases you, or any number of times, but this is different. You are smiling just because."

"And is that now a crime in Venice?"

"Good lord, I hope not, but it does make me wonder. What has gotten into you of late?"

"Nothing has gotten into me. I'm just in a good mood."

"Hmmn," Giacomo intoned suspiciously.

"Besides, aren't you the one who keeps telling me to wake up and re-enter the world? Maybe I am just taking your advice."

"Hmph!" Giacomo grumped. "It would be the first time."

"That's not true and you know it."

Giacomo smiled.

"I know. It is good to see you happy."

He continued to watch Zanetta as she puttered around the room making busy work out of straightening things she had straightened a dozen times before and did not really require her attention. He waited for her to finally come to a rest and sit in the chair beside his bed.

"Giacomo, I need to ask you something."

"Anything."

"Some time ago you told me you had a mission you had to fulfill, something you still needed to do. I thought at the time that you were talking about Lorenzo. I thought that was what all the stories were about."

"And?" Giacomo prompted.

"And then a few days ago you talked about guides and I knew."

"What did you know?"

"It wasn't Lorenzo you were really worried about. It was me."

Giacomo closed his eyes and breathed deeply several times before answering.

"Lorenzo is young. He has his whole life ahead of him, and yes, there is much I want to tell him before, well, while I can, but there are many who will help him along his way when I cannot. But you my dear, there is still much for you to do, and you must be prepared. There are others waiting for you. Their lives may depend on it."

"You don't have to worry about me Giacomo."

"I can see that," he replied gently.

Giacomo felt suddenly tired. It was more than the physical exhaustion that plagued his every waking hour. It was the exhaustion of one who having climbed a mountain does not know if he has the strength to go back down. Not that it really mattered any more. Zanetta was here. Really here, not in some world of apathetic slumber, hiding from her destiny after having been pierced by the loss of love. Her husband was her Longinus, wounding her at the very moment of her atonement. At-one-ment. There it was again Giacomo mused.

"You are so like your mother," he said, not knowing how much time had lapsed in his reverie.

"Do you think so?" Zanetta asked.

"In all the important ways, yes, I do. But you are also stronger than she."

"What do you mean?"

"Your mother had a great heart, as you do, but she was innocent in her compassion. It was part of her. She was born with it and it was who she was. For her there was no other way. You and I, however, we understand the world. We see the wasteland for what it is and choose to see what dwells beyond.

"The innocents, like your mother, are like the angels, ever rewarded but never knowing fully the transcendence in which they dwell. The rest of us must choose, but first we must be able to see past the dualities of life, and that can be a painful venture, and so most will not even try. Oh, they will accept and even seek the joys of life, never knowing that the greatest joy comes from seeing beyond the dualities into the kingdom that is one. And without a guide we flounder about saying 'here it is' or 'there it is,' but it is never so. The kingdom is spread upon the earth, and men do not see it."

"You are a strange man, Giacomo Casanova. You write a biography that takes up an entire bookshelf, in which you sound to the world like rake, while in private you speak like a cloistered priest reciting passages from hidden gospels."

"I suppose I do. And which do you prefer?" Giacomo asked.

Zanetta arched an eyebrow at him. "Truth be told? I am rather fond of the rake."

"Ah! I knew it! Then you don't think I am going to Hell?"

"I didn't say that." Zanetta laughed.

Giacomo put on a crestfallen expression.

"But you aren't sure?"

"Well," Zanetta said in a slow measured tone, "I suppose anything is possible."

Giacomo shrugged.

"I was hoping for something a little more definitive."

"Sorry. I can't help you there."

"Just the same," Giacomo continued, "I wouldn't mind seeing Heaven one more time before I am sent off to the ultimate wasteland, if that is where I am to be consigned."

"One more time? You have seen Heaven before, have you?"

"Of course," Giacomo replied confidently.

"Really? And what does it look like?"

Giacomo raised his hands as if to indicate the answer was obvious.

"Venice."

"Of course," Zanetta laughed. "How could I have not known?"

Zanetta's tone sobered slightly as she continued.

"You know, I have seen it too."

"Heaven?" Giacomo asked.

"Yes."

"And what did it look like?" he asked.

"As it turns out, you were right. It looks like Venice."

Now it was Giacomo's turn to laugh.

"Would you like to hear about it?" she asked.

Giacomo's eyes crinkled in delight.

Zanetta proceeded to describe her venture out into the city just days before, knowing Giacomo would savor each and every detail.

"...and as I sat in Piazza San Marco, sipping a *limoncello*, which came all the way from Sorrento by the way, I felt as if I was seeing Venice, your Venice for the very first time. I felt connected."

Giacomo's eyes began to feel heavy, but he was not ready to abandon his niece's journey.

"Did you stay there long?"

"Just long enough to finish my drink" she said. "After that I strolled around the Doge's Palace and to the Grand Canal. I caught a gondola and had the gondolier take me beneath the Bridge of Sighs."

"I have been there, you know," Giacomo said sleepily. "I looked out from the bridge and thought I would never see Venice again."

"So I have heard."

Giacomo listened as she continued her account, a leisurely float across the canal and a visit to Santa Maria della Salute.

"To enjoy the Titians?" he asked, now barely awake.

"Yes. And to say a little prayer."

Giacomo was no longer aware if he was hearing Zanetta or reliving the splendors of his beloved Venice himself. Not that there was much difference. In his dreamy state, it was all real to him. He was happy and the pain of his failing body did not touch him here. All was well. Zanetta was awake now, for the both of them, and all was well. There was nothing more to trouble him. Zanetta would be fine. Lorenzo was set on his way. Through his stories he had told Lorenzo the truth that would guide him. All was well. Nothing could go wrong. Lorenzo was on his way. Nothing could go..."

The door to Giacomo's room opened with a bang, the neglected sword and scabbard hanging behind it clattering at the impact of heavy oak against plaster. The abrupt thunder of the flung wide door startled Giacomo out of his hovering slumber, somewhere between wakefulness and dream.

The old man jumped and stiffened with the sudden commotion, his body instantly rebelling in a spasm of pain at the undue demands the unbidden reaction exerted on his aged frame. Fleeting and floating images of pretty girls on velveted swings kicking high their stocking-clad legs or as reclining odalisques exotic in their splendor, initiating nuns and Madonnas with child, absinthe numbed ghosts and young women reflecting in a night creek all gave way to the muddled confusion of consciousness pushing its way into Giacomo's thoughts.

"What?" he rasped somewhat groggily as he struggled to focus his eyes upon the source of the noise. A figure, lost in the shadows of the hallway, stood confronting him. "Lorenzo, is that you?"

The younger man filled the doorway, his body quivering in rigid indignation.

"Grandnephew?" Giacomo asked, now alert to his surroundings and his abrupt visitor. "What's wrong? What has happened?"

The suddenness of the entry and the strained expression on Lorenzo's face arrested him and raised an alarm in the old man. What was it? Why was Lorenzo here, now, in such an agitated state? Was it Zanetta? Had something happened to her? His mind struggled to catch up to the possibilities that were racing through it, none of them fully comprehended or considered.

Lorenzo stepped forward, hesitated, and then stalked to the foot of his uncle's bed.

"You!" Lorenzo screamed. "You lied to me! It was all lies!"

Giacomo was taken aback at his grandnephew's outburst.

"What? Zanetta? Is she alright?"

"Liar!"

Giacomo realized belatedly that Lorenzo was confronting him, not talking about some imagined calamity.

"I don't know what you mean. Please, what's happened?" he implored.

Lorenzo's voice was choked with emotion. "You know damn well what happened! You lied to me. All of it, your stories, all of your conquests, they was all a big lie!"

Giacomo struggled to push himself up a little straighter in his bed, all too aware that Lorenzo, in his anger, was not inclined to help. He tried to make sense of what his grandnephew was saying.

"I don't know what you are talking about. Lorenzo, I never lied to you. Never!"

"Really?" Lorenzo asked with acid-laced sarcasm.

"The great Giacomo Casanova! Cocksman and lover, that's your claim, isn't it?" He didn't wait for an answer. "Only it isn't true, is it? Any of it?"

Giacomo read the condemnation and fury on his grandnephew's face.

"No," Giacomo said a little too harshly, the edge to his denial fueling Lorenzo's already hot anger. "No," he repeated, "I did not lie. What makes you say such a thing? Tell me, who says I lied to you?"

"This does" Lorenzo spat as he held up a worn leather-bound volume. "This book tells me of your lies!"

Giacomo quickly looked up at the twelve volumes of his life sitting atop his chest of drawers. All were still there, so what was this book his grandnephew was wielding with the damning finality of an Old Testament prophet?

Lorenzo advanced to the side of the bed, his chest heaving in great gasps as his body vented the fury that had been building within him since understanding replaced the worship he held in his heart for his uncle and the adventurous exploits he recounted so convincingly.

"Did it make you feel good, Uncle, to make such a fool of me? Did you laugh when I was gone at the great joke you spun at my expense?"

"Lorenzo, please, calm down. Tell me what it is that burns you so. I don't understand."

"Did you think I wouldn't find out? That's it, of course, isn't it? How could anyone ever question the renowned Giacomo Casanova?"

Giacomo was at a complete loss in the face of his grandnephew's anger.

"That book," he asked, "what is it?"

"I think you know it well, Uncle. It sits on your bookshelf downstairs. It's one of yours."

"Is it?" Giacomo asked, still not comprehending.

"See how it is worn? You must have looked at it thousands of times!"

"I, I don't know," he answered, suddenly feeling older than his near-death body could ever feel on its own.

"Of course you know, Uncle. See? It is your book of great art."

Lorenzo yanked opened the oversize book, displaying a large page with an engraving affixed to it.

"*Masterworks of the Great Artists*, it is called. Now do you see?"

Giacomo stared in confusion. Certainly he knew the book. It was one of his favorites. It contained etchings reproducing one hundred of the greatest paintings ever created. It was a treasure of the world's great art, many of which he had seen in his travels. So many nights Giacomo had poured over the pages, the images having been hand colored with aquatint bringing them to life, reliving the beauty and magnificence of the originals. But why was this book of such import to his grandnephew?

"You see, Uncle?" Lorenzo continued, flipping pages as he spoke. "Here they are! Your conquests!"

"My what?"

"They are here. Right here!" he said, stabbing a shaking finger at one of the prints, a reproduction of Botticelli's *Birth of Venus*. Giacomo tried to clear his mind, to comprehend whatever it was Lorenzo was trying to tell him. He peered more closely at the book, shaking unsteadily in Lorenzo's grip.

"But that doesn't any make sense," he said, looking up to search the young man's face.

"Doesn't it?" Lorenzo spat the retort. "Here!" he exclaimed. "Here," he rushed on in his excited recitation, "Botticelli's *Venus*. There she is, your beloved Simonetta just as you described her. And here," he indicated another print as he nearly tore it out of the book to thrust the image towards his uncle's face, "Carracci's fresco in the Palazzo Farnese. Only you might remember her better as Juno. Oh, and let's not forget Sibyl. You'll never know a greater love than this!"

The familiarity of the words hit Giacomo, but he still could not fully appreciate why.

"How fortunate for you that Michelangelo painted her, right on the Sistine ceiling!"

Understanding began to dawn on the old man. The book. The paintings. Lorenzo was of the belief that he had described these paintings when recounting his experiences, but how could that be? It made no sense.

"But, Lorenzo, that's not…"

"Uncle! Stop lying! They are in this book, just as you described them. Vermeer, Lippi, Rembrandt, Titian, Caravaggio, and the list goes on. Oh, I understand they are not all in here. Some of your descriptions are great sculptures, aren't they? Bernini's *Saint Teresa* in the Cornaro Chapel, *Queen Uta* from the Naumburg Cathedral. They aren't in this book, but once I caught on to your charade it wasn't that difficult to figure it all out. And then there are others I haven't placed yet, but I will. Some sound as if they haven't even been created yet, other than in your twisted feeble mind, but I'll figure it all out. I'll know every one of your lies!"

Giacomo shrank back from his grandnephew's verbal assault.

"The pictures," Giacomo exhaled in a weakened voice.

"Yes, Uncle, the pictures. Oh how you must have laughed every time I left your room. Your stupid, gullible grandnephew. He likes a girl so let's have some fun at his expense. After all, he'll never measure up to the great Casanova, will he?"

"No, Lorenzo, no. You don't understand."

"I understand perfectly well, Uncle. You lied to me. Every one of your great loves was actually just some work of art you recalled and described. Nothing more"

Lorenzo lowered his voice to a choked whisper.

"The great Casanova is nothing more than a curator of memories. There's more book than bed about the famous lover."

Tears were streaming down Lorenzo's cheeks as he closed the book and laid it beside his uncle on the bed.

"Lorenzo, I..." The words were not there. For the first time in his long, long life Giacomo Casanova was at a loss for what to say.

"Forget it, Uncle. No more of your stories. I don't want to hear any more."

"Please, Lorenzo. Let me explain."

"Save it for an art student or someone else gullible enough to believe your tales." Lorenzo turned his back on his uncle and walked towards the door.

"Wait," Giacomo pleaded.

Lorenzo halted and turned back, not wavering from his uncle's gaze.

"I believed you. I believed in you. Maybe I was the only one who did." Lorenzo exited, leaving the door open behind him.

Giacomo heard his grandnephew's descent down the stairs followed by a slam of the front entry door echoing through the halls. He was alone.

"The pictures," he said in a weak whisper. "I remember the art, yes I do, but that's not…

"Lorenzo," he called to the empty room, "let me explain."

Deceiving Women

Agnolo Bronzino
Venus, Cupid, Folly, and Time (The Exposure of Luxury)
1546
oil on wood

She is a caution, this wanton maid of alabaster glow. In cold brilliance she sits, a Mannerist allegory I labor to define. Of her allure, there is no denial, but she is a dangerous shoal to be avoided. Beneath her becalmed surface lies a torrent that will destroy me if I am not wary. Already I have waded into the inviting waters. Now I must find my way out.

"Come," she commands with the exaggerated elegance of an immortal. Her voice is cool and inviting.

I urge to rush in as if struck by love's arrow, but I am halted by uncertain restraints. She is too complex, too inventive to be the easy love she pretends to be. I am torn between relish and dismay. I stand my place.

"What holds you back?" she asks, as if affronted. "I am here for you, breasts bared, yours for the taking."

It is an inviting tableau as she stretches and purrs. I resist its carnal pull.

A sudden thought darkens her brow, "Don't you want me?" she asks.

I do want her. She is Venus and lust. I crave and hunger for her. I long to touch the smooth perfection of her skin, but I remain still.

"You entice me," I say at last.

She stretches and strikes a pose. My hunger swells.

"Then come to me and let your enticement be satisfied."

"Shall I rush in like a youthful Cupid, callow and blind" I inquire warily.

"Cupid and Venus," she purrs, "mmm, an illicit love." She licks her lips invitingly.

All ends for her are but a sating of the animal. Alimentation, gratification, and empowerment are her only desires and she will use any means to see them filled.

"You would see me as a child of deceived will, rushing in to pleasure's lure," I say in my resistance. "I would be little more than folly lobbing petals at your feet."

She cannot see beyond her wants, so cannot hear beyond her argument.

"You know my pleasure," she says. "We are a good match, Giacomo. We know what each other desires. Come, taste me."

I have tasted before. But she is not what she seems. She conceals. Behind her womanly allure is the daughter of her conceit, fraud, a girl of innocent countenance, but with a serpent's tail. She proffers honeyed dalliance, but there is a sting in her. No, she is not what she seems.

"Why do you resist me, Giacomo?" she asks in a hurt and petulant voice.

She cannot understand why I deny her. I want life, not just the pretense she offers.

"I have not resisted you, not in the past," I answer.

"No, you have not." She closes her eyes as if recalling the joys of romantic interludes long ago. She opens her eyes of a sudden and fixes me with a calculating stare. "We had something good."

We didn't. What was between us was shallow and selfish. There was no union of two, just the taking of another.

"What we had was mutual," I say.

"So what halts you now? I am here for you."

I endeavor to see behind the deceptive plane, where bearded time hovers, revealing all. He holds back the pale blue veil of her staged set, where truth abides at his right hand. Beneath them, anguish lurks, the syphilitic outcome of an unwise choice.

I shrink from the ugliness her beauty seeks to hide.

"What is it, Giacomo? Why do you look at me that way?"

I cringe within. I have been susceptible to her enamel charm. Have I also partaken of the venom tail?

I see reflected in her flawless countenance my own shame. Have I not spoken her words before? Have I not seduced for my own gain? It is too easy to blame youthful ambition, as if blind self-interest is a necessary stage through which the young must pass. That is an excuse fashioned by those who wish to excuse their selfishness while living it further if they can.

I have been where she is. "Come," I said, "the pleasures are good and consequences of no concern." But there are always consequences. Life altering consequences. The innocent who succumbs to the polished enticements of the cad gives her heart while his only goal is to take her flesh. The real world of consequence has a way of lasting well beyond the momentary pleasure.

"I'm sorry," I stammer after an uncomfortable pause.

"Sorry?" The word seems to strike her unfamiliar. "Why are you sorry?"

I want to tell her. I want to explain that I can no longer partake of the hollowness she offers. I know her game. I have played it. I will play it no more.

"You are beautiful," I say, looking for a graceful exit.

"What do you mean?" she demands. "Of course I am beautiful!" Her eyes spark with haughty indignation.

"I am sorry," I repeat, not knowing what else to say.

She spits my name, "Giacomo! You pig! You used me and now you are sorry?"

"We used each other," I murmur. It is weak reasoning. I am as guilty as any.

Her expression changes as if a new thought has occurred to her. Hers is not an easy surrender.

"Giacomo," she begins with renewed sweetness in her voice. "Come back to me. It will be as it once was and all will be forgiven."

She is back at her mannered pose and I am tempted, if only for a moment, but I see the fallen masks at her feet, falsities I cannot ignore.

"Goodbye," I say with my head bowed.

"You would leave me?"

"Goodbye," I repeat, confident in the finality.

There is a new tone to her voice. Is it desperation?

"You'll be back," she says. "You will come to me again. You'll see."

I turn to leave. Life has become an allegory I must not ignore.

Renewing Women

Isis and Horus
c. 332 BCE
faïence

Throne of the divine child. Lady of abundance.

I thought I was beyond redemption, but if I can be saved, it will be at the hand of Isis. Even when away, we can never truly be parted. We are alike, she and I. Twinned lovers, each seeing unity with the other, we are paired. She will save me. She must save me, as I saved her.

How long have I been adrift? Once I was dead and now alive again, thanks to Isis, my giver of life.

It is a distant land, far away from the hamlets and capitals of the home that will be in my final days. It is lush with green valleys born from the desert sands and flooding waters, and I have traversed it all, at times with Isis at my side and in my death, alone, for her to search. It is an age of gods and she is the greatest of them all.

And there is a villain. There is always a villain.

Isis never suspects. She does not know. She cannot know. It is, after all, because of her brother, Seth, that I am to be usurped. At least that is his plan.

I dream there is a party. The desert sings with the gaiety of immortals. Even among immortals, though, jealousies breed and infest like a canker over the land.

Isis is not here, in my dream. She is away as is her role. Needed by many she is not one to shirk her responsibilities, and so she is gone for a time. I don't know for how long. Time has lost meaning in her absence. How long have I been adrift? It is hard to remember when no longer in the field of time. Is the search also a hallucination? Be it so, I can still sense her lamenting quest. She will find me. She will save me.

Set is here, in my dream. Or is it a memory? Not that it matters. Each is real when one is lost. He is always here, lurking, lusting, and plotting, he and his followers. There must be seventy-two of them, or so it seems.

It all happens so fast.

"Isn't it beautiful?" Set exclaims to the boisterous crowd.

And it is. A box of exquisite beauty, carved, inlaid, and covered with gold. Only my mind's eye could conceive such magnificence.

The assembled think it is all a great joke, but for Set it is no laughing matter. There is always intent behind his leer.

"It looks big enough to hold a man," someone cries.

"Prove it!" another yells.

"Very well," Set says with a smirk, "I'll prove it, and to make it more interesting, whoever fits this box exactly may have it."

"It will be their treasure chest," a voice calls out of the swirling darkness at the edges of my divining state.

"Or their sarcophagus," another says darkly, and all howl at the morbid joke.

One after another the guests try, each positioning themselves in turn, trying it on for size. One is too small, another too large. Always there is something to disqualify the eager and greedy guests.

Then someone yells, "Let Giacomo try!"

"Yes, let it be Giacomo!"

I am lead, jostled, until I take my place within the coffin walls.

With the speed of jackals the seventy-two rush as one to seal the tomb to be, and with it my fate.

Wake. Wake! I scream. Do I scream out loud, or is that too just a dream? Even dreams must give way to blackness when Set grins his evil grin. His is the last face I see as, in my dream, or is it memory, I am encased.

He aspires to take my place, this much I know. Isis will not have it, or him, but he will try. Jealousy blinds him. Lust consumes him. Arrogance defines him. It is his character.

I am trapped, but where? Time loses all meaning without her, without Isis. This is the true perdition, to be denied one's love.

Cast into Nile waters, I drift alone. I am lost. She will find me, I know. Isis will find me.

She quests and the desert dies in her sorrowful steps.

All is lost.

In my sarcophagus deathdream I come to beach on a distant shore. A tree grows up and around me, a tamarisk tomb, embraced as if by a lover, and here I stay, neither growing, nor living, never becoming, merely being. Still, a sliver of hope kindles inside my lifeless corpse and I remember the love that was. I remember the love that is once again to be. I remember Isis.

I am become the tree of life, holy rood.

She is moved to me. All roads lead to the world tree when one truly seeks their heart. In the dimmest light she circles this central pillar as a swallow in heavenly flight, while the embers of immortality burn. Even kings dare not stand in way of our reuniting.

Isis has found me. I am certain of this as my dreams turn to light. Hope kindles.

In my dream I drift again, but this time not alone. She is with me on this sarcophagus turned ark. Surmounted by Isis we pair as consorts do and I am reborn. She gives life again where there was none. I am of Isis. I am resurrected.

Of that union comes a child. He too will fight against the evil one and castrate time. He too will surpass the polarity of forms and in so doing he will become anointed, sanctified, the redeeming Son. He will become the father of the father son.

Isis sits enthroned, proud, straight, sanctified, and he is at her lap, the virtuous child, the giver of life and redeemer of death. Our son.

She is the throne. In many guises she and our child will be remembered. Maya and Mithras, Calliope and Orpheus, Demeter and Dionysus, Madonna and Child, all find their forms in her. She is the renewing principle. She is Isis. And she has saved me.

Damaged Women

Artemisia Gentileschi
Judith Slaying Holofernes
c. 1612
oil on canvas

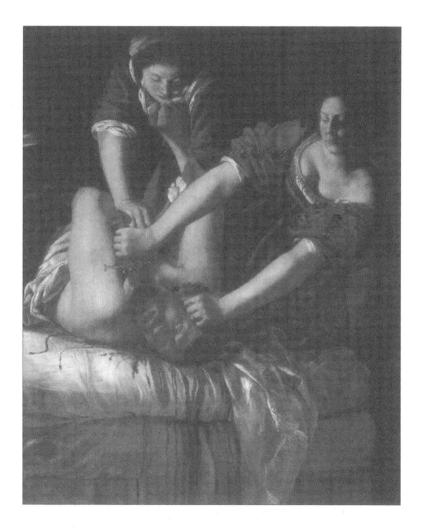

Again and again the scene repeats, like a painted refrain on a succession of canvases. Artemisia screams, and I know she is reliving the assault.

Thrashing legs and helpless arms flail against her attacker in a recurring battle against a memory. Covers cling to her, enveloping her, drowning her as she battles to escape what she can never escape. In the chiaroscuro night the darkness of the room, like a battlefield tent blackened against a moonless sky, is shattered by illuminated figures frozen in horrific action. I cannot see what she sees in the nightmarish darkness. I feel her, though, as she fights the unseen.

Her nightmare is familiar to me, though I can never really comprehend the full devastation of the violence she endured. The damage is unseen, only to reveal itself in these moments of horror sleep.

I want to stop the dreams, stop the screaming. I want to take away her pain. I want to repair her, to fix her, to heal her, but I am impotent to do so.

How many nights have we lain here, Artemisia covered in fear sweat and trembling from an event long past?

"What can I do? Tell me what I can do," I implored more times than I can remember.

"Nothing," she repeats, with increasing frustration. "Nothing."

I have not always been understanding, to my shame. In moments when calm prevailed I thought to reason, as if reason alone could somehow trump the trauma she endured.

"It was so long ago," I said. "Surely you can let it go. Why don't you just let it go?"

It is a stupid question, I know. It was a shattered calm.

"It isn't something I can just let go," she cries. "Don't you think I would if I could?"

I cannot fix her.

I should be able to fix her.

Why can I not fix her.?

Why won't she let me fix her?

"Dammit Artemisia! This has to stop! I can't take it anymore!" I said at last.

To my shame.

"Don't make me feel bad for feeling bad," she cried.

I am ashamed.

In my impotence I made it about me. I blamed her for something of another's doing, as if I was the one assaulted, but from the hurt look in her eyes I realized I was more like her attacker than the attacked. In dismissing her pain, in losing my compassion, I raped her again, as surely as the one who committed the crime.

Over the years I have learned the details of what Artemisia hauntingly refers to as the event.

Hers was to be a future of brightness and joy, a girl brimming with talent, learning under her father's guiding hand, working in his studio among the most gifted of students. That she would be an artist, there never was any doubt. That she would excel in a time when women were denied such equality was yet to be seen. Her skill, even as a youth, was recognized by all, envied by some, hated by one.

What obscenes the jealous mind?

Tassi was his name. A student of promise and gift, a bright future ahead. But for some it is never enough. He could not accept that another, a girl possessed equal, or even more talent than he. And if he could not possess Artemisia's talent, he would possess her. Possession is the true obscenity. Tassi plots and rapes and young Artemisia will never fully heal.

I swallow the venom I feel at this coward's theft. Would that vengeance was within my grasp, to chase him across Phlegithon to the

Plain of Fire, in the seventh circle to forever burn. But who am I? I am no Dante able to consign a sinner to an eternal poem and everlasting infamy. I cannot fix this. I cannot go back in life and stop the crime, though I would if I could. I cannot punish the less than man that committed this crime, though I would do so with my bare hands were it given me, even if it meant I would burn in Hell for delivering vengeance not mine to give. It is a past I cannot reach, but for now, Hell is here and Artemisia screams its terrors.

I call her name, never touching, lest in her dream my caring hand becomes Tassi's raping claw.

"Artemisia," I whisper, "Artemisia, it's all right. I'm here. It's all just a dream, just a dream."

She awakens, eyes wide, sweat glistening on her brow.

"I, I was dreaming," she stammers.

"I know. It's over." I touch her now and she folds into my arms, her body convulsing in sobs. "It's over," I repeat, though I know it will never be over.

I have learned. There are some things I cannot fix, and my impotence is not Artemisia's fault. What she needs from me is to be there for her, to comfort when I can, to understand when I must.

After a time we both lie back, quiet in our thoughts. Artemisia's breathing is labored and hard, but it will ease with time. Her hand touches mine, and when she is ready she holds it, accepting the reassurance of the now. Neither of us sleeps, but there is comfort in not sleeping.

In the dawning light of day the nightmare recedes. Artemisia wills it back into the deepest recesses of her consciousness as she imagines herself assailing her assailant. As Judith she avenges.

Tassi's crime is visited upon him as sure as Holofernes met his end. In her waking dream she leaves the general's bed, and with swift descent she strikes. Death is instant in this Baroque theatre, a single candle lighting Judith's deed. A maidservant gathers the bloody trophy, Artemisia's revenge.

I am there for her. Simply there to understand as she repeats the Judith scene over and again. The dreams do not rule her, but they remain a part of her.

The nightmares are fewer now, coming less frequently with the passing of time, but never quite gone. Artemisia lives Judith still.

Women Unfulfilled

Jan van Eyck
Giovanni Arnolfini and His Bride
1434
oil on wood

A promise is witnessed. I take her hand in mine, a symbol of our wedded vow. With an open palm she receives me, a union to be consummated. Ours will be a sumptuous wedding, with expectations of happiness to reign for all of our days together.

Demure Giovanna, daughter of the Cenami is resplendent in her gown of ermine-lined green velvet, holding the abundant folds to her womb, a portent of life yet to come. She wears the green and white of hope and purity, but her hopes entail more than I, or this Flemish frame can give. I would see her hopes fulfilled.

"It is the way of the world," she resigns.

"Who's world?" I protest.

"Giacomo, it's alright. We will be married and all will be well."

"How will all be well when your family dictates the bride you are to be?"

"They did not choose you, I did."

"Yes, against their preferences as I recall."

"At first, but once they got to know you they changed their minds."

"Once they got to know my accounts, you mean. How is it your sister described me? A profitable catch!"

"Is that so bad? I mean, you are successful after all."

"Yes, but what if I wasn't? Would I still be a good catch?"

"You would to me."

"And that is my point, Giovanna. You love me for who I am, not for what I can provide. Just as I love you for who you are. Everything you are. Not only the dutiful bride they expect you to be."

"It is the way of the world," she repeats.

Our good friend Jan witnesses our vows. It is as if his portrayal is a reflection of our promises to one another. Like an all-seeing creator he composed our day and no detail has been omitted. I can learn from him. His is a new way of seeing. Glaze upon oiled glaze adds depth to the world he portrays. It is not unlike Giovanna, my bride to be. There is richness in the layers of her mind yet to be revealed.

Her family is quite pleased. Jan has created a showcase of commodities and Giovanna is to be the chiefest of commodities, a bauble to be bartered for standing in a wealthy household. My household.

There can be no mistaking their hopes. They want their daughter to expand the family. It is the norm for the times. I hope in my heart of hearts Giovanna does not find it too confining. Their wishes are not hers. She has a keen mind and quick wit, when privately she reveals it. Hers is an intellect that is no man's lesser.

"And you, my brilliant love, are you satisfied with the bargain?"

"I am pleased to become your wife."

"As I am your husband. But what of your happiness? You have so much more to offer than servant bride. I want more for you."

Today, however, she lowers her eyes, acting the role her family defines. Today she assumes her place.

The reception room is transformed for the vows. It has become a bedchamber. Giovanna stands next to the bed denoting her new station. It is a short-sighted waste. She is to be domestic and produce the heirs to the family fortunes, while I stand next to the window, for my world is not confined to the sole comforts of home. Oranges of the Medici proclaim my profession as a man of banking, a man of industry. I am free to pursue any interest, any education, any accomplishment I set my mind to, as Giovanna is not. Does her family know of Giovanna's wish to be a part of what lives out there? Do they understand her need for challenges of the mind?

"There is no place for me out there," she says.

I know she is right.

"And there never will be, unless we change it."

"We can't change society."

"Why not?"

"It just isn't done."

"It will be," I say with determination.

A cherry tree is in full fruit, a symbol of love, but love for what? Love of man and wife? My love for the world of accomplishments I am to dominate? Or is this an unrequited love, opportunities to be denied my bride?

Flanders sees no such ambiguities as far as Giovanna is concerned. She is to be bride and birthmaid. Saint Margaret, patron saint of fertility and protector of laboring women presides over the consummating bed like a towering finial.

Her family cannot comprehend Giovanna's dreams, only the limitations of an era. Bruges is not ready for a woman of Giovanna's gifts. She will be constrained, wielding brush and broom rather than pen and power. It is not her time. We must change the time.

"It doesn't have to be like this," I say. "You can be as you wish to be."

"I wish to be your bride."

"You can be that and more."

Hope flickers in her eyes as if catching a solitary flame.

A single candle burns in the ornate brass chandelier. It is tradition, a mystic light to be extinguished once she is a maiden no more.

Fido, fidelity, plays at her feet, another symbol of expectation. Patten clogs kicked aside, we stand in a hallowed room, on the sanctified ground of matrimony. Is Giovanna happy? Will she find fulfillment in the role she is to play?

"Do you really think so?"

"I believe you can do anything you choose to do. I believe in you."

The desire is clear. Giovanna and her sisters deserve all that I and my gender enjoy. Gender, skin, inclination, all are and must be equal or we will never see our full potential.

"My sister is right. You are a very profitable catch."

With northern clarity I view my bride. The world is not ready for her. We must change the world. Together we present an ideal wedding portrait, but what of the woman who is not of her time? The bedchamber awaits, potential unfulfilled.

Women Who Support

Porch of the Maidens
From the *Erechtheum*
421-405 BCE
Acropolis, Athens, Greece

I long for a home I no longer know. Not the home of childhood play and nurtured comfort. I remember such a place, where I once ran and learned and slept and read and feared and sang and all manner of things, but this is not what I long for. The home I seek is one of belonging. It is a feeling I have long past abandoned, or rather, it has abandoned me. This place of childhood memory was comfort, and it was the home to which I belonged if only because I was of that place, as children are. Belonging flees when one leaves the child abode to seek the world and it can only be found again when the heart has found its place. I have stayed in many houses, called many cities my land, but none of these were homes of belonging.

I am tired. So very tired. It is not the seeking that wears one so, it is not finding.

There is something familiar here. Not the scenery. I have never been here before. The buildings are not unlike others I have seen, though perhaps older, more majestic in their stand. It is something else, or rather, someone else. She catches my eye and holds it, and I belong.

"Nice view," I say as I take in the magnificent sweep of the valley below and the Aegean blue sea stretching into the horizon.

The view is breathtaking, but not so much as this woman sheltered on the porch.

She speaks.

"We like to think so, my sisters and I." She gestures to the other young women at her sides. "I am Clio."

"I am Giacomo," I introduce myself to her and to all.

"You are not from around here," she says.

"No," I reply.

"Where do you call home?"

I am taken aback by her question. It is as if she can read the weariness of my mind.

"I don't have a home."

Clio tips her head and gives a little shrug.

"You will."

I look off into the valley, wondering if that is so.

Clio follows my line of sight and holds it, her sisters also setting their eyes on the distant horizon, as if they were seeing farther in the distance, and deeper into the past than I can even imagine.

"We like to come out here," she continues, "onto this porch to take it all in."

She exudes the satisfaction her words imply and I am envious of the stability her connection to this place gives her. They belong.

"Have you lived here long, you and your sisters?" I ask.

I cannot imagine her anywhere else, her or her family. Her head turns ever slightly towards me, a kore grin still on her lips.

"Clio can tell you all about our family," one of the sisters says, rather enthusiastically. "She is the historian among us."

"Indeed," I say, glad to have my attention directed again towards Clio.

"Our family has been here since classical times," Clio says, assuming the role her sister described. "Tradition has it all the way back to the reign of Erechtheus, a legendary king, so they say, but who really knows? We are a very old family," she concludes.

"And yet you look as young as you must have the first day you stood here as the maidens of this porch," I flirt, as much to compliment her as to win the approval of her sisters who seem to be ever-present, and ever listening.

"Thank you, Sir, though it is hard to be here in this place and not feel the tremendous weight of time," she says almost wistfully.

"I suppose it is," I agree.

Young Calliope, standing behind her glows a bashful sunburnt red, like a sunset ending an epic poem, on her sister's behalf. The others react each according to their personalities. Erato, her lovesong twin, standing next to her, echoes her Polykleitian pose and mirrors the same knowing look, as if a compliment to Clio is one to her as well. Elegiac Euterpe, farther right, wants to hear more of my words, eager for any new gossip to spread and discuss among them when they are next alone. Urania, the oldest, is positioned away on the opposite corner of the porch, a constellation unto herself. I hear the slight dismissive click of her tongue, as if she has heard it all before and is yet unimpressed. She looks the other way, absorbed in her own thoughts and ignoring me. As far as she is concerned, I am just another passing traveler, here for the sights before I am once again on my way. And then there is Polyhymnia, mysterious Polyhymnia, always in shadow like a solemn hymn. Each of them, in their own way, is as much a part of this place as their sisters, but it is Clio who attracts me now, here.

I catch sight of her in the setting rake of the sun and feel both the strum and craving tug of my heart. She, like her sisters, is clad in traditional Athenian garb. Chitons of clinging white, aged like marble, once multi-hued and worn pure by passing winds of time, cling to their legs to reveal their slender solidity. A thin peplos molds against Clio's breasts, each passing breeze shaping the fragile cloth.

"An impressive family," I say.

"We are not all here," says Calliope.

"We are sisters nine," explains Erato.

"Three more?" I ask. "Is it possible to have so much beauty in such abundance all in one family?"

The sisters giggle and Clio smiles.

"Where are the others?" I ask.

Clio responds, "Two are off laughing and dancing who knows where."

"And the last?"

Clio turns serious.

"Well, every family has its tragedy."

She does not explain further. I think it best to change the subject.

"And yet the rest of you call this home," I say.

"There was a contest here, once upon a time," she says.

"A contest?"

"At least," she continues, "according to myth. It was said to have taken place between Poseidon, the Olympian who rules the sea, and wise Athene. Each was to bestow a gift upon humankind. Poseidon struck a rock with his great trident and it poured forth water fresh and pure."

"It was a nice trick," Calliope interjects, wanting to get into the conversation.

"Very showy," Erato declares, adding her own observation before again assuming her echoing position.

Clio continues as if she had told this story a thousand times and these comments were now a featured part of the rendition. "But it was, in the end, just a show of his power. 'See what I can do? Don't I impress?' was all it amounted to."

"So Athene won the contest?" I ask, jumping ahead.

"Her gift was the olive tree, with all of its abundance. It was a gift to support an entire city. That is why it is named for her. Athens."

"Is that why you, and your sisters, stay at this place? Is that why you are such pillars here?"

"That is one reason," she says.

"Do you stay for love as well?"

"That is what makes it home."

"Love of this place?" I ask.

"Yes, but home can be any place."

"Love of family?"

"My sisters and I, we do share great love, but each can come and go, according to her desires, and home it will still be."

"Love of another?" I ask with hope in my voice.

"We are Athene's daughters," Clio answers. "It is not enough to impress. Any nubile nymph can turn a man's head. It is genuine support that counts over time. That is where love of the ages is found."

She turns her head to match the others, looking out to the sail dotted sea like classical caryatids standing from another time. I sit on the porch's edge beneath Clio's shade. I am falling in love. I am finding a home. I will stay for a time to gather my strength on this porch of the maidens.

Chapter Eight

The sharp report of the bronze knocker at the front door startled Zanetta out of her solitude as she sat by the now smoldering embers of the fire in the front receiving room. She had been absently stitching on her embroidery, savoring the few moments of relaxation after seeing Giacomo settle in for the night and before the enticement of sleep overtook her. Now she was suddenly alert and alarmed.

The rapping at the door sounded again, this time more urgently.

Zanetta quickly rose and pulled her robe tightly around her, resecuring the sash at the waist. She hastened to the entrance hall and stopped at the front door.

"Who is it?" she called out loud enough to be heard on the other side. Her senses were on alert. It was late, well beyond the time for visitors, and one never opened a door to the unknown in the blackness of a Venetian night.

"Signora!" a deep and vaguely familiar voice called back. "It is I, Foscarini. Your neighbor!"

What? Foscarini? Here, at this hour? Zanetta was lost in confusion as she tried to make sense of the unexpected intrusion.

"It is your son, Signora! I have Lorenzo with me," the voice called through the door again.

Lorenzo?!

Zanetta forgot her caution and clumsily fumbled with the latch, pulling the large heavy door open to peer out. Muted candlelight from the entrance hall cast an angled illumination on the figure of Signore Foscarini, standing on the front step, holding onto an arm cast over his shoulder with one hand while the other supported the slumping figure of another man. Lorenzo!

"What happened?!" she exclaimed.

"Please Signora, if I may?"

He stepped forward, not waiting for an answer, half carrying half dragging the unconscious, or semi-conscious young man at his side.

Zanetta stepped back from the door, pushing it farther open to make room for their passing.

"Through here," she exclaimed, indicating the front receiving room. "There is a settee."

Signore Foscarini carried her son past her and into the receiving room. She quickly closed and secured the front door and rushed to follow them. She entered to see Signore Foscarini lowering her son to the settee, then lifting his legs into a laying position.

"What happened?!" she asked again, her fear sounding in her voice as she rushed to her son's side.

Foscarini stood and immediately faced her, raising his hands to both halt and calm her.

"It's all right, Signora, your son will be fine."

Her eyes were on Lorenzo, collapsed on the settee, his face bloodied and his clothes disheveled and stained. Signore Foscarini's reassurances did not comport with the fright of seeing her son injured and unconscious before her. She knelt by him, quickly examining his blood-stained face.

"What happened?" she repeated, fighting back the panic she felt and that clearly came through in her voice.

She tentatively touched her son's face, then she tilted his head to the other side, examining him in the process. The blood that was smeared across his face gave him a frightful appearance, but on closer inspection seemed to have come as the result of a bloodied nose. She saw no cuts or evidence of current bleeding.

Just then her son stirred, and a slight lopsided grin curled his mouth. He mumbled something incoherent. Zanetta leaned in closer to hear.

"I'll teach you, you," Lorenzo slurred through his slack mouth. The pungent odor of stale liquor and vomit accompanied the mashed words, causing Zanetta to pull back sharply, covering her nose.

"He's drunk!" she said with some disbelief.

"Quite so," Foscarini confirmed. "As I said Signora, your son will be fine, though I suspect he is in for a none too pleasant morning."

"He's drunk?" Zanetta repeated, a question edging its way into her voice. "Please tell me what happened?" she asked again, this time without the alarm or fear of her earlier queries.

"I will tell you all I know, Signora, but perhaps you will permit me to sit momentarily," Foscarini said while gesturing to his knee.

Zanetta's eyes followed his hand movement to see that his breeches were torn at the knee and a small amount of blood stained the fabric.

"You're injured," she said, a degree of alarm rising in her voice once more.

Foscarini waved his hand dismissively.

"It is nothing, Signora. Nothing. I stumbled while helping your son and my knee had an unfortunate encounter with the pavement. A small scrape, nothing more, though a bit tender from the impact. If I may?" he indicated the chair by the fire.

"Yes, yes, of course!"

Zanetta hurried over and grabbed her embroidery from the chair where she dropped it when rushing to answer the door.

"Please, Signore, sit."

She noticed Signore Foscarini limped as he made his way to the chair and sat heavily."

"Umph," he grunted involuntarily as he lowered himself. "Much better, thank you."

"You are cut," she said. "Let me have a look at it."

"That won't be necessary. It's just a scrape. Like your son, though, I think I may feel it more in the morning." He let out a short laugh.

Zanetta relaxed a bit at the ease of tension and took a seat in the high-back settle angled from the fireplace, facing Signore Foscarini.

"Please, how did you come to be here with my son, drunk and injured?"

Foscarini took a deep breath and let it out before speaking.

"A fortuitous happenstance, actually. I was working late at my warehouse and just happened to be on my way home when I encountered your son."

"Encountered?"

"I was on my way home, not my usual route, but shorter, and I was eager to end my day. As I entered the Piazza, I heard a commotion outside of one of the taverns, Caravaggio's it is called. I didn't pay much heed. Just a couple of drunken patrons. Voices were raised and I saw one of them, Lorenzo it turns out, take a wild swing at the other. He missed and nearly fell over in the process. The other fellow was a little more lucky in the return punch and managed to find Lorenzo's nose. They both went down and, quite frankly, I don't think either of them will remember the altercation, if you could call it that, clearly in the morning."

"My Lorenzo was in a drunken brawl?" Zanetta said, the incredulity revealed in her voice.

Foscarini laughed again, this time more sustained and relaxed.

"I would hardly call it a brawl," he said. "More of a misunderstanding fueled by mistemperance resulting in mild misfortune."

Zanetta was taken aback by Signore Foscarini's casual dismissal of the events that led her son to his current state.

"You call this," she indicated Lorenzo's prone body, "a mild misfortune?"

Foscarini nodded.

"Nothing more," he said, smiling.

Now it was Zanetta's turn to take a deep breath.

"I see."

She pulled her robe more tightly around her collar, trying to make sense of what he was telling her.

"What was the fight about?" she asked.

Foscarini let out another short laugh. "Who knows? A spilled drink? An insult? An argument over artichokes?"

"Artichokes?" Zanetta was perplexed.

"It's possible. That particular tavern makes excellent artichokes, but some people prefer oil and others butter. How they are cooked is a matter of some pride to the owners and patrons of the tavern. It wouldn't be the first time such things rose to altercation. I myself am partial to butter," he said somewhat whimsically.

"Signore Foscarini, are you making light of these events?"

"Only because they are light, Signora. No real harm has befallen your son, and the aftermath will provide a lesson he won't soon forget."

"But he was drunk, and fighting, in public!"

Foscarini shrugged a bit while absently rubbing his knee, apparently not feeling that a response or further explanation was necessary.

"Well, I, I don't know what to say. I am so embarrassed," she said.

"You needn't be, Signora. Truly. Lorenzo is a fine young man, but he is young. And like all young men, he has much to learn."

"But drinking and fighting in public?"

"Well, yes, but he isn't the first young man in Venice to learn that lesson the hard way. I recall in my youth a couple of, um, embarrassing situations."

"Signore?"

Foscarini laughed. "It's true! I remember one particular notorious incident in which a bunch of ruffians I thought were friends dared me to swim across the Grand Canal. Naked! Suffice it to say a great deal of wine was involved."

"Signore Foscarini!" Zanetta exclaimed.

"I wasn't much older than Lorenzo is now. And to make matters worse, I was more than half way across when my so-called friends grabbed up my clothes and ran away, leaving me high and, well, wet. That was a hard thing to explain to my father when I showed up at our home wearing nothing more than an apron I stole from the back of an inn as I wound my way home through the dark alleyways."

Foscarini was now laughing so hard that Zanetta could not help but join in.

"You're lucky you weren't arrested," Zanetta said, amused.

"I'm lucky I didn't catch some horrific disease. The Grand Canal. In summer!"

Foscarini composed himself and continued.

"My point is, Zanetta, your son is a fine young man. He is trying to figure some things out, as all young men do, but you have raised him well. He will make mistakes, but in the end he cannot deny being the man you have helped him become."

Zanetta stared at the man sitting before her. It was the second time in recent weeks he called her by her given name and though it was more familiar than social mores dictated, she was warmed rather than offended by the familiarity.

"Thank you Signore Foscarini."

"Sebastian, please," he responded.

"Sebastian," she tentatively repeated, inwardly pleased.

She continued, "It seems you are always in the right place at the right time to help the men of my family at their times of need. Thank you."

"As your uncle once was for me," he said thoughtfully. Their eyes locked before each looking away into the fire.

"You know," she continued almost conspiratorially, "I got drunk once when I was young."

She could feel herself actually blushing at the revelation. Blushing! Zanetta surprised herself by confessing this to the man sitting across from her.

Foscarini raised an incredulous eyebrow. "You?"

"It was during Carnival and my girlfriends and I decided it would be a good idea to stage our own masked ball. No boys of course! That would have been far too scandalous! Just the four of us. We waited until my friend's parents were away for the evening and their maid had retired, then we locked ourselves in her parlor and did what we thought happened at masked balls. We danced poorly and practiced our flirting. As you said, a great deal of wine was involved."

"What happened?" Foscarini asked eagerly.

"My friend's parents returned home to find four thoroughly silly girls that could barely stand. After a sound scolding, her father walked me and the other two girls to our respective homes, explaining to our mothers what had occurred."

"Did you get into trouble?" he asked.

"Oh yes. More chores. I couldn't leave the house for what seemed like forever, though I think it was really only for about a week. Mother never did tell my father. At least, I don't think she did. He never said anything about it."

"And you were probably no older than Lorenzo is now."

"Oh, much younger. Thirteen," Zanetta was chagrinned to admit.

"So, we each have our stories. And we survived."

Zanetta looked back across the room to the settee with Lorenzo now passed out upon it.

"I do worry about him, though. Things have not been easy for him. Not lately, anyway."

"Hmmn. Well, now that you mention it, I haven't seen him about of late. That is, we managed to run into him quite often over the past few months. He even came to our home for a Sunday dinner, as you know."

Zanetta looked away, not wanting to meet Foscarini's eyes at this observation.

"Ahhh. I see," he said at last. "Costanza."

"You know then, of Lorenzo's feelings towards her?"

"Hah! I would have to be a blind man not to know. The entire neighborhood knows, what with the two of them mooning at each other whenever he passes by her window. Why do you think I invited him to that Sunday dinner? Not to see some dusty old book, certainly. It was at Costanza's urging."

"You mean she," Zanetta cut herself off. "If I may be so bold, Lorenzo seemed to think her affections were directed at another."

Foscarini appeared to consider this for a moment. "You mean Carlo? My cousin's son?"

"I don't know his name. Lorenzo just said there was another."

"Carlo. He's, well, he is family, but Carlo and Costanza? No, there is no interest, or rivalry there. Frankly it was all we could stand to have him visit for a month. I think my cousin was hoping I would put him to work in one of my warehouses, but that will never happen. You don't maintain a successful business by hiring arrogant fools, family or not. I apologize if I'm being too candid."

"Not at all," Zanetta replied, surprised and relieved at the information.

"Is that the problem facing Lorenzo? Is that why he has not come around?" Foscarini trailed off, looking over at the young man.

"That's part of it," she said. "And then of course, there is Giacomo. Lorenzo idolizes him. He is taking it hard."

Foscarini sat rubbing his chin, staring again into the fire. Zanetta wondered what this strange caring man was thinking. Here was a man she had known as a casual neighbor for years, one greeted in passing or at Mass on Sundays or on holidays and at fairs, but now he seemed so much more. He saved Giacomo's life and carried her son home in the pitch of night, protecting him. But there was more to him than just that. He understood. He seemed to know the right things to say, even if his words did surprise her and move her in unexpected ways. It was a quality Giacomo possessed, only now, to her, so much more unsettling.

When at last he spoke again, it was while looking directly into her eyes, and she could not look away.

"Zanetta," he began. "I never had a son, but I know a good son when I see one. Lorenzo is a good son. *Bella figura.* He is smart. I know he gets this from his mother and his great uncle. You have prepared him well, and he will be a success. Of this I have no doubt. But most importantly, he has a good heart."

"He takes after his grandmother," she said, almost involuntarily.

"He takes after Giacomo," Foscarini returned simply.

"Ah, yes, Giacomo, well…"

"Well nothing. That old man laying upstairs has the greatest heart I have ever known," he said firmly. "And Lorenzo shares that heart, as do you.

"I told you before, I owe much to your uncle. He made possible the greatest joys of my life." Foscarini hesitated before continuing. When he did, he spoke while staring back into the fire. "My wife, Costanza's mother died in childbirth. I never had the chance to witness what a wonderful mother I believe she would have been, but when I see the fineness of your son and the way you have raised him, I think I know." Foscarini looked up to meet Zanetta's eyes.

Zanetta could feel the heat rising to her cheeks and her breath catching in her chest.

Foscarini continued.

"I have done my best in raising Costanza. I love her with all my heart and have devoted my life to her happiness and well-being."

He broke off as if speaking had become difficult for him.

"I guess what I am saying is," he continued, "if I were to ever have a son, I would hope and pray he would be like Lorenzo."

He stopped, as if embarrassed by his own admission.

"Signore, Sebastian, that is the kindest thing anyone has ever said to me. Thank you."

Zanetta was unsuccessfully fighting the emotions from overcoming her. She did her best to compose herself.

"Then Costanza and he?" She left the sentence unfinished.

"Ah, that I cannot say," he said, waving his hand. "I think it would be wrong to try and engineer. Love is a thing those involved should work out on their own, I think. It may not hurt to ease the process, however, as your uncle once did for me. Learning the true status of a cousin's son, for instance, could help, but ultimately, they must find their own way. We cannot deny our children that."

Zanetta marveled at the man before her. He sounded so much like Giacomo. Emotions were colliding inside her and she struggled to sort them and to contain them.

"Thank you, Sebastian." She now wanted the closeness of calling him by his given name, just as she felt when he used hers.

Sebastian seemed to struggle with something, then fixed his gaze again upon her.

"Just as we must find ours," he said.

Zanetta was confused by his words, until it dawned on her to whom he was referring.

"Our way?" she asked, the heat burning her cheeks once more.

Sebastian rose to his feet.

"Zanetta. I realize the burdens upon you at this time are great. If there is anything, anything I can do for you as you care for your uncle and your son, please, it would be my greatest honor to help you, to be with you when you need me. I would like, that is," he seemed to consider his words.

"Costanza and I prefer to walk home after Sunday Mass by way of the Rialto. Perhaps, if you are of a mind, you would join us?" he said.

Zanetta was elated to see the color rise in his cheeks as he spoke. She felt happy and excited for the first time in a very long time. She couldn't help but smile.

"At Costanza's urging?" she teased gently.

Sebastian reached down and captured Zanetta's hand.

"No," he said, "not hers."

He pressed her hand to his lips, then quickly turned and exited the room as if afraid he had gone too far.

Zanetta stood and took a few steps towards the door. So much was happening so fast, but she felt ready for it. She thought of all Giacomo had been telling her these last few months, and for years actually, and now she finally understood. She had been where Lorenzo is now, and beyond. She had loved, lost, suffered and endured. She experienced the wonder of this world and she had been to the skies of fulfillment and to the underworld of despair. She was ready for the return. She was the master of two worlds, and now she could choose, just as Giacomo told her she would.

Zanetta crossed the room to where her son lay. She looked down on him with a tinge of frustration, but more so with new understanding and hope that he too would find his way. She lifted a folded blanket from the back of the settee and draped it over Lorenzo, tucking him in as she did when he was still a child.

Blowing out the candles as she passed through the room, she gathered up the last flickering tallow before casting one last look back at her son. Giacomo was right. She had shut herself off from the world for too long. Now she wanted to see it more as she did just a few days past, and maybe, she thought, maybe she would begin her new journey with a stroll across the Rialto.

Daylight over Venice shortened. Grayness canvassed what little sky Giacomo Casanova could see, though, in truth, he had little desire to gaze out his window. It was more than his recent fall. It was, he thought, the disappointment that he would not be able to repair the damage he somehow inadvertently caused. He no longer worried for Zanetta. She would be fine and, if he was reading these things correctly, she was falling in love once again. Love in second bloom, he mused. It was more than he could have hoped for his niece, so much like his beloved sister. He had a mission to fulfill, and he was successful. When one guide passes it is necessary that another take his place. Zanetta would be that guide. It was her nature. It was her destiny.

No, it was not Zanetta's fate that troubled him so, it was Lorenzo. Their last words were of confusion and inadequacy on his part, and misunderstanding and anger on Lorenzo's. He had long since come to terms with the fact that he would not be around to advise his grandnephew and guide him through the shoals of life, but it tore at him to think that their parting would be as it was. Time was slipping through his fingers like the wet sands of a receding tide.

The days became a season of tormenting pain interspersed by fits of sleep that left him more disoriented and unrested than before. Food lost its appeal and he could feel what little strength he had left ebbing from his body. Daily he grew weaker and he knew that his time was near. What journeys were yet to come remained unknown, but the fear of that unknown paled in comparison to the anguish he felt at the way things were left with Lorenzo. The young man's words had been harsh, the condemnation complete.

Time and again Giacomo sent word through his niece asking Lorenzo to return, but the young man would not come. His mother fretted for him. She told Giacomo her son would not leave the house except at night, though Giacomo never saw him by day. She feared the danger her son might be courting in the denizens of the dark. She feared he had fallen in with a bad crowd.

"What about Costanza?" he asked, only to be informed that Lorenzo all but abandoned the burgeoning romance with the lovely and sweet neighbor girl. Even Sebastian Foscarini was perplexed by Lorenzo's sudden change. Giacomo noted, with great pleasure, that Zanetta now frequently spoke of the good Foscarini in familiar terms, but this did little to relieve his concerns for Lorenzo.

When pressed as to why he refused to see his uncle by his mother, Lorenzo angrily avoided explanation, but did say that he would not fall victim to his uncle's lies ever again. When his niece asked Giacomo what that could mean, Giacomo mumbled an incoherent response about a misunderstanding, but his heart sank. He had thought long and hard about the confrontation and he now knew what led to his grandnephew's anger and now jaded views. If only he could explain, it was not a lie.

Giacomo tried to reassure his niece, telling her it was natural that a young man of Lorenzo's years explore the world, but he too was concerned for his grandnephew. It was easy to fall prey to the careless avoidance of life and its rewards. Too easy to replace love with carnality, effort with gamble, and morality with expectation of desire fulfilled. Giacomo knew this to be true, for he had traveled each of these roads, only to realize there was no easy path to genuine happiness. It took effort, commitment, and giving more than one takes. It required one to see in another not the fulfillment of want, but the recognition of self. It required love.

Lorenzo would need to learn this lesson as well, if ever he was to experience life beyond the terrestrial bonds of passivity. The disillusioned ran in packs with the ignorant and the selfish, each supporting the other in their mutual descent and each denying themselves the experience of being alive. Lorenzo must choose, Giacomo knew, between the ease of unfulfillment and the effort of gaining one's heart.

Giacomo spent long hours examining what brought his grandnephew to this crossroad. He was accustomed to the uninformed stranger and salacious reader seeing in his life only the torrid adventures of a rogue, but that was not necessarily the truth of the matter.

He looked ruefully at the wooden crucifix on the wall opposite his bed.

"Perhaps, Signore, my niece is correct. Perhaps I will go to Hell, but not for the life I led, or rather for the life they read, but for not revealing the whole truth of what I learned in this life's journey. Have I failed as guide? If there is a place reserved in the tormenting dungeons of eternity for withholding the true way of happiness while those around me floundered, then perhaps that is indeed where I shall be consigned."

Giacomo waited for a comforting response from the static figure, knowing one would not be forthcoming. There would be no easy absolution from the crucifix he had come to identify as his confidant and court. He continued with his defense before the suffering judge.

"What is Hell after all, Signore, but the absence of the beloved, and how can I deserve her presence if I deny others the knowledge of finding their own path? If God is love, then love is God. Is this not so?

"It is true, Signore, I have been too selfish with this precious truth. I sought to hold it in my heart for fear of losing it. I concealed it behind adventures of romance, lust, and conquests, never daring to lessen my grip on the eternity I hold most dear, the knowledge that we are all on the same path, if we would but open our hearts. I have tried to fill the role given me, to see and to guide, but I have been selfish with my most treasured knowledge.

"Zanetta was to be my replacement, and my salvation, and Lorenzo was to be my blessing. I tried to tell him, Signore, to prepare him for his own path. He came to me for yarns of a life not lived, and there they sit, bound in twelve volumes, a catalog of lies, so he believes. But what I gave him, Signore, what I tried to give him, was the truth. He did not understand."

Giacomo stretched his hand to the side table and touched the large, well-worn book, *Masterworks of the Great Artists*, still there from his grandnephew's last angry visit. He would not let it be taken away.

How curious, he thought, that Lorenzo mistook his remembrances for descriptions of art. Many times since Lorenzo's confrontation he leafed through the pages trying to imagine what his grandnephew heard that would lead him to those conclusions. Did he speak in the language of art when trying to share the truths of his love? Or is it that artists, like poets, philosophers, and saints all speak the same language when describing the greatest of truths, that I and the other are one.

"Lorenzo," Giacomo cried towards the sacrificing god suspended at his wall, "don't you see? I wasn't spinning tales of bedded victories from some imagined memoirs, nor was I describing paintings and sculptures as you seem to think. Does my aging mind play tricks on me, on my memory? Did I employ imagery of love portrayed to explain my heart? Perhaps, but I would never intentionally be so cruel to the grandnephew I have come to love more than my own eternal destiny. I sought to share with you the truth of my life, not as others read it, but as I know it. I am neither artist nor poet. I am not a philosopher and certainly not a saint, but I have tasted the greatest of truths. Don't you see?"

Tears streamed down the old man's face.

"It was not many women of whom I spoke, but many facets of one woman ... my beloved, my wife, my Katerina."

Preceding Women

Venus of Willendorf
c. 28,000-25,000 BCE
limestone

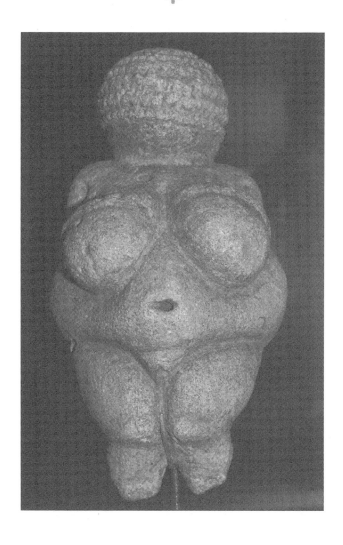

I stand sluttish before her.

She casts a daemonic eye upon me. She draws me down into dank caverns, Mother Nature's open thighs, the bloody depths where truth lies uncorrupted by Apollonian dreams.

I wish to impress her, this primeval great mother. I will present my merits and she will see that I am worthy of her.

I wear clothes of the finest cut, as fitting one of my station. Surely this will convey to her my success. I preen and dash, but she takes no note. Such outer show does not improve her estimation of me. She will not be easily swayed.

I surround myself with riches, gold and the finest jewels. I think that these will turn her head so that she will know I can a provider be, but she does not need these petty things. Baubles of the earth. She ignores their shine and glint and I see their value wash away. These are not the things of human worth.

She will not be moved by my possessions and wealth. She has all that she needs. I understand. It is not what I have, but what I am that counts. My way is clear.

"I have been a warrior," I boast. "Men have trembled in battle against me."

She smiles benignly. It is not the response I had hoped for. When she speaks it is as if her words are heard by the earth itself.

"Men rise, men fall," she says. "In the end they all return to me."

Her calm exceeds time, and yet I can feel the uncontrollable nearness of nature within her. It beckons me. I am small. I wish her to think me grand. To be thought great in battle is nothing to one who is more powerful than these. Soldiers destroy. I will show that I create.

"I have been a builder," I exclaim. "Edifices stand to bear testimony to my genius. They tower above the earth, my designs, and my mastery. They defy the long slow suck of murky ooze in which my forbears lived."

I am puffed with pride.

She closes her eyes and nods her head in slight acknowledgement of my accomplishments.

"Impressive," she admits, and I feel my chest swell with the awesomeness of my achievements.

She glances away, past the trees, to the towering mountain, a nonchalant aim. She gestures to the summit.

"My home," she says simply.

I look, up and up to snowcapped peaks. Massive jagged cliffs thunder with passing winds. Trees, vines, plants, herbs, flowers, and grass crawl over its surface, their roots deep in life infusing fornication. Down it flows, expanding as it nears the flatted plain. Caverns yawn, frightening in their mystery. Within lay treasures unknown, stalactites seeking to kiss the earth, subterranean waters falling and falling to be heated and returned from near a molten core, ores, gems, and remains of lives long past awaiting my discovery.

The works of my hands are puny and transient in comparison. They will fall as men in battle fell. I am a child. Only my pride compels me on. Only if my works can last will she be moved to see the greater me.

"My creations are more than stones and bricks can build. I have crafted words, ideas, poems. Surely nothing can match their eloquence?"

"And of what do you write?" she asks.

My heart hesitates a beat in my realization. I cannot hide the truth from her. Never her. I confess.

"Of you."

"Yes."

I have come all this way to find her. I am not ready to surrender my grandeur. There is one final effort to be made.

"I have served God." My apparent humility in service of a greater power is sure to impress.

"Which God?"

The question confuses me. It is other than I have been taught.

"The God that hovers above all."

She extends her hands, an embracing gesture.

"I existed before the sky-cult came, before daemon became demon, before you left my side."

"I never left your side," I protest.

"Before you were Adam you were also Eve. It was your sky-god that abominated us with a penis womb, a phallic rib come vagina, a severed birth. It is illusion. It is denial. It wishes you to believe you are less than you are."

Her chthonian creed is undeniable, unarguable, and irrefutable. I am but an initiate to her stonetime truths.

"See," she commands with outstretched finger pointing to the ground.

I follow her direction and there, on the scorched earth are two snakes, entwined in copulation.

"See the knowledge that has been denied you and is now revealed. You are as Tiresias."

I fall into a dream and in my dream I have become the holy man of Mount Cithaeron who saw two serpents mating, as I have, and became androgyne for his trespass upon the primordial scene. Changed and seven years he lived as woman, then once again as man. It was his curse. It was his gift. It made him a seer. He knew what I now know, we are not severed, bereft. I do not seek what I do not possess. I am she. I am he.

With my eyes newly opened, I wake from my waking dream.

"I understand," is all there is left to say. It is not wealth or wars or creations wrought that make me who I am, who we are.

Sophia. I study her voluptuous beauty, a bounty-hipped Willendorf, fecund as the elements. We unite as we were before my arrogance divided me away, a caduceus entwined. Wrapped in her legs, chest to breast, I give myself to her pagan force. She receives from me my seed and I am inseparable from her, from all around me.

She will birth a child, a tribe, a civilization. They will wander. Like me they will create their own arrogance. But they will return. In the end, they all return to her.

Women Who Stand

George Rivera
Atonement
2004
oil on canvas

I hold to her, veins heightened, tendons strained with flexing muscles and sinews. I am determined not to let her slip away, yet she abides untouched. She is not bound or captive to my will. She is strong, calm, and confidant gazing up and out, beyond my ken, beyond any horizon. She remains in my embrace of her own volition.

From the north Kristin came, with flaxen hair and ice warm eyes that see distant images I can only imagine. I seek to hold her as if she was some treasure that might slip through my arms, as indeed she is. She is ageless and eternal, the alpha and omega.

"You were unexpected," I say.

"Not unwelcome, I hope," she says.

"Anything but."

"We've known each other forever, or nearly so."

Her eye sparkles with a knowing light.

"I wasn't ready for you. I had too many mistakes I needed to make first."

"We both did." she says.

"It was never the right time," I say. "There always seemed to be someone else in the equation, your equation or mine."

"The timing was a bit off for us over the years. But at least we were friends," she offers gaily.

"Friends," I laugh. "Yes, we were friends at least."

She eyes me quizzically.

"Weren't we?"

"Well, yes, if by friends you mean years of torment from wanting to be with you but always finding one of us in another relationship."

"I see what you mean. So why did it take you so long to ask me?"

"Other than the others to whom we were committed for times?"

She nods.

"I was afraid you would say no."

Now it is her turn to laugh.

"I was waiting for you to ask!"

"You should have said something."

"I did, about a hundred times. I thought you weren't interested."

"I guess I was too good at pretending to be your friend."

We enjoy the moment of revelation, but there is a seriousness to my confession.

"It's true," I continue, "we were, are friends, and the fact of the matter is I didn't want to damage that by…"

"Starting a relationship with me?"

"Something like that. I haven't had the best of luck in that area."

The haunting remains of the past seem to cloud above me, relics and remnants, remembrances of former and failed relationships, skeletal reminders of loves past. I feel the drip of their terminal blood as it lingers at the ends of my pain and guilt. No failed relationship is without its price. It is payment for my past follies, blood payment.

"I am not the others," she says. And you are certainly not the mistakes of my past either. We all have our histories."

"Who was it that said 'History is a nightmare from which I am trying to wake?'"

"Whoever it was, wake and rejoice."

I bear the markings of sacrifice and Kristin is the tree upon which I will find redemption. She is an otherworldly bride.

My hands nurture rivulets of lifeless life, a crimson flow across my wrists, the stigmata of a former existence. Its ribbon arrests me, but it is nothing compared to the power and flow of blood unseen, evident in my pulsing veins. Purpleblue shadows map my flesh in topographical testament of a new force burning within me. It courses with each beat of my heart and I surrender to its steady pulse.

Like my Golgotha forebear, I atone.

"I am glad you asked," she says.

We endure against an unknown plane. It is everywhere and nowhere, the ompholos, the world navel. She centers me. My world has become a great wheel and she is its hub. She centers me in a timeless paradise. Eternity is not a time. Heaven is not a place. Her realm is spread upon the earth and men do not see. But now I see

I am bound to her, an unpierced piercing, suspended on her Valkyrie branch. She is Yggdrasil, the world ash, and I am one-eyed Othin, wounded, speared, impaled on the windy tree for nights full nine. I am a sacrifice to Othin, myself to myself. It is an act of self-annihilation in quest of the greater wisdom that our apotheosis will achieve.

Or is she the Bodhi tree and I the Eastern prince seeking illumination? Away from the comforting confines of the palace keep I have wandered to see the realities and vagaries of life, to end up here beneath the Maya branch.

She is the sublimity of recognition, the truth I seek. She is the found awareness that we are not separate, we are connected, the yin and the yang, on the path to one's true nature and true potential. She is the sacred marriage. I and the bride are one. I am at one. I atone.

"I have never felt so raw," I say.

"And this is good?" she asks.

"I am not used to being seen."

"But you are so well known. You are seen all the time."

I mask. I am concealed. I cannot render the complexities of my mind, but she marks it all. Wearing outward calm and civility, I project an overt expression that does not reach the soul beneath. The pleaser and the pleasured, a mask acquired over time, each past and broken relationship making it more permanent. Nothing holds it there save my own vanity, and shame. It abides on its own volition. It is part of me.

"No, not like this. Not like you see me."

The mask cracks. Fissures appear and it cracks. It is due to her, the becalmed female that what once was steadfast, now crumbles and fails. She will expose me and the true visage beneath. Am I ready for it? For her? This is the impact of the two becoming one. I bear the scars of a life left behind, but they are lessening as the newness of the new bond grows in strength. As our union grows so will the mask fall away, and my singular identity be made known. I will have achieved at-one-ment.

    I atone.

Women Who Dream

Frederic Leighton
Flaming June
1895
oil on canvas

Is she dreaming my dream? Do thoughts of our hands touching, lips meeting, and tender embracing fire her sleep as it does mine? I try to read in her slumbering face the signs of her mind.

I wasn't looking to find her. At least this is what I tell myself. I wasn't seeking more than a friend to share a dinner, a walk, maybe more, but what I found was friend and more. And then, suddenly, there she was, as if waiting for me all the while. We laugh and share, each marveling at the divergent path that lead us to this place. There is comfort as if we have known each other forever, and excitement as if we have yet to touch the fires we both feel. And now she sleeps.

She drifts in languid repose.

I find her at the marbled balustrade from which she likes to watch the setting sun across a becalmed silverblue sea. It is her favorite perch, and mine, so long as she is there, beside me. A thousand times I gazed across the mirrored waters, imagining lands beyond, but never imagining her. The air is perfumed by white oleander and trade wind spices and the subtle intoxicating fragrance I find nowhere else but in the soft curve of her neck and between her flesh warm breasts.

She has fallen asleep at her pleated nest like a torsioned heroine, like Michelangelo's *Day* giving way to weary *Night* atop a Medici bed. I marvel at the evocative power of her sensuous limbs, a hedonic somnolence.

Arrayed like Parthenon deities in recline, she is bathed in apricot splendor, her diaphanous gown like a flickering blaze that consumes me in erotic longing. Her very name, June, evokes the summer warmth of this Mediterranean clime and summer dreams.

As if I were drifting on the lighted sea I return to a time of my own dreams, the quixotic journeys that have led me here to this flaming June.

As a child I dreamed dreams of adventure and daring and lands far away. I was a pirate braving the vastness blue, plundering my way to unknown treasures. I was Aladdin coursing above the Orient on a magic carpet or El Cid battling at the gates of Valencia. I was invincible with the invincibility of childhood dreams. But sooner or later all childhood dreams come to an end. The hero fades and adventures change.

With maturing youth came new dreams, disturbing dreams. As young men do, I learned there was more to life than novel plots and battles fought. I dreamed of girls and little understood their effect on me, girls walking the promenade, turning shyly away from my curious gaze, their downturned eyes new treasures yet to be discovered. I would see them in the market or from far away, adolescent girls massed in packs, pointing and pirouetting, and new visions were born. There were dreams that aroused me in the depths of night, pleasured and embarrassed, and that kept me up, eager to dream some more.

Then came the dreams of new grown man, callow yet confident without the right to be so. I dreamed of she who would make me whole. It was an unfair dream. I gave her my heart, but in my driven state I did not realize the individuality of hers. And once I found her my dream dreamed me until I became lost in the confusing mist. I thought in my jealous pride that she was the one who would complete me, and when she did not, we both were lost.

Such expectations could never be filled. To expect that she would complete me was to think her an extension of me. My plans, my ways, my dreams, but what of her dreams? Did she act the way I wanted her to act? Speak as I would have her speak? Was she there when I wanted, or away when I demanded solitude? These were the concerns of one who does not understand the nature of sharing love.

And then she left to seek herself, and my dreams turned to dreams of despair. What would I do without her, this one who was never her own in my eyes? There were no more unfair dreams of a lost half that never existed. There was no longer a girl who once strolled through an open market confusing an awakening boy. There were no more heroes to take me on adventures beyond the sky. So I left off dreaming and dreamed no more.

Was her heart as broken as mine, I wondered, hoping it was so. Unfair dreams. I did not stop to think that her pain preceded mine. Expectations can be a severing blade, one I wielded with the skill of a selfish man.

Seasons passed, and I walked among men without them knowing I was devoid of that which visited them nightly. But it was a purposeful walk, a walk of discovery, a walk of determination. In my dreamless state I found myself repaired, but alone.

Then came life's summer with its warming rays and perfumes of oleander blossoms and trade wind spices and fragrances I never smelled before. Then came June.

I did not expect her. How can one expect a dream never dreamed before? She is a new dream, a waking dream, a summer dream.

Gone is the need of childhood escape, gone is the confusion of youth and gone are the unfair dreams which cannot be fulfilled. They have been replaced by a dream of sharing, a touch, a kiss, an embrace, a dream that asks nothing but to let me be a part of it, to give myself to it, to her.

I watch silently as she sleeps in gentle hues of sheer orange glow. I cannot guess the fires that flame in her. Is she dreaming my dream?

June stirs and whispers my name. She sets my heart aflame. She dreams of me.

Women of Self

Cuong Nguyen
Ophelia
2013
pastel on sanded paper

There is a willow grows aslant the brook, and nearby in the winding wake fair Ophelia lies, mad dreams lost in currents of time.

"Where is your father?" I ask, knowing his dark hand has twisted her serviceable heart.

"My father? Why, he's ... he's at home," she dissembles.

A mousetrap set and sprung.

"Indeed. I expected otherwise." And otherwise I know.

"I don't understand," Ophelia smiles, and in her smile I see the seeds of regret. A trust now lost.

I am not her father's choice for his daughter's love. What he sees in me does not comport with his plans for his daughter. Fulfillment of such expectations are beyond a princely task. And now we are caught, she and I, in dramas not of our devising. Though I have travelled the world, our own little hamlet has now become the center of all.

"He sent you here, did he not? With a message to deliver? A heart to wound?"

There is is, all laid bare. The father would convert daughter to accomplice in his efforts to dissuade. Does she understand?

"Giacomo," she continues. "I am afraid."

There's the rub!

"Of what are you afraid?" I ask.

"My father, and my brother. They do not approve."

"Of us? Of me?"

Ophelia casts down her eyes.

"Yes," she replies, her voice a brittle breeze barely heard across the distance that now divides.

Our love was once sure, as love in youthful promise always seems to be. Is it a father's plot that will drown our love in order to meet his expectations? Ophelia has become a mere extension of the father's pride. She is not of herself. I ponder in my ruminating soliloquy.

Fathers and daughters. Fathers and sons. Where does the parent end and the child begin? Is Ophelia to be a single discordant note in her father's composition, or will she find her solo song to sing her own life? In the latter way is hopeful love; in the former madness lies.

And what of me? Am I so different? Am I not but a hand of my gone father's ghostly return? Does his vengeful voice so different than that that of Ophelia's family?

My own father's fears invade me. They rumble through Elsinore's misty night, like a spirit shone and I am bound by his sorrowful tale. It is an old story.

It is a tale of an uncle's betrayal and a wife's deceit. Was this love gone awry, or merely lust taking command of weaker hearts? It is a story oft told, but it need not be our story, Ophelia's and mine. Am I to be some melancholy prince, in servitude to histories past? *Avenge,* my father cries, but should I do as he commands I will lose my soul. History repeats, and hearts are stilled in the repetition.

Is this who I must be? I am caught in the pride that comes with pain, and I am not ready to let it go. I place on Ophelia the unjust holds on my own humanity.

Deceived. I have been deceived, and in duty to my ghost father's commands, I lash against she who is herself under a father's venomous spell.

"Why would you lie to me?" I demand. "How could you lie to me?"

"I didn't lie," she cries. "I didn't..."

"Your father aims to prevent what we seek to have. He manipulates and unwittingly you follow his lead."

Ophelia finds her voice.

"And you, sweet prince, are you not a pawn in your own father's sordid tale? You chastise me for obeying my father when you plot and plan and play a ghost's revenge?"

She has seen through my hypocrisy.

My words are now swords, unfair in parry and thrust.

"Lies! Is what we had nothing but lies?" I seek to inflict a vital wound for the pain I feel.

"That is unfair, Giacomo. I never meant to lie to you. My father… I did not understand his ire and goal."

I know what she says is true, but generations of pain and fear and drama and doubt plague me.

"You lied to me," I repeat, as a schoolboy reciting by rote my only defense.

Ophelia rests her hand on mine, and my wrathful pride is consumed in her tender touch.

"Yes," she replies, "but the lie was not mine. We are victims, you and I, both of a parent's design."

"Then this is it?" I ask. "Are we destined to play roles of others' designs?"

A silence passes and breaks between us.

"Would you have me a cloistered nun?" She asks. "Would you have me turn mad in my despair? Without you, madness lies."

Madness and despair. These are things I now understand.

The thought of life without her is a poison chalice.

"I have hurt you," she says. "I sought only to love. Oh, what a noble mind is here overthrown."

Ophelia is my Elsinore dream and I cannot let her flee. It would be my undoing. It would be my crime.

Ophelia waits for our next act, like actors strutting upon a globe.

I see her now, as if fallen, petals pressed against her breasts, each rising breath challenging their delicate hold on tightly clasped stems. Ice blue eyes upwards gaze, lost between duty to home and the perils of love unknown. Auburn hair splays her crown, like a ministering angel, while I liest howling at my importune crimes of demanding fealties.

Will Ophelia forgive me? My once noble heart is cracked, and no flights of angels arrive to sing me to my rest. Is this then to be my lonely freedom, to be shy of want or need of love? It cannot be so. Ophelia is my salvation and I must atone. Without her life is a wasteland, an undiscovered country from which I may never return.

I lift a single delicate petal of yellow hue from her ivory flesh and press it to my beating heart.

"Ophelia," I begin, "I will not my father be. His life was his and his sins his own. His loss of marriage bond is not cause to deny ours. As for you and yours, can you ever find a life with me, away from a father's disapproving stare? Can you deny his ire and be with me, as I must find my own self away from those who would fit me to their mold?"

She closes her eyes and time stands as still as chilled air in hollow halls of a castle keep. When at length she opens her eyes, she looks at me. History repeats, but we can make history of our own.

"I love you, Giacomo," she says, and vengeance dispels like a virulent wisp of an apparition from the past. My heart begins to heal, and two fathers' plans are no longer ours.

There is a willow grows aslant the brook, and nearby in the winding wake fair Ophelia lies, mad dreams lost in currents of time.

She has chosen me.

We are to be.

Tender Women

Rembrandt van Rijn
The Jewish Bride
1667
oil on canvas

It is the tenderest of loves. It is love in second bloom.

Rebekah nestles close as I wrap her in my embrace, my arm around her shoulder, holding her to me as though I might lose her if I ever let her go. But she is no possession, this bride of second life. I do not hold to possess for I have long since learned that this is the fastest way to lose the one you love. I hold to touch, to feel the oneness we have found and forged, to draw from this woman who gives so much. All that came before is but a shadow of now.

Having once loved and once lost and believing love was an illusion relegated to some distant past, I had given up hope of ever finding it again. Shock gives way to pain, pain gives way to acceptance, and acceptance to the loss of dreams. It is a poor man without a dream. How was I to know then what I know now, that I was not so poor after all? I dared to dream once more. I dared to believe once more. And then came Rebekah and love was reborn, as if I needed to go through all that had gone before in order to prepare myself for the fullness that was to come.

"It took me a long time to find you," I say.

She smiles, dimples creasing her flush cheeks.

"What took you so long?" she asks.

"I wasn't ready, was not yet deserving of you," I reply, "but I was searching all the same."

"And now that you have found me?"

I gently squeeze her shoulder.

"I don't plan on ever letting you go."

She tilts her head, resting it on my arm.

In truth, we found each other. Her path was much the same as mine and though we would each have denied it at the time, we were each seeking the other. One must be ready for the quest, whatever the age.

Set against a chiaroscuro Amsterdam night, the renderings of Caravaggisti past read as a single journey to this moment in time. The voices of saints and kings are made personal in the lighted figures of me and my bride, a couple celebrating the wonder of finding one another at a maturing point in life.

"You foolish man," she says. "You wonderful, foolish man. You gaze at me like a moonstruck boy. It has been a long time since anyone looked at me that way."

"I don't believe that."

"Hah," she laughs, "it's true. Oh, there was a time, I suppose, when a head or two turned my way, when such things really mattered to me. It seems silly now, the whims of a young girl, and yet here you are."

"Here I am, head turned."

She slaps at my chest playfully, a gesture more loving than scolding.

Neither of us is in the first blush of youth, but Rebekah's beauty surpasses time. I still see in her face the bloom of earlier days, only now it is layered with tiny lines at the corners of her eyes and the fleshy contours of her jaw. Each minute wrinkle is evidence of experiences and events, lessons and loves, and each mapping crease adds beauty as can only come from life lived. Hers is a beauty more profound than youthful charm. She smiles again, and the tiny lines deepen at her eyes and mouth. Her beauty celebrates life.

My hand is at her breast. A gentle touch. I feel and hear the subtle intake and exhale of each breath. It is the sound I listen to in the stillness of night, its rhythmic warmth calming me, drifting me, lulling me. It is both comforting and reassuring. Her breath echoes my own as we fall into a silent harmony, each sensing the other. It is the sound of life found.

"You are the most beautiful woman I have ever known," I say.

Rebekah shoots me a doubtful look.

"I am not so young anymore," she says.

I see her in her finery, a gown of luscious cadmium red, opulent lace, pearls at her neck and circling her wrists. On another these might be distractions. On Rebekah they are lovely, but far from necessary.

These are but decorations afforded by the labors that have brought us to this moment, but they are not her. Even without such elegance she would still be just as lovely. She is radiant.

Rebekah too, I believe, sees beyond an expensive suit of gold and silk. I never thought to be seen with loving eyes again. Life tires and wears. Where once I hoped to catch the eye of some young beauty, I had long since comforted myself with the realities of passing time. The knees are not as forgiving as once they were, the walk not so steady. There was a day when run and walk were each brushed aside as just another means of getting from here to there and I never thought to measure my pace, but now all things are measured, all things come in their proper stride. Where once I heard the tiniest notes of a bird's song, I now must listen and strain to capture the music it sings, and in the effort, I hear more than before.

Rebekah sees my thinning hair, more gray showing with each passing day, and a careworn face full of tired lines, and still she looks at me as at a virile lover. She sees me for who and what I am, not for the unguaranteed potential of what youth might become. Now we both know that lasting love is not a race towards an end called pleasure, as we did in our youth, but that the greatest pleasure is enhanced by the knowing of souls, the experience of age, the sharing of the tenderest of loves, the love of my tender bride.

Questioning Women

Diego Velásquez
Venus at Her Mirror
1650
oil on canvas

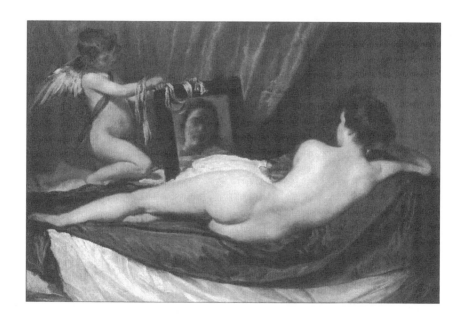

I enter to see Katerina reclining on midnight sheets, seducing me with her languored charm. She has been waiting for my return.

"Tell me Giacomo, what is it you see when you walk the streets of Rome. You disappear for hours on end and when you return you are both excited and exhausted. Should I fear a rival lover?" Katerina asks playfully. "Where do you go for such lengths?"

I collapse with amused satisfaction into a chair facing the bed to regard Katerina, lounging like a snow-white cat warming by a fire.

"No. No rival lover," I say. "You are more than enough for any man, certainly this man, who is but mortal after all. You have nothing to fear, for I am yours alone."

She raises an eyebrow as if assessing my humble assertion.

"As for where I go," I continue, "I wander."

"And where do you wander?"

"Through time," I say without irony.

"That would explain the exhaustion," she concludes with pretend gravitas.

"It's true. Rome is the city of creation. Strike a course in any direction and history unfolds before your eyes."

"Well, we do have our fair share of things to see in this city," she agrees. "So, when you wander through time, what do you seek?"

I think about her question before answering.

"I seek beauty."

"And did you find it?"

"Yes."

"Will you tell me where?" she asks.

"I will give you a clue."

"Is it a puzzle?"

"More of a reward after a long journey's quest."

"Ooh, I like rewards," she says.

"Shall I give you the clue?"

"I will guess the answer as soon as you give it!"

"Very well. Here it is. Beauty greater than any other art is not of the eye, but of the heart."

"That's it? That's your clue?"

"There you have it," I say.

"That isn't a clue. It's a line from a bloody poem or some sugared song."

"Do you give up?"

"Not so fast," she cautions. "Let me think about this a bit. Let's see, the beauty you found is greater than any other art. That must mean it is the *greatest* work of art in all of Rome. Let me guess, you have been to the ceiling, Michelangelo's ceiling? You would not be the first visitor to Rome who found the Sistine to be the city's crowning jewel."

"Justly so," I agree. "It is the genius of Rome's greatest master. I stood directly below the *Delphic Sibyl* and felt as if I could hear the rushing of leaves, as if the prophetess could peer into me."

"I know the one. She is majestic, and beautiful."

"Yes," I say, "but she is not the perfect beauty I found."

"Hah! You reveal more, Giacomo. Not only the greatest beauty, but the perfect beauty. The challenge grows."

Katerina is warming to the game.

"Then certainly," she continues, "you must have visited the Cornaro Chapel in the Santa Maria della Vittoria. Bernini's *Saint Teresa* is a theatre of ecstasy, a Baroque saint of sensuosity. Perfection itself."

"True. I have visited her as well. I stood before her for hours, learning much about love. I felt as though I could pierce her heart with my longing."

"And she swoons in such ecstasy!" Katerina says. "I heard it told that when Bernini first unveiled his masterwork, the French Ambassador, who would know such things, being French, took one look at Teresa's climactic expression and said that if that is spiritual ecstasy, then he experiences it nightly. Hah! Sounds like you! She must be your perfect beauty."

"She is exquisite, but she is not the beauty to whom I refer."

Katerina licks her lips seductively and extends across the satin black of the sheets.

"Ah, who could be more beautiful than Venus, the goddess of love? And of all the Venuses none is lovelier than Botticelli's. She resides in a Medici palazzo. She is perfection on a scalloped shell," Katerina says.

"So she is. I was seduced by her as she set ashore. I shall remember her in a moment of forever, yet it is another beauty, a perfect beauty, greater than any other art, not of the eye, but of the heart that captures me."

"Giacomo, you are not making it easy for me. There are hundreds, no, thousands of beautiful works in Rome and your wanderings are so extensive. You must have seen them all!"

"Many, but not all," I counter.

"What then?" she pleads. "I've got it. I have heard it said that Fra Filippo Lippi's Madonna is one of the most beautiful women who ever lived. She was a real woman, you know? Lucretia Buti was her name. She was a nun, but that didn't stop her and Filippo from living as man and wife. They even had a child, Filippino. He was an artist too."

I shake my head.

"Oh, Giacomo, tell me!"

I leave my chair and circle the bed to face her, a cherubim reflecting back so she can see the obvious.

"Do you give up?" I ask.

"Fine!" she pouts prettily.

"In Madrid," I begin to explain, "I was a painter of the royal court. Honors were heaped upon me. I was made Court Chamberlain and was even named to the Order of Santiago."

"Yes, I have heard these things about you. Your reputation preceded your visit to the Venerable City."

I continue. "During my time in Madrid, in my heavenly Venice, and throughout all of my travels I have seen much beauty, from the innocent charm of the Infanta and *Las Meninas* to the greatest works of art by the greatest masters."

"And?" Katerina asks.

"And none come close to you, my Katerina, my opulent beauty of Rome."

Katerina gasps, and then blushes deeply at the compliment.

I continue, "You possess the beauty of all the masterpieces you named, and many more, and while you are indeed the loveliest of women, your true beauty, your perfect beauty is of the heart, which transcends all."

I slide my hand over her arching hip, across her bottom and onto her thigh. Katerina responds and I know my wanderings are over.

*G*iacomo Casanova lay dying. An oppressive cloud-shrouded night limited the view beyond the high window. Darkness permeated the room, battling against the waning light of a single candle.

The sounds of his beloved city seemed distant now, and remote, the splendors of the Venetian sun now long set. Giacomo could distinguish neither voice nor howl nor the lapping water of the canal against stone. All was but a muted hush, though he knew life in his city would go on as ever it had. Markets would bustle, babies would cry, and youths would run to spy the pretty girls. And at night, as on this night, there would be gamblers and drunks, whores and thieves. Laborers would return to their homes and ruffians would brawl, and someone would certainly die.

It isn't so bad, Giacomo thought. He said his goodbyes. Over the past days his niece was as protective and disapproving and caring as always. Together they enjoyed the tug of wills, to which she always relented. She was finding love. There would be no void.

It was she, in a final gesture, who demanded of her son that he visit his uncle one last time.

Lorenzo came earlier that day, anger and hurt defining his young, handsome face.

"Come, sit," Giacomo invited, his voice a weak rasp.

Hesitantly Lorenzo approached the bed and took the chair as instructed, keeping his head down, refusing to look his uncle in the eye.

For a long time Giacomo merely watched his grandnephew as he tried to read the conflicting emotions he must be feeling. It was not the time for the telling of tales. He had but one chance to convince Lorenzo, so he would speak of the one thing he knew was weighing on the boy's soul more than anything else.

"This girl, Costanza, do you love her?" Giacomo asked at last.

Lorenzo's head jerked up in surprise, and then slowly nodded, as if unable to conceal the truth of his feelings.

"Is she the love of your life? The one that makes you feel as if all the others combined could never fill your heart so full? The one by whom you touch the transcendent?" Giacomo asked.

Lorenzo remained silent, but his coloring face was answer enough.

Giacomo grunted in understanding. "Then we are once again more alike than not. Let me tell you a story. A true story."

Lorenzo seemed to bristle at his uncle's suggestion, but the calm insistence of Giacomo's words halted him, and he listened.

For the following hour and with clarity of mind and memory, Giacomo told him of Katerina, his wife and one true love. He told him of their years together, and the myth of his life, written in twelve volumes, which was but a trope for the truth of his love.

"I was not lying," he explained. "There was ever but one woman. I made her my wife. She illuminated my life." He then shared with Lorenzo the story of this woman with whom he found oneness. He spoke of joys and sorrows, happiness and pain, and he told him of how he would give anything if only to be allowed one more kiss, a touch of her hand, or a glance of her eye that allowed him a peek into eternity.

"Do you understand, Lorenzo, there were never many women. There was always only one, my Katerina. The others," he said, gesturing towards the twelve volumes of his biography sitting on the chest of drawers, "they are but fictions devised by one poor man at a loss for how to explain the universe in a single woman."

Lorenzo hung to his every word, his countenance softening with each new revelation.

When he was finished Giacomo again asked, "Do you love Costanza?"

"Yes, Uncle, with all my heart," Lorenzo replied.

"Then go to her. Tell her you love her. Never let a day pass without showing her, and someday, when you are old and worn like me, you too will look back and realize that your one love was every love. Together you will be one, and that is enough."

Tears streamed down Lorenzo's face as he thanked his uncle, kissing him on his cheek before dashing out of the room.

It was the best of goodbyes.

Night arrived as it inevitably does.

Somewhere outside, in his beloved city, a woman laughed, and Giacomo heard it clear as it drifted through his window on an unseasonably warm fall breeze.

Giacomo was content. He closed his eyes and whispered to the shadowed walls, "Katerina…"

Then, as gentle as a woman's laugh trilling through a window high, Venice breathed, and the candle sputtered into darkness.

Gianlorenzo Bernini
Costanza Bonarelli
1636-37
marble

For More Information

For historical information and color renditions of the art portrayed, along with artist information and explanations by the author on how they relate to the vignettes in *Casanova, Curator of Memories*, please visit
PrestonJamesMetcalf.com.

Art and Photo Credits

Works in the Public Domain

Artworks listed as being is in the public domain are designated as such because their copyrights have expired. This applies to the United States, The European Union, Japan, India, Greece, Egypt, and those countries with a copyright term of the life of the author or artist plus 100 years or less. These works are in the public domain in the United States because they were published (or registered with the U.S. Copyright Office) before January 1, 1923. Faithful reproductions of two-dimensional public domain works are also considered to be in the public domain.

Beardsley, Aubrey, *Salome with the Head of John the Baptist*, illustration from *Salome* by Oscar Wilde, 1892. Ink on paper. Aubrey Beardsley Collection, Manuscripts Division, Department of Rare Books and Special Collections, Princeton University, New Jersey. This artwork is in the public domain.

Bernini, Gianlorenzo, *Costanza Bonarelli*, 1636-37. Marble. Muzeo Nazionale, Florence, Italy. This artwork is in the public domain. This image is licensed under the Creative Commons Attribution Share Alike 3.0 Unported license. Image by sailko and retrieved from https://commons.wikimedia.org/wiki/File:Gianlorenzo_bernini,_ritratto_di_co stanza_bonarelli,_1637-38,_02.JPG. This photographic reproduction has been released into the public domain on Wikimedia Commons and may be used for any purpose without any conditions.

Bernini, Gianlorenzo, *Ecstasy of Saint Teresa*, 1645-52. Marble. Cornaro Chapel, Santa Maria della Vittoria, Rome, Italy. This artwork is in the public domain. This image is licensed under the Creative Commons Attribution-Share Alike 4.0 license. Image by AlvesGaspar and retrieved from https://commons.wikimedia.org/wiki/File:Ecstasy_of_Saint_Teresa_Septembe r_2015-2a.jpg. This photographic reproduction has been released into the public domain on Wikimedia Commons and may be used for any purpose without any conditions.

The Birth of Siddhartha, 2nd–3rd Century CE. Stone, Zen You Mitsu Temple, Tokyo, Japan. This artwork is in the public domain. This image is licensed under the Creative Commons Attribution Share Alike 3.0 Unported license. Personal photograph, 2005. Released under GDFL. This photographic reproduction has been released into the public domain on Wikimedia Commons and may be used for any purpose without any conditions.

Botticelli, Sandro, *Birth of Venus*, c. 1482. Tempera on canvas. Uffizi Gallery, Florence, Italy. This artwork is in the public domain.

Boucher, François, *Diana Resting After Her Bath*, 1742. Oil on canvas. Louvre, Paris, France. This artwork is in the public domain.

Bronzino, Agnolo, *Venus, Cupid, Folly, and Time (The Exposure of Luxury)*, 1546. Oil on wood. The National Gallery, London, England. This artwork is in the public domain.

Buonarroti, Michelangelo, *Delphic Sibyl*, from the *Sistine Ceiling*, 1508-1512. Fresco. Sistine Chapel, Vatican City, Rome, Italy. This artwork is in the public domain.

Caravaggio, *Medusa*, c. 1590. Oil on canvas mounted on wood. Uffizi Gallery, Florence, Italy. This artwork is in the public domain.

Carracci, Annibale, *Jupiter and Juno*, from *The Loves of the Gods*, 1597. Fresco. Ceiling of the Farnese Gallery, Rome, Italy. This artwork is in the public domain.

Chassériau, Théodore, *The Toilet of Esther*, 1841. Oil on canvas. Louvre, Paris, France. This artwork is in the public domain.

Correggio, Antonio Allegri da, *Jupiter and Io*, 1530. Oil on canvas. Kunsthistorisches Museum, Vienna, Austria. This artwork is in the public domain.

Degas, Edgar, *Glass of Absinthe*, 1876. Oil on canvas. Musée d'Orsay, Paris, France. This artwork is in the public domain.

Fragonard, Jean-Honoré, *The Swing*, 1766. Oil on canvas. The Wallace Collection, London, England. This artwork is in the public domain.

Fuseli, Henry, *The Nightmare*, 1781. Oil on canvas. Institute of Fine Arts, Detroit. This artwork is in the public domain.

Gentileschi, Artemisia, *Judith Slaying Holofernes*, c. 1612. Oil on canvas. Museo Nazionale di Capadimonte, Naples, Italy. This artwork is in the public domain.

Goya y Lucientes, Francisco José de, *The Clothed Maja,* 1808. Oil on canvas. Museo del Prado, Madrid, Spain. This artwork is in the public domain.

Goya y Lucientes, Francisco José de, *The Naked Maja,* 1808. Oil on canvas. Museo del Prado, Madrid, Spain. This artwork is in the public domain.

Hogarth, William, *Breakfast Scene*, from *Marriage à la Mode*, 1745. Oil on canvas. The National Gallery, London, England. This artwork is in the public domain.

Ingres, Jean Auguste Dominique, *Odalisque with a Slave*, 1842. Oil on canvas. Fogg Museum, Harvard University. This artwork is in the public domain.

Queen Uta, 1249-1255. Painted stone. Naumburg Cathedral, Germany. This artwork is in the public domain. This image is licensed under the Creative Commons Attribution Share Alike 3.0 Unported license. Image by Linsengericht and retrieved from https://commons.wikimedia.org/wiki/File:Naumburg_Ekkehard_und_ Uta.jpg. This photographic reproduction has been released into the public domain on Wikimedia Commons and may be used for any purpose without any conditions.

Rembrandt van Rijn, *The Jewish Bride*, 1667. Oil on canvas. Rijksmuseum, Amsterdam, The Netherlands. This artwork is in the public domain.

Rembrandt van Rijn, *Woman Bathing in a Stream*, 1654. Oil on canvas. The National Gallery, London, England. This artwork is in the public domain.

Rivera, George, *Atonement*, 2004. Oil on canvas. Collection of the Artist. © 2004 George Rivera. Used with permission.

Snake Goddess, c. 1600 BCE. Faïence. From the *Palace at Knossos*, (Crete), Greece, Archaeological Museum, Herakleion, Greece. This artwork is in the public domain. This image is licensed under the Creative Commons Attribution 2.0 Generic (https://creativecommons.org/licenses/by/2.0/deed.en) license. Image by George Groutas (https://www.flickr.com/photos/22083482@N03) and retrieved from https://commons.wikimedia.org/wiki/File:Snake_Goddess_- _Heraklion_Achaeological_Museum_retouched.jpg. This photographic reproduction has been released into the public domain on Wikimedia Commons and may be used for any purpose without any conditions.

Spranger, Bartholomeus, *Vulcan and Maia*, c. 1585. Oil on copper. Kunsthistorisches Museum, Vienna, Austria. This artwork is in the public domain.

Theodora and Her Attendants, c. 547. Mosaic. From the south wall of the apse, *San Vitale*, Ravenna, Italy. This artwork is in the public domain.

Thutmose, *Nefertiti*, Dynasty XVIII, Egypt, c. 1353-1335 BCE. Painted limestone. Ägyptisches Museum, Berlin, Germany. This artwork is in the public domain. This image is licensed under the Creative Commons 2.0 Generic license. Image by https://www.flickr.com/photos/icelight/ and retrieved from https://commons.wikimedia.org/wiki/File:Wiki_nefertiti_icelight.jpg. This photographic reproduction has been released into the public domain on Wikimedia Commons and may be used for any purpose without any conditions.

Titian, *Danaë*, 1554. Oil on canvas. Hermitage, St. Petersburg, Russia. This artwork is in the public domain.

Utamaro, Kitagawa, *Lovers in an Upstairs Room*, from *Utamakura (Poem of the Pillow)*, 1788. Woodblock print on paper. The British Museum, London, England. This artwork is in the public domain.

van Eyck, Jan, *Giovanni Arnolfini and His Bride*, 1434. Oil on wood. The National Gallery, London, England. This artwork is in the public domain.

Velasquez, Diego, *Venus at Her Mirror*, 1650. Oil on canvas. The National Gallery, London, England. This artwork is in the public domain.

Venus of Willendorf, c. 28,000-25,000 BCE. Limestone. Naturhistoriisches Museum, Vienna, Austria. This artwork is in the public domain. This image is licensed under the Creative Commons Attribution Share Alike 3.0 Unported license. Image by Don Hitchcock and retrieved from https://commons.wikimedia.org/wiki/File:Willendorf-Venus-1468.jpg. This photographic reproduction has been released into the public domain on Wikimedia Commons and may be used for any purpose without any conditions.

Vermeer, Jan, *The Letter*, c. 1666. Oil on canvas. Rijksmuseum, Amsterdam, The Netherlands. This artwork is in the public domain.

Waterhouse, John William, *Circe Offering the Cup to Ulysses*, 1891. Oil on canvas. Oldham Art Gallery, England. This artwork is in the public domain.

Yakshi bracket figure, on the East *Torana* of the *Great Stupa* at Sanchi, Early Andhra Period, mid-1st Century BCE. Stone. Sanchi, India. This artwork is in the public domain. This image is licensed under the Creative Commons Attribution Share Alike 3.0 Unported (https://creativecommons.org.licences/by-sa/3.0/deed.en) license. Image by Vu2sga and retrieved from https://commons.wikimedia.org/wiki/File:Nymph_of_Sanchi.JPG. This photographic reproduction has been released into the public domain on Wikimedia Commons and may be used for any purpose without any conditions.

About the Author

As Chief Curator and Deputy Director of the Triton Museum of Art in Santa Clara, CA, Preston Metcalf has worked with many of the most renowned artists in the country, showcasing their works in exhibitions and publications. In addition to his curatorial role, he helped create innovative art and art history education programs for public schools and children's hospitals, providing free programming and classes for thousands of kids, teens, and adults. He has lectured internationally on art and art history and published more than sixty essays and articles on artists and their work. He is a regular lecturer of Art History at colleges and universities throughout the region. To learn more visit the author at PrestonJamesMetcalf.com.

Cuong Nguyen
The Curator
2017
graphite on paper